Wedding
Interrupted

Gwen Andrews Mystery #4

Michel ~
Great to
meet you...
enjoy Gwen's
4th story!

Debi Graham-Leard

Debi
Oct '21

Riverhaven Books

Wedding Interrupted is a work of fiction.
Any similarity regarding names, characters,
or incidents is entirely coincidental.

Published in the United States by Riverhaven Books, Massachusetts.

ISBN: 978-1-951854-13-3

Printed in the United States of America
by Country Press, Lakeville, Massachusetts

Author photo credit: Ria MacKenzie

Edited by Riverhaven Books
Designed by Stephanie Lynn Blackman
Whitman, MA

Previous Gwen Andrews Mysteries

The Uninvited Guest
Introducing Gwen Andrews
2015

Where There's Smoke, There's Trouble
Gwen Andrews Mystery #2
2017

Bed, Breakfast, & Blackmail
Gwen Andrews Mystery #3
2019

Acknowledgements

The following people graciously shared their individual expertise as I created *Wedding Interrupted.* My sincere gratitude to them all.

Pam Loewy
Plymouth Writers Group

Ralph Arguin
Country Gardens Wedding Venue

Deputy Chief Thomas Petersen
Norton Police Department

Chief Shawn Simmons
Norton Fire Department

Heather Daniel
NP, Norton Medical Center

Ria MacKenzie
Wedding Photographer

Patricia C. Graham
Master's Degree Student

My sister **Jerri Graham Burket**
who inspires me daily

And the most important person of all…
my husband **Vinnie Leard**

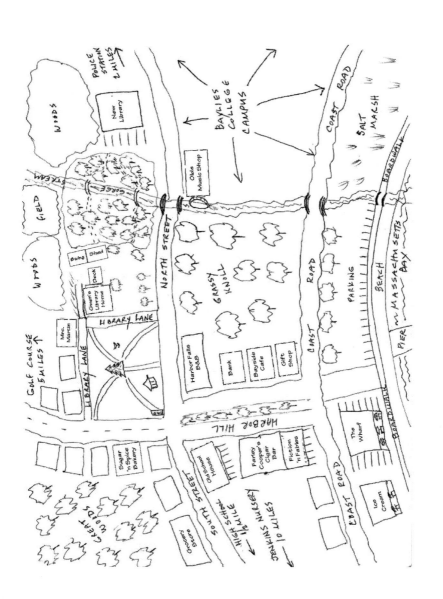

Not all good deeds go unpunished.

Chapter One

… late afternoon, Saturday, mid-June

Gwen Andrews came to regret writing '*backyard wedding*' on her summer calendar. The trouble began weeks earlier with the arrival of Cousin Sally's handwritten note:

> *Cousin Gwen… so sorry I've been out of touch since your sister's reunion dinner this past Christmas. Tess's description of your picturesque gardens brings me to the purpose of this letter.*
>
> *Would you allow my granddaughter's wedding in your back yard? Allison has her heart set on a simple ceremony at sunset in mid-June. I know this is short notice, but your consent would mean so much to us.*
>
> *I'll handle all the details. I await your reply.*
>
> *Hopefully yours, Cousin Sally*

Gwen had stared at the note. Until Sally's return to her New England roots the previous autumn, she'd lived on the west coast for decades. Why was Sally – as opposed to her granddaughter's parents – planning the wedding?

Did the reason matter? The request hadn't been complicated... Would Gwen permit the nuptials in her back yard? By mid-June, her flowers would be bursting with color, thrumming with life. She had to admit, her gardens would provide the perfect spot for a wedding.

And how intrusive could a simple ceremony be? Deciding the one-evening event would require no more than a few hours, Gwen penned a note – adding a P.S. that Sally should visit for a tour of the property – and snail-mailed her assent.

Within a few days, Sally had driven to Harbor Falls from Cape Cod. "I didn't realize you live in a converted library, Gwen," Sally had cooed as she gazed up at the brownstone and brick facade. "And on the edge of the village green to boot. How very New England. Allison will be thrilled with this setting for her wedding."

Over the next three weeks, Sally had called, emailed, and texted to advise Gwen that another guest or two had been invited. Day by day, the number of attendees increased at an alarming rate. Understandably, Gwen worried about parking limitations because Harbor Falls – a quaint college town on the east coast of Massachusetts – did not offer the plethora of public garages like Boston to the north. The parking spots on the village green would be insufficient for the expected number of vehicles.

To avoid frustration, Gwen asked Sally to instruct the guests to park behind the bank on Harbor Hill as it would be empty on a Saturday evening. The short walk across the village green to Gwen's shouldn't create a hardship for anyone.

In case any of the guests missed the instructions, Gwen cordoned off the length of her side yard – where it stretched to

North Street – with white nylon rope attached to wooden stakes. She didn't want to deal with tire ruts in her lawn and counted on respect for her makeshift barrier.

Now that the wedding day had arrived, she was beginning to regret her consent. First thing that morning, the bride's twin sister Ashley – in the spontaneous role of event decorator – had affixed multiple strings of overhead bulbs to every available structure in Gwen's back yard.

In the upper section of the side yard – now filled with rented tables camouflaged with Ashley's pastel paper coverings – the young woman had dangled dozens of luminary bags from the low-hanging branches of Gwen's red bark maple trees.

Folding chairs crammed the lower deck. Gwen wondered if Sally had ordered enough. A center aisle led toward the trellis where the ceremony would take place.

A salty breeze from Massachusetts Bay swirled up Harbor Hill and across the village green to ruffle Gwen's hair. Pushing the errant strands from her eyes, she half-tripped over extension cords snaking in and around the flowering bushes, browning lawn, and wooden deck.

As Gwen drifted through her gardens, every possible concern shadowed her steps. Usually the burst of floral colors and scents would soothe the retired music professor. Not so much on this special day. The event had expanded way beyond the promised simple wedding.

The size of the event didn't bother Gwen. Over the years, she'd hosted many outdoor gatherings for friends, neighbors, and the Harbor Falls garden club. But she'd know virtually none of the people traipsing around her property that evening.

Again, Gwen questioned her agreement to her cousin's plea for a wedding venue. Had she simply wanted to share her picturesque gardens? Or did she want to encourage her recently renewed relationship with the estranged Sally?

Gwen's rationale was irrelevant. At this late hour, she couldn't renege on her consent. Sweeping aside her apprehensions, she stepped onto the upper deck and entered her kitchen through the French doors.

A loud squeal erupted from the second-floor mezzanine of the converted library. A thunder of feet scrambled down the staircase. First to appear was the auburn-haired bride-to-be Allison – her baby bump straining against her tee shirt – followed by twin sister/maid of honor Ashley, and bridesmaid Jenna Jenkins, Gwen's summer houseguest. Beaming, the trio scrambled toward her at the kitchen island.

Breathless, Jenna said, "I still can't believe my college roommate is your cousin's granddaughter."

Gwen smiled and glanced from one young woman to the next before addressing the bride's twin. "Ashley, I'm concerned about the wax candles you'll be lighting in those paper luminary bags. Are you sure they won't burn?"

"The package says they're flame-retardant," Ashley answered, her tone all-knowing like most young adults. "Real candles give off a shimmering glow, Mrs. Andrews. It'll be okay. Nothing will go wrong."

Gwen could only hope Ashley was right.

Allison came up beside Gwen and held out a CD. "This is the song Cole and I chose for my sister and Jenna as they walk down the aisle ahead of me. And then Jenna will play the traditional wedding march on her flute." Allison pressed the sleeved disk into Gwen's hand. "Thanks for taking care of the music. By the way, I love your home."

Flattered by Allison's appreciation, Gwen said, "Thanks. I love it, too."

Nearly a dozen years had flown by since Gwen's architect husband Parker had converted the abandoned village library into their one-of-a-kind residence. A few years after they moved in, Parker had been killed by a freak storm. Abandoned, Gwen had struggled with her grief for years.

When she was at her lowest point, Parker's good-natured spirit had shown himself to Gwen, assuring her all was well in the afterlife. Her mourning abated. She participated in life again, all the while eagerly awaiting his next manifestation.

Parker's spirit had appeared repeatedly. Several times when she called his name. Once during a séance. Whenever she was upset or emotional, it was as if he sensed her anguish and materialized accordingly. Their shadowy encounters eased Gwen's ache for Parker. Within this unique library home, her memories of their thirty-seven-year marriage endured. She would live nowhere else until the day she died.

Her mood bittersweet, Gwen jolted that she was ignoring the bridal party. "When are your parents arriving?"

Allison fielded the question. "Mom and our stepfather are caught in Cape traffic."

The French door surged inward, catching them all by surprise. Breathless, Sally barreled in, her gray curls bouncing. "I made it, Gwen. Traffic on the Sagamore was horrendous for a late Saturday afternoon."

"It still is, Grandma," Ashley offered. "Mom thought the Bourne Bridge might be less crowded, but she texted they're stuck at the Bourne rotary."

Cousin Sally flipped her hand in dismissal and changed the subject. "Gwen, I've said this to you more than once, but it bears repeating. The girls and I can't thank you enough for hosting our wedding. And Ashley did a terrific job with the decorations. I'm so proud of my granddaughters."

When both young women stepped around the island to hug their grandmother, Sally continued her monologue. "Oh, by the way, I posted a sign in your front yard that the wedding is in the back yard. I hope you don't mind."

Gwen opened her mouth to protest, then decided the flow of foot traffic up the left-side driveway was preferable to the guests traipsing through her home. Although, at some point, someone was bound to need the bathroom. Not until that moment did Gwen realize Sally hadn't rented one of those portable potties. She shivered, grateful that an ugly monstrosity was not plopped unceremoniously among her flower beds, though she might regret her disdain when guests lined up to use her indoor facilities.

The banging of hammers, the clunk of cinder blocks, and the zing of power tools – the sounds of Gwen's long-overdue garage being built at the top of the driveway – intruded through the open French door.

Spring rains had delayed all outdoor projects. The construction crew had arrived much too late to finish the job before the wedding. Gwen informed the foreman that when the guests began to arrive, the men would have to halt their racket.

Cousin Sally kept talking. "I brought lots of food for the reception. Cooked all day."

"Does anything need warming?" Gwen asked.

Sally waved aside the suggestion. "I'll reheat small batches in your microwave while the photographer is snapping pictures after the ceremony. We'll serve family style at each table. I don't want to babysit the food during the wedding." She smiled at her granddaughters and Jenna. "Can you girls help me carry in the feast?"

***

Cousin Sally's many pans of lasagna, meatballs, and salads would not all fit in Gwen's fridge, so she walked to her neighbor's house and knocked on Mrs. Miller's kitchen door.

Before Gwen could utter a single word, elderly Mrs. Miller launched into an apology. "I'm so sorry, dear, but Henry and I can't come to the wedding this evening. He's eaten something that's upset his stomach, and I don't dare leave him alone."

Gwen had learned years ago to always invite her neighbors to any large party. Whether the elderly couple attended or not,

7

they'd be less likely to complain about the noise level. "What a shame, Mrs. Miller. Let me know if there's anything I can do for Henry. In the meantime, I hope you can help me with a short-term problem."

The older woman dried her hands on her apron. "What problem, dear?"

"Well, my cousin brought food for the reception, but my fridge can't hold it all. Do you have extra space in yours?"

Mrs. Miller laughed. "Oh, my, yes. We installed a second unit on the back-porch years ago. Henry wants to throw it away, but I've told him repeatedly it'll come in handy one day. And here you are."

Chapter Two

… early evening, Saturday

After stowing away Sally's food, Gwen went home and dropped onto an island stool, contemplating the wedding with both dread and relief. Thankfully, the event would conclude within a few hours.

Jenna scurried down the staircase and twirled in her bridesmaid dress. "What do you think?"

Gwen fingered the exquisite fabric. "The dusty rose color blends beautifully with your skin tone. You and Ashley were fortunate to find similar dresses so close to the wedding."

Jenna swirled again, floating the chiffon skirt. "Ashley's is this same style in lavender, which looks very smart with her auburn hair. We avoided the bridal shops and stuck to regular stores. Much cheaper and less hassle." She intertwined her arm with Gwen's. "Thanks again for your invitation to stay here this summer while I begin the classes for my master's degree."

Repositioning a strand of Jenna's errant hair, Gwen said, "I love having you here. With your grandfather moving to Florida, his farmhouse isn't an option. No sense in you making other arrangements when I have a perfectly fine guest room."

Jenna smiled. "Still, I appreciate your generosity." She walked to the sink for a glass of water.

Gwen considered her connection to Jenna's grandfather Hal Jenkins. Several years earlier, he'd hired Gwen to prepare his granddaughter for a music competition. As the weekly tutoring progressed, Gwen and Hal had become friends and eventually almost inseparable companions. That is, until a few days before Christmas Day.

With no warning or discussion, Hal had presented Gwen with a plane ticket to Florida, explaining he was tired of New England winters and planned to move south. He expected her to fly down with him to house hunt.

When she reminded him of a rare family reunion dinner at her sister's home in the Berkshires – to which he and Jenna had both been invited – he'd insisted she sacrifice her plans for his. When she handed back the plane ticket, he'd hurled words that hurt her deeply. Their friendship crashed and burned.

Jenna eased onto an island stool, suspending Gwen's unpleasant memory.

"How's your granddad adjusting to his new life?"

"He likes it. I talk to him every weekend. He finished a few projects in his little cottage and made some new friends. To tell you the truth, I think he misses the activity of the nursery."

Jenkins Nursery and Garden Shop had been a mainstay in Harbor Falls for decades and Gwen's go-to source for seasonal flowers. "Does he regret selling the family business?"

Jenna rotated a vase of blue delphinium, orange poppies, and white sweet peas from Gwen's gardens. "Actually, he hasn't sold it."

This news came as quite a shock. A month before, when Gwen had bought summer annuals, she'd assumed a new owner had taken over. "I thought his foreman Oscar bought it?"

"He's trying to, but he and his brother are having trouble getting their loan. When Grandad moved to Florida, he hired them both to manage the greenhouses and tend the fields until they can resolve the bank delay and close the sale."

"Well, judging by the well-stocked sales tables when I was there a few weeks ago, the brothers are doing a great job. Your grandfather must be discouraged by the delay, not to mention the financial strain of owning two properties."

"He's never mentioned money problems."

"That's good," Gwen said, genuinely relieved. "Before you run back upstairs, there's something I need to ask you."

Jenna's blue eyes – the exact color of her grandfather's – widened with interest. "What is it?"

Gwen retrieved a manila envelope from a lower cabinet. "I need to update my will. Would you agree to be co-executor with my sister Tess?"

"I'd be honored," Jenna answered. "Do I need to sign a document?"

"I'll let you know after I meet with the attorney."

"Okay." Jenna glanced at the staircase, apparently listening for activity from either Allison or Ashley. "Did you want to ask me anything else?"

"Not ask but tell." Gwen fingered the envelope. "This may come as a surprise, but I plan to leave you my home."

Jenna's jaw dropped. "Are you kidding? Why me?"

Gwen rested her forearms on the island countertop. "Are you aware my husband and I never had children?"

"No," Jenna answered. "I assumed your kids were grown and gone."

"It's not that Parker and I didn't want children," Gwen explained. "We tried, but the pregnancy tests always came back negative. My music students have always filled the void."

"Is that why you're leaving your home to me? Because I was one of your music students?"

Gwen laughed. "You weren't just a student, Jenna. You're my competition-winning flute protégé. Who better to inherit?"

Jenna's gaze swept the unique spaces of the converted library. Her eyes misting, she grasped Gwen's hand. "Saying thank you sounds so inadequate. But living here without you will be nearly unbearable."

"Your sentiments are sweet," Gwen murmured, "and another reason I'm so fond of you."

"I'm lucky to have you in my life, Gwen. You mean more to me than you'll ever know." Throwing her arms around Gwen's neck, Jenna whispered, "Don't you worry. I'll treat your home with the respect it deserves."

"I never doubted that for a second," Gwen said.

Jenna pushed her to arm's length. "Wait a sec. You're not sick, are you?"

"Oh, goodness, no. I'm due for my annual physical this week, but for the most part, I feel fine."

"For the most part?" Jenna challenged.

"Now and again, I get a little light-headed. I'm blaming stress from the wedding and the garage construction. I'm sure it's nothing."

"Why don't I drive you to your appointment?"

"Not necessary, but thanks for offering."

"Well, if you change your mind, let me know."

The two women – one preparing for the end of her life and the other at the beginning – embraced each other.

Female voices echoed down from the second floor. "Jenna, we need you."

Warmed by their evolving bond, Gwen said, "Scoot. You're being paged."

***

As Gwen daydreamed about the peace and quiet after the wedded couple and guests had departed – at least until Matt's crew returned on Monday morning – Sally tottered through the kitchen and out the French door, calling over her shoulder, "I have one last special food item to bring inside."

Two minutes later, she returned with a cake plate balanced in her hands. Placing it on the island countertop, she removed the cover with a flourish. "What do you think?"

Gwen moved closer to view Sally's creation.

The wedding cake was edged with pink roses, grape vine tendrils, and green leaves, topped with the requisite bride and groom statuettes.

"This is stunning, Sally. Did you bake it?"

"You bet I did. This spring, I enrolled in a cake decorating class. Until Allison announced she was getting married, there were no special occasions that required my new skill."

"Well, I'm impressed," Gwen cooed and meant it. The cake was gorgeous.

Sally reached into her pocket and withdrew a card. "Here's my contact info. If you hear of anyone who needs a decorated cake, send them my way. I'll deliver to Cape customers and this side of the bridges, too."

As Gwen tucked the embossed card into her jeans, the French door swung open and smacked Sally in her ample backside. Her arms flailed in a vain attempt to remain upright, but still she landed with little grace on the kitchen tiles.

Not caring who had entered, Gwen squatted beside her cousin. "Are you hurt?"

"I don't think so." Sally reached out. "Help me up."

When both cousins stood again on their feet, they looked toward the open doorway to see a middle-aged woman supporting a disheveled man. Shifting his weight, she glanced at Sally. "Sorry, Mother. I didn't see you standing so close to the door. Are you okay?"

"Yes, yes, I'm fine, Robin." Sally glared at the man, her irritation obvious. "You're drunk, Frank? Can you even walk your stepdaughter down the aisle?"

Frank lifted his head, his bloodshot eyes searching for his inquisitor. "I'm not drunk," he slurred. "I took something for my stomach. I get car sick."

14

Exposed to alcoholics during her lifetime, Gwen knew the difference between medication and liquor. Avoiding Sally's family drama, Gwen edged to the other side of the island. Even from several feet away, she could smell the whiskey fumes wafting from Frank like a fog bank. His sagging eyebags, red nose, and distended belly confirmed his addiction.

Sally glared at her daughter. "Is that true, Robin?"

Robin rolled her eyes. "Yes, Mother. Frank does get motion sickness." She shifted her attention. "You must be Gwen. Sorry to arrive in such a state. Is there somewhere Frank can rest?"

"Of course. The sofa in the living room. Go past the staircase and take a right." Gwen waved in that direction.

After Robin and Frank were out of earshot, Sally muttered, "Something for his stomach, my rear end. He'd better not make a spectacle of himself."

Gwen's innate curiosity surfaced. "Sally, we've been out of touch for decades, so I don't know your family. I hate to be nosey, but if Frank is the stepfather to Robin's daughters, what happened to her first husband?"

Sally plopped onto the nearest stool. "Now, *Kyle* was a good man. I couldn't have chosen better for my girl. Robin met him at a USO event. They fell in love and when they discovered she was pregnant, they got married. Not long after the wedding, he was deployed overseas and was killed months later. Robin was devastated. Allison and Ashley never met their father. Why Robin chose Frank as her second husband is beyond me. He's a poor substitute for Kyle."

15

The ever-increasing chatter of voices outside confirmed the arrival of guests. Gwen hopped off her stool. "Excuse me, Sally. I'll be right back." She hurried along the length of the upper deck, bounded down the end steps, and was about to descend onto the pavement when a voice called, "Watch out!"

Gwen caught her forward motion in time to avoid a beefy man pushing a dolly over-burdened with cinder blocks.

"Sorry, Mrs. Andrews," the man said on his way by. "Can't stop now or I'll lose my momentum." He maneuvered his load to the left edge of the new garage and added his blocks to a growing pile on her lot line with Mrs. Miller.

Spotting the foreman, she yelled, "Matt, I appreciate your men working overtime, but they need to stop. The wedding guests are arriving." To confirm her statement, several more people skirted past them, speaking in overly loud voices. They ignored Gwen, probably because she was wearing jeans and they thought she worked with the construction crew.

Matt headed her way. "No problem, Mrs. Andrews. I apologize again for our late start on your garage. We're behind on all our projects."

"You can't control the weather, Matt. Mother Nature dumped a lot of rain on us this past spring."

He consulted his clipboard. "And then sent us a drought. I'm expecting a water ban any day now." Matt tucked his clipboard under his arm and put his hands to his mouth to amplify his voice. "Time to quit, guys." He switched back to Gwen. "We poured your concrete floor earlier today. It'll cure overnight." He waved toward the half-built wall. "After we install the rest of the cinder blocks, the support wall will be twice as high and ready for the upper frame."

Gwen pointed. "What's that metal sticking up?"

"Rebar. It strengthens the base so it can hold the weight of the wooden walls and roof." Matt waved as he explained. "On Monday, we'll slide the rest of the cinder blocks into place. Then it's just a matter of attaching the frame, running the wiring, adding the roof, installing the garage doors and windows, and affixing the siding. Sorry we didn't have enough time to finish before the wedding."

"Not your fault, Matt. I'll see you and your men on Monday morning."

"We'll be here no later than eight." Matt led his men down the driveway, passing four more arriving guests.

Nodding at the newcomers, Gwen waved them toward the back yard with minimal conversation.

Chapter Three

... early evening, Saturday

Because Gwen had been wearing her usual jeans and loose top, the guests had no idea she owned the property. Beyond a polite smile, they paid her no attention. As Gwen climbed the end steps from the driveway to the upper deck, snippets of conversations floated on the breeze.

'What a beautiful garden.'

'This is a perfect spot for a casual wedding.'

'I hope Allison's stepfather isn't drunk.'

Doing her best not to stare, Gwen noted their apparel. Most men wore pale summer jackets. One a collarless shirt. A dapper old man leaned on a silver-tipped cane. The women's summer outfits ranged from flippy dresses to slacks with matching tops in every color. Some wore strappy sandals, others more sensible flats.

A group of twenty-somethings gathered near the huge field boulder at the back of Gwen's yard edging the wooded lot. Middle-aged invitees strolled among her flower beds. The older guests were seated in the rented chairs on the lower deck.

Gwen halted her observations and re-entered the kitchen. "Sally, do you know if the justice of the peace and the groom have arrived? The sun will be setting soon."

Sally peered out the bay window above the sink and pointed toward the end trellis where a trio of men stood. "The justice of the peace is the hefty fella in the black robe. The tallest young man with black hair is the groom Cole. The blonde next to him is his best man Brodie. "I'm not sure Cole is a good match for our Allison. He's handsome and seems nice enough, though he's not as serious. With her pregnant, I guess I should be relieved he's willing to marry her – not typical these days."

Gwen gazed at the three men. As Cole and Brodie shadow-boxed, the justice looked on, his facial expression revealing disapproval of their youthful antics.

Then Gwen noticed a man near her potting shed at the woods, clicking away with his camera. "Who's the guy taking pictures?"

Sally focused. "He must be the photographer Robin hired. I'm sure she told me his name, but I don't remember." Squaring her shoulders, she did an about face. "I guess it's time to get this show on the road." She strolled to the staircase landing and yelled up, "Allison, Ashley, Jenna. It's nearly sunset. Make your final touch-ups. We'll get your stepfather on his feet."

Gwen followed Sally into the living room to find Frank positioned on the sofa, his head clasped between his big hands.

He mumbled the obvious. "I don't feel good."

When Gwen switched on the nearby lamp, the light revealed a bald spot where the man's hair had thinned.

Standing in front of him, Robin touched her husband's shoulder. "Do you want an aspirin, Frank?"

"Quit babying him," Sally demanded as she approached. "He's drunk. Aspirin won't help."

Frank eyed his wife. "Listen to your mother and leave me alone." He gripped Robin's wrists and shoved her. When she stumbled, the backs of her knees bumped the coffee table.

Instinctively, Gwen gripped Robin's arm to keep her from falling. Receiving a nod of thanks from the woman, Gwen noted a bruise on the mother-of-the-bride's cheek that wasn't quite concealed with makeup. Was her husband an abusive drunk? Robin's jacket and pants concealed every inch of her skin. Was she hiding other bruises?

After Gwen's near perfect marriage to Parker, she couldn't grasp the concept of one spouse abusing the other. How gloomy to be trapped with such a partner.

Cousin Sally glared at her son-in-law. "The ceremony is about to start. Get up, Frank, get up." She plunged her hand beneath his armpit and yanked.

He didn't raise a hand to his mother-in-law.

Robin and Gwen trailed behind Sally as she hauled Frank to the kitchen and parked him on an island stool.

When someone knocked on the French door, Robin admitted a frizzy-haired woman and introduced her as the mother-of-the-groom Kathleen.

"Is there any way I can help?" Kathleen chirped.

Behind her, the groom Cole entered, glancing around at the collection of women. "Sorry, ladies, but the JP sent me in to find out how soon we're starting." He noticed Frank sagging against the granite island and stepped closer. "What's up, Frank? Have a few too many today?"

Glaring sideways at his soon-to-be son-in-law, Frank hissed, "Watch yourself. When you've been married to the wrong woman for as long as I have, you'll be drinking, too."

Cole shook his head and laid one arm across Robin's shoulders. "Guess that goes both ways, huh?" He thumbed back at Frank. "Is he going to make it through the ceremony?"

"We can only hope, Cole. You're sweet to be concerned." Robin said these words with no glance at Frank. "Tell the justice that Allison and the girls will be along any minute."

As Cole attempted to exit, he backed inside to allow entry of the man Sally had identified as the photographer.

"Jeremy," Robin called over. "So glad you were able to squeeze our little wedding into your schedule."

The broad-shouldered man with a military crewcut stepped inside, his camera slung around his neck. "Would you like some photos of the bride as she gets ready?"

A startled look overtook Robin's expression. "Great idea. I should have thought of that myself."

The photographer glanced over at Frank. "Is he walking her down the aisle?"

Blushing, Robin said, "He's supposed to." She tucked her hand through Jeremy's arm and moved him away from her husband. "Let me introduce you. This is Jeremy, the photographer I hired. Mother-of-the-groom Kathleen, the groom Cole, my mother Sally, and our hostess Gwen."

Gwen thought it a bit odd that Robin clung to the photographer but chalked it up to the woman's desperate need to put a hopeful spin on the event.

A female voice echoed down the staircase. "We're ready!"

Jeremy glanced at Cole. "Sorry, young man, but you're not supposed to see your bride until she walks down the aisle."

Without saying a word, Cole saluted and flew out the French door.

Jeremy stepped to the lower landing, adjusted the camera settings, and aimed his lens up the stairs.

"Okay, girls," Robin chirped, "the photographer's ready. Come on down."

Jenna peered over the mezzanine rail before descending to the mid-way split. In one hand, she carried her flute. In her other, a bouquet of pink hydrangeas and purple irises. She paused and posed as Jeremy clicked away.

Next came Ashley, her halo of auburn curls framing her face, wearing the lavender version of Jenna's dress with identical flowers.

As those two young women floated down the staircase, the two mothers, one grandmother, and Gwen clapped and cooed. Jeremy's camera captured each radiant expression.

Robin glanced to the top of the staircase, her eyes bright with moisture as she half-sang, "Here comes the bride."

Resplendent in an off-white knee-length gown hiding her baby bump, Allison swept down in slow motion. Her wavy auburn hair had been pulled into a classic chignon topped with a short veil. She clutched a bouquet of pink hydrangeas and white begonias, her expression confirming her nervousness.

"You look lovely," Robin remarked as Allison came to stand beside her, moving in for a mother-daughter embrace.

Allison's laugh belied her jitters. "I can't believe I'll be marrying Cole in a few minutes."

Snapping away, Jeremy backed into the kitchen until he bumped into Frank. Letting go of his camera to dangle from the neck strap, Jeremy grabbed Frank to keep him from slumping to the floor. Unphased, the stepfather appeared oblivious to the activity around him.

"Oh, damn," Ashley blustered.

Robin regarded her other twin. "What is it, sweetie?"

Ashley's face pinched with distress. "I forgot about lighting the candles in the luminary bags. Can you do it, Mother?"

At first Robin seemed flustered, but she quickly squared her shoulders. "Of course. I'll go out the front door and walk around so I don't confuse the guests."

"I'll help you," Kathleen offered.

Jeremy straightened. "I have enough indoor pictures. I'll go out and take more candids before the procession begins."

After the two mothers and the photographer disappeared, Sally once again took charge. "Let's give them a few minutes to light those wicks before we send you out, Jenna."

Hearing a grunt, they all swerved. As Frank struggled to his feet, he grabbed a hand towel and wiped sweat from his brow before tossing the damp cloth to the kitchen floor.

Sally stomped to his side and rapped his arm. "It's almost time, Frank. Can you stay on your feet long enough to walk Allison down the aisle?"

Hearing no sympathy in Sally's command, Gwen sensed the family had tired of the stepfather's battle with booze.

Chapter Four

... near sunset, Saturday

For the past hour, Gwen's sound system had been broadcasting Vivaldi's *Four Seasons*. She'd opened a mullioned window in her music studio and placed the detachable speaker on the sill, keeping the volume mid-range so the guests could talk to each other without screaming.

With the procession about to begin, Gwen inserted Allison's CD. The singer Train crooned "Marry Me," the plea drifting out and floating above the heads of the guests.

Gwen peeked around the speaker. Despite her irritation with Ashley's decorating technique, she had to admit the girl had transformed the back yard into a fantasy. As the sun approached the western horizon, the candles in the luminary bags cast a soft glow upon the surroundings. A breeze moved the overhead bulbs back and forth, creating a flicker of shadows. At ground level, the timed landscape lights blinked on, further illuminating the area. The tiny lights tucked into the trellis vines beamed down on the groom, best man, and justice of the peace. After the ceremony, Gwen would flip on her backyard spotlights to brighten the area for the reception.

Jeremy positioned himself adjacent to the justice, his lens aimed toward the French door.

Gwen strode to Sally's side. "You go take your seat. I'll send out the girls and Frank."

Sally dabbed at a tear. "This is lovely, Gwen, just lovely. Thanks for all your help."

"You're welcome," Gwen said, finally pleased she'd agreed to her cousin's request.

Waiting until Sally made her entrance, settled in the front row, and turned to watch the procession, Gwen ushered Jenna to the French door, murmured words of encouragement, and gave her summer guest a gentle push. Jenna winked at Gwen before strolling the makeshift aisle toward the trellis. Flashes recorded her journey.

Ashley stepped in measured time to the music, smiling at the guests until she paused beside the best man Brodie and reached over to relieve Jenna of her bouquet.

When Jenna raised her flute to her lips, Gwen pushed the remote in her hand, silencing Train's plaintive words.

The dulcet notes of the classic bridal march filled the summer air with anticipation.

Behind Gwen, Frank made a noise and she pivoted to see Allison pulling at him, anxiety souring her expression. The stepfather looked none too ready for his part in the ceremony. Nevertheless, he struggled to his feet and offered his arm, leading his stepdaughter through the French door.

Gwen waited until they stepped onto the lower deck before she moved to the upper deck rail to observe the ceremony. As she'd suspected, the number of rented chairs was insufficient to seat everyone. Many guests stood on either edge of the deck, shifting their weight from one foot to the other.

Frank swayed.

Allison stretched her arm around him in an obvious attempt to support her stepfather.

Two beats later, Frank shuddered and fell, all but taking the pregnant Allison down with him as he crashed into chairs.

Guests scattered in all directions. The domino effect forced many to jump into Gwen's hosta beds. Luckily, no one landed in the small fishpond.

Allison stared down at her stepfather and screamed, "What's wrong with him?"

Robin and Sally jumped to their feet. The justice of the peace didn't move, his face contorted with disgust.

Cole flew to the side of his almost-bride. "Allie, you okay?" He touched her belly. "Is the baby okay?"

Sliding her hand across her baby bump, she gazed at him with grateful eyes. "We both seem to be fine. I don't know about Frank though."

Frank twitched, then lay still.

Robin squatted down and brushed her husband's thinning hair from his sweaty brow. "He's only fainted."

From the deck rail, Gwen called, "Should I dial 911?"

"No, no, don't bother," Robin insisted. "This has happened before. He'll be fine." She struggled to her feet. "Cole and Brodie, can you carry him to that chaise lounge?" She pointed to the upper deck.

Cole's body language suggested his reluctance to leave his bride-to-be. When Allison tilted her head in her stepfather's direction, Cole whispered, "I'll be right back."

With little effort, the bridegroom and best man deposited Frank on the lounge chair. They dusted off their hands as if they'd been plunged into a dirty bucket of slime.

Frank moaned and blacked out again.

Robin grasped Allison's hand. "I'm so sorry, sweetie, but your stepfather won't be able to walk you down the aisle." She surveyed the faces surrounding them. "I'm sure one of these men will be happy to take his place."

Before any of the male guests had a chance to volunteer, shouts of "FIRE! FIRE!" ripped into the sultry evening air.

Chapter Five

... mid- evening, Saturday

Gwen whirled toward the shout.

Burning fragments from the swaying luminary bags had dropped onto the rented tables, setting fire to the paper coverings and stacks of napkins. Flaming chunks of the bags clung to the lower branches of the red bark maples, touching the dry leaves which flared but burned themselves out. The breeze sent other bits of burning embers in all directions.

Ignoring the hysterical guests, Gwen dialed 911 as she rushed inside. Cupping the cell phone between her cheek and shoulder, she yanked her kitchen fire extinguisher from its wall bracket near the stove. After yelling her address and a quick explanation to the dispatcher, she dropped her phone on the island countertop and bolted outside, recalling the acronym PASS from the community safety course. She pulled the pin, aimed the nozzle, squeezed the trigger, and swept the contents at the base of the nearest flames.

Some of the men stomped on burning tufts of dry lawn grass. Others had removed their jackets and were swinging at the smoldering table covers, heedless of damage to the fabric. Some fires fizzled in a puff of smoke; others were whisked by the air current into the taller ornamental grasses in the flower beds. Flames found dried leaves and twigs captured beneath the lower deck overhang. Luckily, the deck boards were too thick to catch on fire, but some edges appeared singed.

Gwen aimed her nozzle into the branches of her red bark maple trees where burning luminarias had not yet dropped. The branches were too thick to feed the flames, but she'd rather prevent damage than wish she'd done more. She hustled from one outbreak to the next. Her efforts combined with those of the wedding guests met with partial success.

Without warning, Gwen's extinguisher stopped spitting its contents. Empty. As she panicked, sirens announced the arrival of emergency vehicles.

Half a dozen firemen rushed around the side of the old library, pulling their hoses into position. Some concentrated on the flames while others raked through the smoldering debris to expose cinders. The wedding guests scattered into the far reaches of the back yard to escape the pulsing streams of water.

EMTs circulated, asking if anyone had been injured.

Ten minutes later, as the firemen rolled up their hoses, the fire chief ambled toward Gwen. "You were lucky we hadn't been called to other outbreaks. I don't like to lecture, but you should have known better than to light candles in your trees. Especially since we're in a dry spell. Besides, aren't you aware those paper bags are illegal for exactly this reason?"

Ashley hurried over. "Don't blame Mrs. Andrews, Chief. I'm the one who hung the luminarias. The packaging said they're fire resistant. I didn't know they were illegal."

"Young lady, fire resistant doesn't mean they won't burn."
He held out his hand. "I'll take the rest now."
"There are none left, sir. I hung all three dozen." Ashley
slunk away to join Cole, Allison, Jenna, and Brodie standing
dejectedly beyond the dripping trellis. The dimming light of
dusk shadowed their faces as they stared across the ruined
remains of the wedding venue.

Even from this distance, Gwen could see the wet fabric of
Allison's wedding gown clinging to her swollen body.

Guests ambled about, avoiding the puddles. The sound of
dripping water added a note of sadness. The overhanging light
bulbs gave off no glow. Forceful water from the firemen's
hoses must have shorted out the extension cords.

Robin made her way to the upper deck and clapped her
hands repeatedly until everyone faced her. "Sorry, folks. This
won't come as a surprise, but our wedding isn't going to take
place this evening. Thank you all for coming."

Cole and Allison stood near the garage entrance,
murmuring their apologies as the guests exited. The women
hugged Allison, the men pressed envelopes into Cole's hand.

Sally appeared at Gwen's side. "Your yard is a mess. I'll
come back tomorrow and help you clean up."

The justice of the peace appeared, his face frowning.
"Which one of you is paying me?"

"But you didn't perform the ceremony," Sally pointed out.

His wooly head shook side to side. "Doesn't matter. I was
here as promised. The bride's father collapsed before he

31

delivered her to me. Your candles caused a fire. You cancelled the wedding. Those events are irrelevant." He held out his hand, palm up. "I'll take cash, please. No personal checks."

"You're a piece of work," Sally snarled and headed inside, returning seconds later to slap the fee into his outstretched hand. "We won't hire you when we reschedule the ceremony."

"Good," he scowled, grasping the cash, and hurrying along the upper deck. He hopped down the end steps and disappeared down the driveway.

Snapping her purse closed, Sally said, "Gwen, I'm going to check on the kids and suggest we all retreat to the B&B. I'll see you first thing tomorrow."

"What about Frank?" Gwen asked, glancing at his prone body slumped and unmoving on the chaise lounge.

Robin struggled to her feet from the adjacent deck chair, her outraged expression distorting her face. "I'm sorry, but I can't do this anymore. I have to get away from him."

"But what about Frank?" Sally repeated.

"I don't care what happens to him." Robin stomped along the upper deck and down the end steps. Before she had a chance to escape, a man's voice called her name. Robin either didn't hear him or ignored the call.

As Gwen watched, Jeremy rushed from the back yard and caught Robin's arm.

While Sally poked at Frank, Gwen didn't move her focus from the bride's mother and the photographer. Though she couldn't hear their words, their conversation appeared intense.

Gwen spoke sideways to Sally. "What's going on between those two?"

Sally looked where Gwen pointed. "No idea. I only met Jeremy an hour ago, same as you."

As the two women watched, Robin pulled her arm free of Jeremy's grasp and disappeared around the corner.

"It certainly looks like they're more than recent acquaintances," Gwen ventured. "Where's Robin going?"

"Probably our rooms at the B&B." Seemingly unconcerned about her daughter's destination, Sally's focus toggled from Gwen to Frank and back again. "I hate to saddle you with my sorry excuse for a son-in-law, but I need to see if I can calm everyone down. When Frank wakes up, can you send him to the B&B?"

Gwen nodded in disbelief as Sally turned to depart. "I'm sorry about everything, Gwen." She scurried past the upended chairs and through the trellis toward the bridal party gathered near the bushes at the side of the new garage.

In the fading light, Gwen could barely distinguish Allison, Cole, Brodie, Ashley, and Jenna as they huddled. She could make out only a word or two as Sally spoke to them.

Gwen surveyed the ruined landscape that used to be her beautiful gardens. Water dripped at an ever-slowing pace. Trying to distance herself from the fiasco, she stepped off the deck and through the rented tables toward her side lawn.

Expecting the guests to have crossed the village green by that point, she was surprised when their chatter grew louder.

Two couples and a single man passed within feet of her without acknowledgement. They entered one car, an SUV, and a pickup truck, threw their gearshifts into reverse, and backed off her lawn, avoiding the stakes and white rope they'd run over when they'd arrived. The vehicles soon disappeared.

Gwen fumed, ashamed to wish them flat tires on their way home. She squatted beside the tire ruts and groaned. Those deep gouges would require topsoil and reseeding if she expected them to eventually blend into the rest of her lawn.

Trying to calm down, she approached the North Street birches, grateful the fires had not come anywhere near those majestic trees. She leaned against a slim white trunk and watched the remaining clusters of wedding guests as they crossed the village green, heading for their cars parked behind the bank. She doubted any of them would revisit Harbor Falls.

Lingering in the descending darkness, Gwen's heart sank. What a failure she'd been as a hostess. She'd been powerless to prevent Frank's collapse, but she should have put her foot down and forbidden Ashley from lighting wax candles in those damn luminary bags, flame-retardant or not. The resulting fires had dealt the final blow to the ceremony. Thankfully, the firefighters had arrived quickly and prevented the flames from causing even more damage. She'd send a note of thanks to the fire chief.

As the roar of escaping vehicles faded, the plaintive cry of seagulls echoed up from the harbor, creating the only sounds. The sudden quiet was a stark contrast to the recent hubbub.

When Gwen left the serenity of the birches and hiked back up her side lawn, she considered grabbing a flashlight from her potting shed for a closer look at her flower beds. Having no stomach for another disappointment, she opted to defer her inspection until the morning. The effort required to replant the annuals, perennials, and grasses would be punishment enough for her good deed.

As she passed the bare tables and approached the trellis, the landscape lights blinked off, withdrawing what little light had brightened the back yard.

She ducked through the trellis and was side-stepping the upended chairs when she remembered the unconscious Frank. Had the man woken up? Would Robin find him help for his drinking problem or file for divorce? Considering the woman's desperate escape earlier, the latter seemed more likely.

Gwen placed one foot on the upper deck and glanced over. The chaise lounge was empty.

Chapter Six

… early morning, Sunday

As the soft light of dawn slanted through the bay window in Gwen's kitchen, she filled Amber's food and water bowls. The golden tabby had been banished to the basement for the duration of the doomed wedding, so Gwen made sure to give the cat a few extra pats.

Carrying her first cup of coffee outside to the deck, Gwen winced at the scene before her. Her back yard looked more like a Halloween setting than a wedding venue.

Her carefully tended flowers had been trampled underfoot by fleeing wedding guests and the force of the water from the firemen's hoses. Debris littered the entire property.

The scorched branches of Gwen's red bark maples stood bravely above the bare rented tables. Would those trees recover? She'd need to contact the local arborist and let the experts determine the best course of action.

"Good morning," a youthful voice called.

Gwen wheeled around to greet her summer house guest. "Good morning yourself, Jenna. What time did you get back from the B&B last night?"

"Around eleven," Jenna answered, pulling the sash of her robe tighter. "I tip-toed so I wouldn't wake you."

"I didn't hear you, so you succeeded. How was everyone holding up over at the B&B?"

"Allison couldn't stop crying about her ruined wedding. And poor Ashley kept apologizing over and over for the fires. Robin never came out of her room. Allison told me she and Cole might elope. After I shower and get dressed, I'll walk over there. Maybe I can help them decide." Jenna glanced around the back yard. "It probably looks worse than it is," she said, optimism in her tone. "Have you inspected the damage yet?"

"Not up close. Walk with me." Gwen hoisted her coffee. "Do you want a cup to carry with you?"

Jenna shook her head and led the way through the upended chairs on the lower deck. Folding each one, they made quick work of stacking them in short piles. "Who's responsible for the rentals?" Jenna asked.

"Sally handled all the details," Gwen answered. "She said she'd come over this morning and help with the clean-up."

When they reached the trellis, Jenna untied the white bows and stared at the drooping ribbons. "This is heartbreaking."

Stepping through the gardens, they inspected each row and border, each cluster and patch of flowers. Crushed annuals, broken perennials, and bent grasses tugged at Gwen's sadness.

Jenna bent down and fingered mushy blossoms. "Is it too late in the season to replace your flowers?"

"I don't know. I may need to visit your grandfather's garden shop. If Oscar and his brother secure their loan, will they keep the name Jenkins?"

Jenna straightened. "Hard to predict. Granddad hasn't decided whether to wait for Oscar's loan to come through or search for another buyer."

Gwen empathized with Hal's plight but was powerless to resolve his predicament so made no comment. "After I clean up this yard, I'll drive over there and check the plant tables. Maybe they have enough leftover flowers to fill my beds."

They circled the huge field bolder and headed toward the top of the driveway, stopping along the way to inspect the forsythia bushes that concealed the beginnings of the garage.

"What's that?" Jenna asked, pointing.

Gwen followed Jenna's finger. "No clue. Let's go see."

As they rounded the final bush, they came upon a black loafer poking out from beneath one leg of black slacks, then a suit jacket, and finally a man's face. He laid belly-up atop the cinder block half-wall.

Gwen gasped. "Frank?"

Jenna screamed.

Moving closer, Gwen touched her fingers to the cool skin of the stepfather's throat. No pulse. His chest didn't move. A rancid smell wafted from his body.

Jenna's voice quavered. "There's a rod sticking out of his chest, Gwen. Is he dead?"

"I think so, but I'm calling 911. Don't touch anything."

This was not Gwen's first encounter with a corpse, but she hoped it was her last. Without evaluating her calm reaction, she punched 911 on her cell phone.

Waiting for the call to be answered, Gwen glanced at Jenna. "Why don't you go inside and take your shower?

Jenna said nothing but hurried to the end steps and sprinted the length of the upper deck, the tail of her robe flying.

When the dispatcher picked up, Gwen reported an unconscious man and provided her address.

The instant she disconnected, she dialed the Harbor Falls police department, all the while staring at Frank's unmoving body. When the desk officer answered, she forced herself to look away from the disturbing sight. "Ben Snowcrest, please."

She'd met the white-haired detective more than a year before and bumped into him a second time that past December. For the past six months, they'd been dating now and then. But there was no regularity due to the combined demands of her private music students and Ben's police work. With her young musicians on summer break, Gwen would have more free time. But would Ben?

"Sorry," the officer on the other end advised. "Ben's not here. Is this Gwen Andrews?"

"Yes, it is. I'm flattered you recognize my voice."

A chuckle escaped the officer. "You have a distinctive soft tone. Do you want to leave a message for Ben?"

"No, thanks. But I do need to speak with someone."

"Hang on, I'll patch you through to the chief."

Seconds later, Chief Mike Brown picked up. "Hello."

"Hi, Chief, this is Gwen. Ben's not there?"

"Afraid not. He's in Oakfield presenting seminars on

domestic violence. He's due back sometime today. I realize I'm a poor substitute, but what can I do for you this morning?"

Swallowing to break the tension in her throat, Gwen proceeded. "A few minutes ago, I found an unconscious man in my new garage. I've already called 911."

"Never a dull moment, Gwen. Do you think he can be revived or is he too far gone?"

Gwen forced herself to look at Frank's body. "I didn't feel a pulse, but I'd rather let the paramedics decide." Based on the dried blood staining Frank's white shirt where the rebar spike emerged from his chest plus the dark trail that had dripped down the cinder blocks, she concluded he'd died hours before.

"No pulse is not a good sign," the chief commented. "I'll have dispatch alert the medical examiner."

In Massachusetts, Gwen had learned, a death without a doctor in attendance would be treated as suspicious until the medical examiner declared natural causes. Gwen was quite certain natural could not be applied to Frank's demise.

The chief's voice interrupted her amateur analysis. "Does it look like an accident or something more sinister?"

Invisible to the police chief on the other end of the call, Gwen shrugged one shoulder. "Well, the new garage is only partially constructed. The man is belly-up on a cinder block half-wall that's only two feet high. A length of rebar is sticking out of his chest. Last evening, he was drunk as a skunk. He passed out during his stepdaughter's wedding, nearly taking her down with him. I guess he could have fallen backwards."

"Are you thinking someone helped him onto the spike?"

Gwen didn't think anyone could fall backwards with enough force to impale himself, especially a man who was as plastered as Frank had been, but she kept her opinion to herself. "Hard to say, Chief. The last time I saw him, he was passed out in a lounge chair on my upper deck."

"But he ended up in your garage?"

"That's where I found him this morning. When I headed inside last night, the lounge chair was empty. I assumed he had woken up and walked to the B&B to join his family. I had no idea he'd wandered over to the garage."

"Why not?"

"For one thing, it was growing dark by the time I went inside. For another, there's a row of bushes blocking the half-wall. Jenna and I didn't come across him until we were inspecting the damage to my flowers a little while ago"

"Damage to your flowers?" the chief repeated, his tone skeptical. "Can't wait to hear this story, Gwen. I'll send a detective to get the details." The chief broke the connection.

Gwen hurried to the bottom of the driveway to wait for the 911 responders. She dialed Sally's cell phone, grateful to be sent to voicemail. "Sally, this is Gwen. I'm sorry to be the bearer of bad news, but I found Frank in my garage a little while ago, and he doesn't look good. I've called 911."

The wail of approaching sirens confirmed Gwen's message. "I have to go, Sally. It's probably best you keep Robin and the girls away from here. I'll call you when I know more."

41

A patrolman arrived as two paramedics slid a stretcher from the back of their ambulance. Gwen waved the three men up the driveway. They hustled to Frank's body and performed several tests before shaking their heads and backing away, speaking to each other in voices too low for Gwen to hear.

The taller paramedic strode down the driveway to where she waited. "Sorry, but there's nothing we can do for this fella. The patrolman is requesting the medical examiner."

"No need," Gwen was quick to say. "I spoke to Chief Brown a few minutes ago. He's alerted the medical examiner and is also sending a detective."

The paramedic lifted one eyebrow. "Sounds like you've done this before. The M.E. will take charge of the body." He and his partner packed their equipment. Within minutes, they drove off, their ambulance siren silent.

When Gwen was about to step into the garage, the youthful patrolman rushed over to her. "Ma'am, you need to keep your distance until we know whether we're dealing with an accident or a crime."

Chapter Seven

… mid-morning, Sunday

From her stance at the garage entrance, Gwen spotted a man moving along the sidewalk toward her front door. She hurried down the driveway to find a curly-haired man standing on her top granite slab, his finger aimed at the bell button.

She called over, "Hello. Are you the detective Chief Brown sent over?"

The man waved and ambled along the front walk, stumbling over an uneven crack, his unnecessary trench coat blowing in the warm morning breeze.

Gwen couldn't stop herself from comparing him to TV's Detective Columbo.

"Sorry, ma'am. I didn't realize you weren't inside." He extended his hand. "You must be Mrs. Andrews?"

She returned his handshake. "I am."

"Detective Perry Warren, ma'am."

During the past year or so, because of her connection to the police department through Ben Snowcrest, she'd met every Harbor Falls detective, but she didn't recognize either this man or his name. "You must be new, Detective."

He shook his head. "Temporary assignment from another precinct, ma'am. Now, where is the victim?"

Wanting to be helpful, she waved toward the garage, saying, "A patrolman is guarding the body. The paramedics left a few minutes ago. The chief alerted the medical examiner."

Detective Warren glanced up the driveway. "Thank you for those details, Mrs. Andrews."

A van emblazoned with 'Medical Examiner' pulled to the curb. A tall silver-haired man emerged and hurried toward them. "I'm Dr. Otis, the medical examiner."

Detective Warren introduced himself and then Gwen.

She had met Dr. Otis at the B&B in December, but he obviously didn't recognize her. She didn't take it to heart.

The distinguished doctor nodded at her before addressing the detective. "Please take me to the body."

Detective Warren touched Gwen's elbow. "You stay here."

Ruffled at taking orders and being left out of the loop, Gwen stayed put and observed the two men.

Squatting beside Frank's body, Dr. Otis performed a series of assessments, his head shaking ever so slightly. He snapped photos from various angles then conferred with Detective Warren, who pointed at the newly poured concrete floor. They waved the patrolman closer and spoke in low tones.

Dr. Otis beckoned two men in white coveralls who had been leaning against the medical examiner van. They removed a stretcher from the back and wheeled it up the driveway.

The young officer, speaking into his shoulder mic, popped the trunk of his cruiser. Clutching several rolls of yellow crime scene tape, he returned to the garage.

After Dr. Otis followed Frank's body to the van, the officer draped the tape from one rebar spike to the next until he'd cordoned off the entire garage perimeter, surrounding the spot where Frank had died.

To Gwen's way of thinking, their assumption was unmistakable. Both officials had deemed Frank's death suspicious. The investigation had begun.

The detective signaled Gwen to join him outside the crime scene tape. He pulled out a small notebook and began patting his pockets, tossing her a half smile. "Sorry, ma'am, but do you have a pencil I could borrow? I can't seem to find mine."

"I have several inside. I'll get one for you." She stepped around him and climbed the end steps to the upper deck.

When she was halfway to the French door, he called, "Never mind, Mrs. Andrews. I found it."

Was he playing games? Gwen took a deep breath and retraced her steps to rejoin him.

Detective Warren licked the end of his pencil, preparing to take notes. "We've initiated a preliminary inquiry into this man's death. I need to ask you a few questions."

"I'll answer what I can," she replied.

He shifted his weight. "Tell me what you know about the deceased man."

Gwen hesitated. "His name is Frank. I don't know his last name." Despite her low opinion of the stepfather, she was overcome by the finality of his death. Maybe Frank could have pulled himself from his addiction. No one would ever know.

The detective wrinkled his forehead. "Can you tell me why he was on your property?"

"Of course, I can," Gwen snapped, her reply overly sharp. "Sorry. Finding his body was deeply upsetting."

He gave her a lopsided grin. "People react differently."

Gwen swallowed to calm herself before speaking again. "Frank was here to walk his stepdaughter down the aisle last evening in a garden wedding."

Detective Warren stepped around the forsythia bushes until he had a clear view of her gardens. "I'm sorry, ma'am, but I've been to a few of these backyard events, and they looked nothing like that. Tell me what happened. From the beginning."

Folding her arms, Gwen summed up the events of the previous evening, ending with her early morning discovery of Frank's impaled body.

Detective Warren scribbled furiously until the pencil lead snapped. Giving her a puppy dog expression, he said, "Sorry, ma'am, but I need to borrow your pencil now."

Controlling her annoyance, Gwen once again headed for the French door, half expecting him to call her back because he found a second pencil hiding in a pocket. But he didn't. In the kitchen, she rummaged through a drawer until her fingers wrapped around a half-used red pencil.

When she handed it to him, he immediately licked the point, then looked at her apologetically. "Sorry, force of habit."

"Not a problem. You keep it," she insisted.

"Thanks. Now, when was the last time you saw Frank?"

"After the firefighters left. He'd been carried to a lounge chair on my deck."

"And you have no idea how he wound up in your garage?"

"None at all. Last night, when I saw the empty lounge chair, I assumed he'd woken up and stumbled to the B&B where the rest of the family was staying."

"You didn't realize he'd ended up over here instead?" He waved toward the blood-stained cinder blocks.

"No, I didn't. Let me show you why." She crooked her finger for him to follow her. She led him past the forsythia hedge and into the back yard where she turned and indicated the bushes. "Because the unfinished wall is so low, Frank's body wasn't visible from my back yard. I couldn't see him from the upper deck or my kitchen earlier this morning either." She waved at her bay window.

He lifted one eyebrow and made a note. "Show me the lounge chair, ma'am."

They ducked through the trellis and onto the lower deck, sidestepping the stacks of folded chairs. Pausing, Gwen pointed. "After Frank collapsed, the groom and best man carried him to that chaise lounge."

Detective Warren glanced along the upper deck as it hugged the back wall of the old library. "So, you think he woke up, walked all the way to the other end and down the steps to the top of the driveway before he entered the new garage?"

"That's the route I'd take to get from here to there."

"Did you see anyone near him?"

"Not really. His wife sat in the adjacent deck chair until the fire trucks drove away. She cancelled the wedding and left."

"You're saying Frank's wife deserted him." Detective Warren flipped to a new page and continued to scribble. "What's his wife's name?"

"Robin."

"Last name?"

"I don't know. The same as Frank's I'd guess."

Again, Gwen felt a bit stupid. In her own defense, she'd thought the entire wedding troupe would show up for the ceremony and depart after the reception, never to cross her path again. So why would she have cared about their last names?

The detective again raised one eyebrow, apparently his favorite reaction. "Where did she go?"

"I couldn't say. My cousin assumed her daughter was walking back to the B&B."

"And your cousin's name?"

"Sally. She was here for a few minutes more, but then she escorted the bridal party over to the B&B."

He stopped writing. "I have to tell you, ma'am, I've never come across a situation quite like this. Can you help me understand why you know so little about the wedding party?"

"Of course, Detective. I only recently reconnected with my cousin Sally at a family dinner last Christmas. She wrote to me a few weeks ago asking if she could borrow my back yard for her granddaughter's wedding. The guests were her family and friends from Cape Cod. I'm not acquainted with any of them."

"Brave of you, Mrs. Andrews." Again, he licked the tip of her...now his...red pencil. "So other than Frank's wife and her mother, no one else came near him?"

"That's right. At least as far as I know."

"And he was unconscious last time you saw him?"

"Yes."

"But later you found the lounge chair empty?"

"That's right." Gwen repeated. She considered mentioning the photographer waylaying Robin as she tried to escape, but the detective hadn't asked if anyone approached Robin. Only if anyone had approached Frank.

"Where were you between the wife deserting him and finding the lounge chair empty?"

Worry crowded Gwen's mind. Did her tone when she described Frank give the impression that she'd arranged his demise? Best to stay calm and answer his questions as simply as possible, like any innocent person. "While the guests were leaving, I walked to the far end of my property."

"And why did you do that, ma'am?"

Gwen hesitated. "Oh, I don't know, Detective. I felt like I was in everyone's way. Maybe I needed to escape the drama."

He flipped back a few pages. "You said the ceremony was planned at sunset. Wasn't it getting dark?"

Perhaps this Columbo look-alike was more on the ball than Gwen had assumed. "It was," she answered. "I had planned to flip on my flood lights for the reception, but with the wedding cancelled, I didn't bother. My landscape lights come on a half hour before sunset and stay lit until ten. They blinked off as I approached the upper deck. If I had to guess the time that lapsed between my stroll to the birch trees and finding that chaise empty, it was a good half hour."

"And while you were at the other end of your property, you didn't see anyone approach Frank?"

"No, I didn't. From my position at North Street, I couldn't see my upper deck. I was watching the wedding guests cross the village green toward their cars behind the bank. Are you thinking one of the guests circled back and relocated Frank to the garage?"

"I can't be sure at this point, ma'am, but it's a possibility. Do you have a phone number for your cousin Robin?"

Gwen scrutinized Detective Warren, her mind ping-ponging from his initial clumsiness to not finding, then finding, his pencil, contrasted with his sharp recall about the timing of the wedding, and now getting the names mixed up. Had he been offered by a nearby town because his detective skills were subpar? She chided herself. Sometimes, the cover is a poor indicator of a book's worth.

"Robin is Frank's wife. Sally is my cousin."

"Yes," he agreed. "Doesn't that make Robin your cousin as well? Second cousin, but still…"

Gwen nodded and looked away with a bit of embarrassment. "I guess she is, but since I only met her yesterday afternoon, I haven't thought of her as my cousin. Sorry, I don't have Robin's phone number. She's also staying at the B&B, so you can probably catch her there." Realizing that she was wearing the same jeans as the day before, Gwen reached into her pocket and removed Sally's business card, holding it out. "Here's her mother's details though."

He copied the contact info into his little book and handed the card back to her.

"And you said the family is staying at the B&B? What's the address, ma'am? I'm not familiar with your town."

Gwen led him into the side yard – skirting the bare rented tables, now divested of their colorful paper covers – and pointed across the village green. "That large white colonial is the Harbor Falls Bed & Breakfast."

"Thank you. Very handy, I must say. I need to head over there to deliver the bad news to this man's wife and family."

As Gwen and the detective circled through the back yard, Jenna emerged through the French door.

Detective Warren cupped his hands around his mouth and shouted, "Young lady, please go back inside."

Jenna froze in the doorframe. "Who are you?"

"Detective Perry Warren, miss. And who are you?"

"I'm Jenna Jenkins. I'm staying with Mrs. Andrews."

"Are you the one who was with her this morning when she came upon the deceased gentleman in the garage?"

"That's right." Jenna glanced at Gwen and back again.

"You seem to be in a hurry."

Jenna waved her arm in the direction of the village green. "I'm walking over to the B&B to check on my friends."

"If you'll hold on another minute or two, I'll go with you. Wait for me out front."

Wincing, Gwen knew she couldn't stop the detective from questioning Jenna. The previous evening, Jenna had walked to the B&B with the wedding party. Not enough time to sneak back and attack the bride's stepfather within the half hour that Gwen was at the birch trees. Besides, with Jenna's small stature, she couldn't do harm to a man Frank's size.

Gwen and Detective Warren kept moving until they reached the garage entrance. He waved to the patrolman. "Call dispatch and request the crime lab team."

The young officer stood stiffly at attention. Whether his response was out of respect or fear of the detective-on-loan, Gwen couldn't tell.

"Yes, sir," the young man replied, stopping short of a salute.

Detective Warren continued his instructions. "I need you to expand the perimeter to include the lower deck, the trellis, the upper deck, those end steps and the top section of the driveway where it connects to the entrance of this garage."

"Yes, sir," the patrolman repeated and began to unroll another coil of yellow tape.

The detective turned to Gwen. "Sorry, Mrs. Andrews, but you need to avoid this entire area until evidence is collected. Lock your French door from the inside and use the front door until you hear from me."

He sidled up to the patrolman. "One more thing. Do you carry a camera in your cruiser?"

"Yes, sir," the young officer replied, halting his task of expanding the crime scene perimeter.

"Good, good. I need you take pictures of those shallow footprints in the concrete floor."

As Gwen overheard the detective's words, her love of mysteries shifted into high gear. Footprints? Was there more than one set? Were they connected to Frank's death?

Detective Warren continued his instructions to the patrolman. "When the lab boys get here, follow them around and record the evidence before they bag it. I'm going over to the B&B to notify the family. I'll be back soon."

"Yes, sir." The patrolman dropped the partially unrolled tape and sprinted toward his cruiser.

Gwen waited until Detective Warren looked her way. "Are you thinking the stepfather didn't stumble onto the rebar spike by accident?"

His expression revealed nothing. "That's one possibility, Mrs. Andrews. I need to follow procedure until we know for sure." He patted her arm. "Excuse me, but I don't want to keep your house guest waiting. I'll walk you to your front door."

Chapter Eight

… late-morning, Sunday

The crime scene van pulled up and two techs emerged carrying satchels. After they introduced themselves, Gwen advised them of the detective's imminent return and directed them to the garage. As they snapped blue booties over their shoes, the techs chatted with the patrolman. When they moved out of the garage and onto the upper deck, the young officer continued his photography duties before they bagged evidence. Gwen had no idea what they were collecting.

A female voice shouted, "Gwen!"

Surprised to hear her name, Gwen pivoted and nearly banged into Sally.

Out of breath, Sally said, "You didn't call me back, so I rushed over from the B&B. What's all this about finding Frank in your garage? Where did the ambulance take him?"

Gwen touched Sally's hand. "Didn't the detective tell you?"

"What detective?"

"His name is Perry Warren. He walked over to the B&B a little while ago with Jenna. I'm surprised you didn't pass each other in the village green."

Sally's face contorted in confusion. "I came around on the sidewalk. What did the detective want?"

Gwen placed her hand on Sally's plump shoulder. "Let's go inside and I'll explain."

Each a captive of her own thoughts, they ascended the granite slab steps, opened the heavy oak door, and passed through the foyer. Gwen guided Sally to the leather loveseat in the living room where Frank had attempted to recuperate the day before.

"I'm afraid the news isn't good," Gwen began. "Early this morning, Jenna and I found Frank in my new garage. I called 911. The EMTs couldn't revive him. I'm afraid your daughter's husband is dead." Gwen didn't share the gruesome detail of the rebar poking from Frank's chest.

For a split second, Sally appeared dumb struck, then she jumped to her feet. "Oh, my God! Is that what the detective is telling Robin right now?"

"I expect so," Gwen answered.

Sally began to pace, seemingly unable to decide whether to stay or go. She made a beeline to the kitchen and peered through the glass of the French door. "Oh, my God, Gwen, your back yard looks even worse this morning!"

Gwen assumed Sally was side-stepping the news about her son-in-law's death.

Sally's eyes brimmed with moisture. "I know I promised to help you clean up, but I have to get back to Robin."

Spotting the wedding cake sitting on Gwen's island counter, Sally picked it up. "I'll give this to Mrs. Owens at the B&B to share with her other guests."

Gwen walked through the foyer and held the front door as Sally exited. "Please express my condolences to Robin."

"I will, Gwen. Call you later."

Gwen didn't expect to hear from Sally any time soon and likened the wedding disaster to an albatross around her cousin's neck. Retreating to the kitchen, she gazed out the bay window and watched the lab techs as they inspected the soaked and soggy remains littering the lawn and flower beds.

The thick extension cords still snaked in and around everywhere. The overhead light bulbs dangled in desolation. With Gwen's recent dizziness, she didn't think it wise to climb a ladder and untangle them. She'd ask Jenna to handle that task.

With the news of Frank's death, Sally and Ashley were unlikely to pitch in for the clean-up. How soon would Gwen be allowed to re-enter her back yard? The crime scene tape would remain an eyesore until it was removed by the police.

Blowing out a noisy lungful of air, Gwen flipped the lock of her French door, apparently triggering her house phone to ring. Though she didn't recognize the caller ID number, it was local, so she picked up the receiver.

"Mrs. Andrews, this is Dr. Otis from this morning. I don't know if you recall, but we met at the B&B before Christmas."

Flattered, Gwen said, "I'm surprised you remember me."

"Your composure back then was appreciated when everyone else was panicking. With all the activity this morning, I didn't have a chance to console you. I'm so sorry you encountered another corpse."

A flashback of Frank impaled on that rebar spike gave Gwen the shivers. She wasn't sure what to say to kindly Dr. Otis. "Thank you for reaching out."

"A simple courtesy. I'm aware you assisted Detective Snowcrest during the Christmas case at the B&B."

Unsure if his statement about her police connection was good or bad, Gwen waited for Dr. Otis to continue.

"Dealing with these tragedies is never easy, even for me."

"I assumed you'd gotten used to it."

"Not really. I distance myself from the unfortunate person lying on my autopsy table. If you'll accept my advice, try not to dwell on the incident."

"I'll try," she echoed.

"My official report will be sent to Detective Warren. Nothing personal, but I hope we don't bump into each other anytime soon. Take care, Mrs. Andrews."

"You, too, Dr. Otis."

***

Gwen again strayed to the French door. The crime scene techs were dusting everything. Unless they found fingerprints inside the garage, they'd be no closer to identifying the person who'd moved Frank to his death. Frank straggling over there on his own was highly unlikely. The shoe impressions were probably the best lead.

But how could anyone determine if his impalement on that rebar spike was an accidental collapse by a drunken man or an intentional act of malice by another hand?

Pushing aside her quandary, Gwen stared at the stacks of rented chairs. She could at least contact the rental company and let them know retrieval of their property would be delayed. Exiting by the front door, she slipped around to the side yard, which was not corralled within the yellow tape.

Ignoring the suspicious glances from the two lab techs, she upended one of the tables, found the rental company label, and dialed the number, not surprised to be transferred to an answering machine, it being a Sunday. She left a message with both her home and cell phone numbers. Back inside, she resumed her surveillance position at the French door.

Though Gwen had risen from her bed mere hours before, her eyes wanted to close. The burden of the impending cleanup, a flower-buying trip to Jenkins Garden Shop, and the exertion of a massive planting effort loomed like a dark cloud. But she could do nothing until the men buzzing around her property finished collecting their evidence and removed the tape. She wasn't about to take her eyes off them.

***

As the clock hands approached noon, Jenna swooped through the front door and plopped on the staircase landing.

Gwen ambled closer. "What's going on at the B&B?"

Jenna picked at an invisible piece of lint. "Before Detective Warren arrived, Allison and Cole had eloped, and Robin had sent Ashley back to the Cape with Brodie. After Robin received the news of Frank's death, she locked herself in her room. There was nothing for me to do, so I came home."

"Where's the detective?"

Jenna shrugged her narrow shoulders.

Hearing a noise, Gwen stepped through the foyer and opened the oak door to find a red-faced Detective Warren leaning against the wrought iron rail.

"Couldn't keep up with your young house guest, ma'am, but I made it back." He rested his hands on his knees and gulped a lungful of air.

While she waited for him to catch his breath, Gwen launched into an update. "Dr. Otis called. He'll submit his report to you. Two lab techs are out back."

"Good," the detective managed. "I'll speak to them before I leave. They're careful with evidence. We'll get to the bottom of this, Mrs. Andrews."

Again, Gwen pondered the detective's easy-going manner. Was he masquerading as a bumbling policeman while being fire-cracker sharp underneath? She'd have to ask Ben's opinion. "When will you remove the crime scene tape? I'd like to begin my clean-up."

The detective's shaggy head moved from side to side. "Can't say yet. Depends on when the lab boys are finished. I'll go talk to them now and let you know."

After the door closed behind him, Gwen swiveled toward Jenna, who'd observed their conversation from the staircase landing. "You left poor Detective Warren in your dust?"

Jenna looked up beneath blonde eyelashes. "I could lie to you and say I didn't realize he was right behind me, but I was tired of hearing his voice. He asked so many questions." Jenna ticked them off on her fingers. "If Allison and I were roommates, why was I only a bridesmaid and not the maid of honor? How well did I know Frank? Did my roommate ever mention that he abused her mother? What was my reaction to his collapse? What did I observe as everyone was leaving after the wedding was cancelled? Did I notice anyone near him?"

Stretching out her legs, Jenna said, "This was my first experience with a real detective. At first, he was interesting, but he became tiresome real fast." She pulled a business card from her pocket. "He gave me this and said to call him if I thought of anything important, but I don't think there's anything else." She rose to her feet and headed for the kitchen. "I didn't eat this morning and I'm starving. What can we fix for lunch?"

They opened the fridge door and spotted Sally's pans.

Gwen moaned. "What am I supposed to do with all this food? Plus, there's more in Mrs. Martin's porch fridge."

Without waiting for Jenna to suggest a plan, Gwen punched in Sally's number and repeated the question to her cousin.

"There must be a soup kitchen in Harbor Falls," Sally suggested. "I'd do it myself, but I can't leave Robin right now. Do you want to borrow my van?"

Sally had just dumped another task into Gwen's lap. Not wanting to appear small-minded, Gwen resigned herself to more unwanted involvement. "Yes, I'll need your van. My car can't hold all your pans." Her real concern was spilling tomato sauce on the pale upholstery of her little sedan.

"Thanks for taking care of the reception food, Gwen. Come over to the B&B and I'll give you the keys for my van."

Gwen hung up and made a face at Jenna. "Sally suggested we donate her food to our local soup kitchen. She offered her van to transport the pans."

"Where's the soup kitchen?" Jenna asked.

"In the lower level of the big church on the corner. I'll call and make sure someone's there to accept Sally's donations."

After speaking to a woman at the church, Gwen shook her head. "They're serving lunch. If we can bring the food within the next half hour, she'll store it in their walk-in refrigerator. Let's hurry over to the B&B and drive Sally's van back here."

Fifteen minutes later, as Gwen parked the van at her front curb, Detective Warren hustled down the driveway, gripping his cell phone. "I'm sorry, but we've been called to another crime scene. The techs will return in the morning. The patrolman is posted to protect the scene. I again caution you to stay away from all the areas within the crime scene tape."

Hustling along the sidewalk, he dropped into the driver's seat of a beat-up car and made his way around the village green. Tossing their satchels into their van, the techs followed.

Glancing at Gwen, Jenna said, "Weird, don't you think?"

"I don't know what to think," Gwen admitted. "I only care about delivering Sally's food to the soup kitchen before they close. Let's unload my fridge before we retrieve the rest from Mrs. Martin's side porch."

Chapter Nine

… late afternoon, Sunday

Detective Benjamin Snowcrest pulled his unmarked sedan into the rear parking lot of the Harbor Falls Police Station, sagged behind the wheel, and closed his eyes. He was exhausted from presenting his domestic violence seminar plus the long drive from western Massachusetts – extended past the usual two-hours by the excess of weekend travelers.

It might be time to give his retirement some serious consideration.

Grabbing his briefcase, he locked up and headed inside. Waving to the desk sergeant, Ben entered the elevator and punched the button for the second floor.

In the detective suite, only one of the desks near the rear windows was occupied. "Hey, Perry." Ben called. "You stuck with on-call duty this weekend?"

Detective Warren smirked. "Afraid so. I'm the new guy, even if I'm temporary. It's been an interesting morning."

"You can tell me all about it after I see the chief. I was surprised to see his car parked out back." Dropping his briefcase on his desk, Ben strolled down the hallway and knocked on the open door of Chief Brown's office. "Working on a Sunday, Mike?"

The chief's head flew up, his expression startled. "Ben, you're back. I want to hear all about your seminar. Were your presentations well received?"

"Seemed to be. I'll adjust for the next round. A few more visuals, additional handouts. Details and more details."

"Next round?"

Ben lowered himself to the hard-bottomed visitor's chair. "Their chief asked me to repeat my seminar for the officers who weren't able to attend the first time."

His eyebrows rising, Mike said nothing for a few seconds. "Are you asking my permission or simply letting me know?"

"I guess a little of both. Can you spare me a few more days this coming week?"

Mike picked up a pencil and tapped his blotter. "I have to admit, it's a feather in our cap to offer a seminar leader to other precincts. There are topics besides domestic abuse you could share. But before you offer to leave town again, you need to hear what happened at Gwen's this morning."

Ben straightened at the mention of Gwen. They'd managed only a few dinner dates during the past six months. The chief had just handed him a great excuse to see her.

"Ben?... Ben?"

The chief's voice jerked Ben from his wishful thinking. "What?"

"Where'd you go? You were staring off into space."

Ben waved off the question. "Tell me what happened at Gwen's place."

Chief Brown outlined the incident, suggesting Ben get the details from Perry Warren.

When Ben jumped up, Mike said, "Hold on there a second." Although younger by more than a decade, Mike treated the lead detective more like a son. "Listen, Ben. I know you're sweet on Gwen, but obligations come first. When does the Oakfield chief want you back?"

Ben heard the disappointment in his own voice. "Tomorrow and Tuesday. Could run into Wednesday."

"Then you should do it. Gwen's case will still be active when you get back on Wednesday."

Downhearted, Ben shuffled down the hallway.

"Perry," he called, approaching the curly-haired man. "Tell me everything you know about the Gwen Andrews' case."

Perry flipped through his notebook, sharing his scribbles with Ben: the wedding fiasco on Saturday evening; the firefighters; Gwen finding the stepfather's body; 911; and the medical examiner. "The cause of death has me puzzled."

"What was it?" Ben asked.

"The man was lying face up on a low cinder block wall with a rebar spike through his chest."

Ben's visceral reaction forced him to sit down. "Inventive."

"I'd never seen anything like that either," Perry corroborated. "I suspect foul play, so I cordoned off the garage, the upper deck, and most of the back yard. Unfortunately, the crime lab techs and I were called to another scene before they finished collecting evidence."

"When are you sending them back?" Ben quizzed.

"First thing tomorrow morning."

Ben murmured, "Who have you interviewed?"

Perry again consulted his notes. "Mrs. Andrews, her house guest Jenna Jenkins, and two family members at the B&B."

"Good start. I'm returning to Oakfield for more seminars tomorrow and Tuesday, back on Wednesday. I'll most likely take over this case."

Perry closed his notebook. "Fine with me. I have a burglary to work on."

Ben swiveled his chair and grabbed his keys, "If the chief asks, tell him I went to Gwen's to find out if any other details have surfaced."

In the parking lot, Ben made sure his detective sedan was locked before dropping into the driver's seat of his red Corvette. This visit at Gwen's was more personal than official.

Chapter Ten

... early evening, Sunday

The day had been an unwelcome whirlwind for Gwen. Except for the original patrolman guarding the garage and cordoned back yard, no other officials remained. The crime lab techs were due back first thing tomorrow to finish up.

Leaving by the front door, she circumvented the yellow tape in the side yard and headed for the swing beside the potting shed. As she dropped onto the cushion, the shock of encountering Frank's body washed over her like a tidal wave. A sob escaped and she dropped her face into her palms.

"Gwen, sweetheart, what's wrong?"

Recognizing that familiar voice, Gwen lifted her head. A man's form took shape, shimmering against the dark wood of the adjacent shed wall.

"Parker," she breathed, quivering with euphoria.

The spirit of Gwen's husband had first appeared years earlier. Her initial encounter with his transparent form convinced her she'd lost her mind from grieving his unexpected death. But before his initial visit ended, she wholeheartedly believed Parker's spirit had indeed found his way back to her from the other side. His subsequent manifestations were usually preceded by an emotional incident

66

in Gwen's life. Regardless of the circumstances, she was always thrilled when he came to her.

Rising from the swing, she scurried toward his gossamer form, stopping short. Though hugging his non-existent body remained a fruitless effort, she stepped close enough to gaze up into his face as she wiped moisture from her cheeks.

"I'm so glad to see you, Parker."

"Tell me why you're upset."

"Oh, hindsight is so clear. I never should have agreed to host a wedding for my cousin Sally's granddaughter. Early this morning, Jenna and I found the body of the bride's stepfather in my new garage."

The ghost indicated the swing. "Why don't we sit while you tell me what happened?" His lightweight anatomy barely dented the cushion next to hers.

Gwen glanced over at the patrolman at the top of the driveway. The distance seemed sufficient that he wouldn't hear their voices, and he wasn't even looking her way.

As she retold the events to Parker, they seemed more like scenes from a novel or movie than Gwen's real-life experience. She relaxed as the tension of the past few hours eased.

"What's next?" Parker asked in his whispery spirit voice.

"The crime lab techs are returning tomorrow to finish collecting evidence. After they're done, they'll remove that horrid tape and I can start cleaning up this mess."

Parker glanced from one littered area to another. "Is anyone helping you?"

"Hard to say. Sally is busy calming her daughter after learning of her husband's death. I'd been hoping the bride's twin sister Ashley would lend a hand, but Sally sent her back to the Cape with the best man so she could report to work tomorrow morning."

"She's the sister who lit the candles in the paper bags?"

"Yep." Knowing Parker's corporeal self was unable to propel the swing, Gwen gave a gentle push with the toe of her sneaker. "Jenna offered to help, but there's nothing we can do until Detective Warren releases my property."

Parker waved his see-through hand toward the flower beds. "Is it too late to replant?"

Her foot pushed the swing a second time. "Depends. I need to visit Jenkins Garden Shop and see if they have any leftover flowers. Perennials should be plentiful, not so much annuals."

"Jenkins Garden Shop?" Parker asked. "I thought your buddy Hal sold the family nursery when he moved to Florida."

"Old habits die hard, Parker. I'll always think of it as Jenkins no matter what the new owners call it. Jenna mentioned her grandfather hasn't sold it yet. His previous foreman Oscar and his brother want to buy it but are having loan issues with the bank."

A veil of melancholy draped over Gwen. Though she hadn't forgotten Hal's hurtful words – or their ruined friendship – she missed their easier early days. Back when they seemed to agree about everything before their clash about life choices caused a permanent rift.

The roar of a sports car out front disrupted Gwen's reflections. Ben's Corvette! She glanced over as the white-haired detective appeared at the top of the driveway. He spoke with the patrolman, then made a quick phone call.

Spotting Gwen sitting on the back swing, he waved. Deterred by the crime scene tape, he retreated down the driveway and popped up seconds later in the side yard. He skirted around the rented tables, his gaze moving from one messy spot to the next. As he made his way toward the swing, he called, "I'm back."

Gwen glanced sideways, surprised to see that Parker's spirit remained by her side. She lowered her voice. "You usually disappear when someone shows up."

"I seem to be gaining control of my comings and goings. Have you told your detective friend about me?"

"Months ago, but he's still somewhat of a skeptic. He came face to face with the B&B's ghost last December, but I don't think he'll believe you exist until he sees you."

Parker floated up from the cushion and paused at the edge of the platform. "In that case, it's time we met."

Understandably nervous about the spirit of her deceased husband meeting the man she'd been dating sporadically for the past few months, Gwen stepped off the arbor platform. Returning Ben's half-hug, she faced him away from Parker. "Welcome back."

He pushed her to arm's length and scanned her face. "The chief mentioned your gruesome discovery this morning. How are you holding up?"

"I'm doing okay."

"Detective Perry gave me the bare facts, but I'd like to hear your version of events. Is now a good time?"

Gwen stepped aside, glancing behind Ben to check if Parker's spirit still waited. Parker winked at her and she glanced up at Ben. "Now is a perfect time, but first there's someone I want you to meet."

Chapter Eleven

… late afternoon, Sunday

Gwen threaded her arm through the crook of Ben's elbow and turned him around to face the swing… and Parker.

Ben dug in his heels. "Oh, my God, Gwen! Who is this?"

She placed her hand on the small of Ben's back and gave him a gentle shove. "When I told you about the spirit of my husband Parker, you only half believed me. Well, now you can witness his reality for yourself." She paused for a beat as she watched the living man and the transparent ghost react to each other. "Parker, this is Detective Benjamin Snowcrest."

Ben automatically extended his hand but quickly let it drop to his side. "Uh, nice to meet you."

Parker crossed his arms, his expression one of assessment. "Same here, Detective."

Stumbling backwards, Ben said, "You can talk?"

"I can," Parker answered, one pale eyebrow lifting.

Ben continued to stare. "When the B&B ghost snuck up on me, she didn't say a word. Christ, I feel like I'm in an episode of *The Ghost and Mrs. Muir*."

Parker's ghostly laugh lacked the deep guffaw of his living voice, but his amusement was unmistakable. "I've often felt that way when I visit Gwen."

Before their conversation could continue, a man's voice shouted greetings across the side yard. Gwen and Ben both turned to see who had arrived.

"Hey there, Ben," Detective Warren called as he zig-zagged through the rented tables and made his way toward them.

Gwen and Ben both whirled toward the swing. Parker's spirit was nowhere to be seen.

Ben gawked at her, his expression unreadable.

As he approached, Detective Warren said, "My shift ended, so I thought I'd stop by on my way to the motel." He nodded at Gwen. "How are you this evening, Mrs. Andrews?"

Though she couldn't fault the detective for being called to another crime scene that morning, he was the only one handy that she could blame for delaying her backyard cleanup. Unable to control her snarkiness, Gwen snapped, "I'll be better when your crime scene tape is removed."

Ben must have sensed her displeasure because he eased between the two of them. "Anything new in the case since we spoke earlier, Perry?"

Apparently tired from a long day of police work, Detective Warren lowered himself to the edge of the arbor platform and stretched out his legs. "Not so much new, but I never explained the final piece of evidence. There are footprint impressions in the garage floor concrete. The lab boys need to make castings."

"You think the indentations are connected to the death of the stepfather?" Ben asked.

Warren answered, "My best guess until I'm proven wrong."

Gwen inserted herself into their conversation. "Don't you think those shoeprints could have been made by my construction crew, or the paramedics, or even the medical examiner?"

"Possibly your construction crew, but if they're seasoned builders, I doubt it," Detective Warren responded. "The concrete was too hard this morning for either the EMTs or the M.E. to sink into it. I'm betting on the attacker."

Gwen pondered those imprints. Detective Warren had decided Frank's death was more than an accident. She couldn't wait to have a look at those shoe impressions.

"Thanks for the update," Ben said. "Let me know if anything else surfaces."

The on-loan detective struggled to his feet. "Sure thing. And I'll stay in touch with Mrs. Andrews while you're gone."

Gwen stared at the Columbo clone and then eyed Ben. Why was he was leaving town again so soon?

Warren shifted away from them. "I'll be on my way. Good evening, Mrs. Andrews. Please call me if anything relevant comes to mind." He retraced his steps through the rental tables and disappeared.

Ben swiveled in all directions. "Did the detective scare your husband's ghost or is Parker hiding?"

Gwen glanced around, seeing no trace of Parker's spirit. "I've never known him to play games. My guess is he didn't want to frighten Detective Warren."

Ben retreated to the arbor platform and lowered himself to the swing cushions. "This has been quite an experience."

Gwen assumed he referred not to Frank's death in the garage, but to meeting her husband's ghost. Her reaction to Parker's first appearance had been equally unsettling.

"Do your husband's appearances disturb you?" Ben asked.

Keeping her distance to give Ben breathing room, she replied, "The first time he materialized, I thought I was losing my mind. Now I find his visits comforting. He's answered my lifelong question of what happens when we depart this earth."

"How often do you see him?"

"No set schedule. He's appeared nearly a dozen times, once during a seance. My sister Tess couldn't see him, but Madame Eudora could. When I was preparing Jenna for the music competition, she spotted Parker at the edge of the woods, but I pretended I hadn't seen him. I was nervous about introducing you to him, Ben, but Parker insisted it was time you met."

Ben's intense grey eyes focused on her. "And he approves of you dating me?"

She laughed. "Parker not only approves, but he encouraged me to develop our friendship. He insists I live a full life."

"How many people know about his ghost?"

"Only Betty and Robert Owens at the Harbor Falls B&B."

"I should have guessed they would," Ben said. "Meeting their ghost Theo last December altered my belief in an afterlife. And now I've met your Parker."

She stepped to the swing and sat down, tucking her hands between her knees. "Let's talk about something else, like Detective Warren's mention of you being gone."

Ben frowned. "Unfortunately, Chief Brown approved my return to Oakfield to repeat my seminars for the officers who couldn't attend the first set. I'll be back Wednesday. I don't like leaving you all alone to deal with Warren's investigation, but I have no choice."

In response to the shivers running down her back, Gwen pushed herself to her feet. "I'm not alone. Jenna moved in after graduation and is living here all summer. She was with me this morning when we discovered Frank's body."

"Must have been quite a shock. How did she handle it?

"Surprisingly well. I sent her inside while I called 911. She hasn't said much about the death of her roommate's stepfather since her interview with Detective Warren this morning."

"Were you with her?"

"Unfortunately, no. When she walked over to the B&B to check on Allison, he tagged along."

"So, you have no idea what emotions Jenna might be keeping to herself?"

Gwen shook her head. "No. I'll see if I can get her to open up."

"Good. And I'm glad someone is here with you."

Gwen gave him a puzzled look. "Am I in danger?"

"I wouldn't go that far. Detective Warren considers Frank Hennessey's death suspicious, but it's too early to say whether it was an accident or intentional. If his death was intentional, then he was probably the target from the start."

"The patrolman photographed those shoe impressions this morning," Gwen offered. "And now the crime lab techs are coming back to make castings. Why would Detective Warren bother unless he thought Frank's death was something other an accident?"

When Ben didn't answer, she asked a different question. "What's your opinion of the detective?"

Leaning his elbows on his knees, Ben took in her ruined gardens. "Why do you ask?"

Gwen tilted her head. "He toggles between incompetence and being sharp as a tack."

"Don't let him fool you," Ben commented. "I've heard Warren doesn't miss much." He pulled out a notebook. "I need your version of yesterday's events and this morning's discovery of the body. Can you walk me through the details?"

"Sure." As she led Ben from one location to the next, carefully avoiding the cordoned-off areas, Gwen identified the people involved and their connection to wedding disaster, finishing with the arrival of Detective Warren.

He closed his notebook. "Thanks for the repeat."

"I'm as curious about what happened as any detective," Gwen admitted as she caught a movement. A second uniformed officer came into view at the top of the driveway.

Ben waved in greeting.

"Why another policeman?" Gwen whispered.

"The first patrolman stayed past his shift, so I called for a replacement when I first arrived."

"How long will this second man be here?"

"Until those castings are made tomorrow morning."

"I should feel safe having an officer on my property, but, somehow, he makes me more nervous." She glanced at Ben. "Is there any chance Frank's death was a random act?"

Ben grasped both her shoulders and turned her to face him. "Doubtful. Based on what I've learned about the stepfather, he may have offended one of the guests beyond reason. With all of them back in their homes on Cape Cod, you can relax."

"That's some small comfort," Gwen said. "I'm also relieved that the local newspaper hasn't shown up."

"Yes, well, the chief received a call from a reporter, but he told the guy this is a typical investigation and he had no comment." Ben glanced at his watch. "I hate to leave, Gwen, but I have to prepare for tomorrow's seminar. Walk me out?"

At the front curb, Ben paused beside his Corvette. "I'll stop over Wednesday when I get back." He leaned down and kissed her cheek. "Good to see you. Sorry we haven't gotten together lately. Soon though. Goodnight."

***

Settling in his leather driver's seat, Ben started the Corvette's engine and zoomed around the village green. As he waited at the North Street traffic light, recent events overlapped, each competing for his attention.

Gwen remained uppermost in his mind. During the past six months, with his hectic police duties plus her bevy of private music students, they'd managed only a handful of dates. He missed her easy smile and thoughtful conversations. Once again, the notion of retirement tempted him.

Gwen finding a dead wedding guest in her new garage had provided Ben with a great reason to see her. But he hadn't been prepared to meet the spirit of her deceased husband.

After he'd encountered the B&B's ghost last Christmas, he'd remained skeptical about spirits until Gwen confided in him about Parker's ghost. Ever since her revelation, Ben had been caught between anticipation and dread.

Finally meeting him, the transparent husband had eyed Ben up and down, taking his measure. To Ben's shock, Parker had spoken, and they'd exchanged a few now-forgotten words. What else might they have said to each other if Detective Warren's arrival hadn't chased Parker away? Now Ben hovered between relief and disappointment.

The driver behind Ben beeped and pointed at the traffic light, now green. Speeding toward his apartment on the south side of Harbor Falls, Ben knew that if he wanted to deepen his relationship with Gwen, he'd have to accept Parker as part of the package. After all, the husband's spirit had calmed the widow, providing comfort about the afterlife. Was this the reason Gwen maintained her composure when encountering a corpse? Or was she simply stronger than the average female?

Resentment overpowered Ben. He hadn't wanted to leave Gwen this evening to prepare his next presentation. Repeating his spousal abuse seminars only served to delay his involvement in the investigation of Frank Hennessey's death.

If Warren's hunch was right that Frank Hennessey's death hadn't been an accident, a guest must have been involved.

In that case, Gwen would be a valuable link to those potential suspects through her cousin Sally, similar to her connection with the garden club members last December. When Ben applied his experience to the evidence, the case would move right along.

After they resolved Frank's death, Gwen would be free from the tension of encountering yet another corpse, and Ben would be free to pursue a romance with the lady.

Chapter Twelve

... early morning, Monday

At eight o'clock on Monday morning, Gwen heard the rumble of a heavy truck and rushed outside. Sure enough, it was Matt and his construction crew.

"Matt," she called to him.

The burly contractor looked up as he buckled his tool belt low around his hips. "Good morning, Mrs. Andrews. We're ready to continue work on your garage. My truck's loaded with your lumber."

"Sorry, but not today." She pointed up the driveway. "See the yellow crime scene tape?"

He removed his sunglasses and stared. "What happened?"

Gwen quivered from an unexpected jolt of adrenalin. "I don't even know how to tell you, Matt." She clasped her hands to keep them from shaking. "Yesterday morning, I found one of the wedding guests impaled on the half-wall."

Matt blanched. "Christ. Was he dead?"

"Yes."

"But how in the world... never mind." Matt stared at her. "How are you holding up?"

Touched by his concern, Gwen kept her answer short. "I'm doing okay. I didn't think to call you."

Matt shifted his weight. "I hate to be mundane, but we were planning to finish the wall and start your framing today."

"I have no idea how soon the police will remove the tape."

"Well," Matt said, scratching his chin. "We'll unload the lumber beside the garage without disturbing the tape. Let me know when we can come back. I'll do my best to fit you in."

"I will, Matt. I'm so sorry."

"Not your fault, Mrs. Andrews. I'll wait to hear from you." His crew backed the truck up her driveway and unloaded the rafters, joists, and 2x4's. Ten minutes later, they drove away.

Back inside, Gwen found Jenna in her pajamas buttering a slice of oatmeal toast.

"Did you stop the construction crew in time?" Jenna took her first bite and chewed.

"I did," Gwen answered, topping off her coffee mug from the carafe. "Matt wasn't nasty about being sent away, but he wasn't pleased either."

"Your clean-up plans are on hold, too."

"True. Yesterday, I left a message for the rental company to delay the retrieval of their chairs and tables. I guess I'll drive down to your grandfather's old garden shop and see what I can buy for replacement flowers."

Jenna swallowed her last bite, swept crumbs into her palm, and dropped them into the basket below. She glanced at Gwen. "Is being there going to bother you?"

"Not bother me, though it will be odd to not see Hal restocking the display tables and chatting with customers."

"I bet he misses his nursery, though I doubt he'd admit it," Jenna speculated. "Next time we talk on the phone, I'll suggest he get a job at the local flower shop down in Florida."

Gwen chuckled. "He might go for your idea."

Jenna let her gaze travel from the music studio to the living room and dining room before focusing on Gwen. "You know, I can't blame you for refusing to move south with my granddad. How could you ever leave your unique home?"

"I don't have a clue." Gwen's more precise reason was Parker's spirit. One day soon, she needed to reveal his spectral visits to Jenna. Coming upon his ghost with no warning would scare the girl. The perfect time would present itself.

Gwen switched topics. "When do your master's courses begin at the college?"

"Wednesday morning. I'll be writing papers all summer. Should be fun." Jenna smirked in a lopsided fashion. "You know, Gwen, since we can't clean up your yard yet, I think I'll take my textbook to the library and read a few chapters."

"Can you wait a few minutes?" Gwen placed her hand on Jenna's arm. "There's something I want to ask you."

"Sure. What is it?"

"How are you doing after we came upon Frank's body?"

"I'm okay," Jenna replied with no hint of deception. "I didn't really know him. Allison told me he never mistreated her and Ashley, but he was always angry at their mother."

Gwen didn't doubt that fact for a second. "You go along to the library and read those chapters. I'll see you later."

Jenna bounded up the staircase to get dressed.

Until Dr. Otis determined if Frank's impalement had been an accident or a homicide, there was nothing to do but wait for an update. If his death had been caused by the hand of another, Gwen worried not only for herself, but for Jenna as well. Hopefully, there was no cause for alarm.

***

Gwen's cell phone vibrated at exactly nine – the man from the rental company. He sympathized with her situation, advising he'd simply tack on additional rental days until the tables and chairs could be retrieved. He'd wait for her call before sending over his panel truck.

A rumble out front urged Gwen to her front windows. A single tech emerged from the crime lab van with his satchel in hand and hurried up her walkway. She opened the heavy oak door before he had a chance to press the button, revealing his startled expression as his finger froze in mid-air.

"Good morning, Mrs. Andrews. Detective Warren instructed me to come back and gather the last piece of evidence. Sorry if I'm interrupting your day. I won't be long." Without waiting for her to respond, he hurried to the driveway.

Settling on the tapestry cushion of the window seat in her music room for a clear view of the tech's activity, Gwen followed his movements as he greeted the posted officer and ducked under the crime scene tape.

He entered the garage and paused near the half wall, leaning down to take photographs. After spraying a liquid onto the

83

concrete, he removed a bag of white powder from his satchel, added water from a bottle, then squeezed and shook the bag. Next, he placed frames in several spots and dribbled the bag's content over his fingers to the surface below. Tucking the empty bag into his satchel, he stood aside and checked his watch every few minutes.

Ten minutes later, he pulled a pencil from his pocket and squatted down to write something, then waited a second time. Another ten minutes passed before he pried the castings from the concrete floor and tucked each into its own evidence bag. Sealing the openings, he stacked them inside his satchel, hustled to his van, and drove away.

Curious about his task, Gwen unlocked her French door and stepped onto the rear deck, intending to inspect the garage floor before ridding her property of the excess litter.

The yellow tape glared at her. Damn it all. Had the tech forgotten to remove the pesky tape or were the police not ready to release her back yard? She saw no sign of the officer who had been posted there. He must have left with the tech.

Gwen placed a call to the police department and was patched through to the detective unit.

Detective Warren answered on the third ring. "Yes, Mrs. Andrews, what can I do for you?"

Gwen controlled her aggravation. "How much longer will the crime scene tape remain in place?"

"Sorry, ma'am. The officer should have taken it down when the crime lab tech was finished. Tell you what… I wanted to have another chat with you anyway. Why don't I drive over now and take care of both?'"

What more could the detective possibly want to ask her? Gwen had no more details to offer. "That's fine."

As she waited for his arrival, she paced past the staircase. Amber strolled down the steps and rubbed against her mistress' ankle. Leaning down, Gwen picked up the cat and straightened. Dizziness overcame her and she felt her way to the landing, sitting down hard, all the while gripping Amber.

"Sorry, sweetie, I nearly dropped you." The feline purred as Gwen's light-headedness receded. "This is only a delayed reaction to the recent turmoil," she whispered in the cat's ear. "Or maybe I stood up too quickly."

Someone knocked on the front door. Not everyone noticed the doorbell button. Gwen released the squirming Amber, who scampered upstairs.

Detective Warren shuffled into Gwen's foyer, gazing at her sideways like a chastised child. "Good morning, Mrs. Andrews. I'm here to remove the crime scene tape. Do you want to talk first or the other way around?"

Surprised by the dual questions, Gwen answered, "The order doesn't matter to me."

Without another word, he backed down the steps and headed around to the side yard.

From the French door, she watched him roll the massive amounts of yellow tape into a trash bag he'd pulled from his raincoat pocket. As he tucked away the last piece and made his way to the upper deck, Gwen stepped outside. "What else do you want to ask me, Detective?"

Dropping the bag to the boards, he pulled out his notebook and repeated his questions of Sunday morning, comparing her answers to his previous scribbles. His final question brought her up short. "When I interviewed Frank Hennessey's wife on Sunday, I noticed some bruises on her cheek and her wrist. Are you aware of any marital abuse?"

Gwen had noticed those same cheek bruises. Worrisome, but if the detective was thinking Robin wanted to do away with her husband, Gwen wasn't about to implicate the woman based on unfounded assumptions.

To avoid an outright lie, and unwilling to influence his conclusions with her amateur observations, Gwen formed her answer with care. "I met Robin on Saturday within an hour of the wedding. If there were any problems in her marriage, she didn't share them with me." Gwen steered him to the question she wanted answered. "Have you learned anything else about Mr. Hennessey's death, Detective?"

"Too early to say, ma'am. I can't go much further until I receive Dr. Otis' report and the lab results." He flipped his notebook closed. "I heard you were involved in several previous cases, so I don't mind telling you there are three possible scenarios. One, Mr. Hennessey was drunk, lost his balance and fell backwards onto those cinder blocks. Two, he decided he was better off dead and threw himself onto that rebar spike, planning to impale himself and end his life. But suicides are not usually so impromptu, and most people leave a note of apology."

When his pause lasted too long, Gwen asked, "And what's number three?"

Detective Warren clicked his tongue. "I'll be honest, Mrs. Andrews. I think his death was the result of foul play."

Chapter Thirteen

… late morning, Monday

The moment Detective Warren drove away, Gwen called Matt to resume work on her garage. He promised to send a partial crew first thing the next morning.

Next, she texted the rental man to pick up the tables and chairs at his convenience.

Finally free to roam about her property, she made a beeline for the new concrete floor. Despite the detective's declaration that the surface was cured, she stepped cautiously. When she glanced behind her, there was no indication of her sneaker soles, so she hurried to the half wall and glanced down.

Multiple sets of footprints indented the concrete's surface. The partial toes of shoes or boots pointed in all directions, simulating a ballet of sorts. Because they overlapped and were mangled, the sizes, shapes, and textures were virtually impossible for Gwen to distinguish one from the other.

Last evening, as Detective Warren updated Ben, he mentioned they could have been made by Frank's attacker. He'd surely have difficulty matching the distorted imprints on the lab tech's castings to actual footwear bottoms.

Gwen held tight to half of the theory she'd expressed to both Ben and the temporary detective. Okay, the concrete had hardened before the EMTs and medical examiner arrived on the scene. But those impressions could have been made by Matt's construction crew. Exactly when had the concrete hardened to the point where nothing could have been pressed into it? For all she knew, those imprints had nothing to do with Frank's death. Gwen might be right. But she could be wrong.

When she and Jenna came upon Frank's body, his legs had dangled downwards so the bottoms of his shoes hadn't been visible. Gwen had no memory of concrete clinging to his soles.

If Frank's death were deemed no accident, could Robin have been the attacker? Gwen peered more closely at the imprints. They all appeared to be flat-soled, with no female heel indentations, unless they'd been smushed. Again, Gwen recalled her limited recall of meeting Robin. The long-sleeved jacket and pants came to mind, but not the woman's footwear. Had she been wearing heels or flats?

Had there been more than one assailant? To Gwen's amateur eye, none of the imprints were clear enough to decide.

Even if the crime lab succeeded in matching those garbled imprints to someone's shoes, how could anyone know for certain if Frank's death had been an accident or intentional?

Not knowing if a record of the mish-mashed impressions would become useful, Gwen pulled out her cell phone, squatted down, and snapped digital images from several angles. Satisfied, she tucked her phone into her jeans pocket, squared her shoulders, and headed off to begin the clean-up of her messy yard.

From the potting shed, she grabbed black trash bags and began collecting the sodden debris. Scorched paper table covers. The remains of luminary bags. Seared napkins. Charred leaves and twigs, every fragment trapped within the tangle of bushes, grasses, and perennials. Gwen stooped and stretched for each piece, putting a strain on her aging knees.

A squeal of tires out front announced a visitor. With a grunt, Gwen straightened and cast a glance toward the driveway.

Cousin Sally barreled into view. Spotting Gwen, she hustled between the forsythia bushes and the fishpond as fast as her legs could carry her, shrieking, "Robin's been arrested!"

Sally threw her arms around Gwen and sobbed.

The trash bag fell to the ground as Gwen patted her cousin's back. "Why?" she asked, though Gwen's answer had already begun to form. "On what grounds?"

Sally sniffed as she pulled away. "The same detective came to the B&B and read Robin her rights about remaining silent and finding an attorney. Oh, Gwen, my girl is being accused of her husband's murder! You have to help me prove she had nothing to do with Frank's death."

Unsure if she wanted to get involved, Gwen countered, "But I'm not a detective, Sally."

Grabbing a tissue from her sleeve, Sally wiped at her tears. "Maybe not, but your sister mentioned during our Christmas dinner that you helped solve a murder or two."

"True," Gwen admitted with caution, "but the police chief doesn't like me sticking my nose into their investigations." She chose not to mention that she'd been enlisted by Ben during December's B&B case.

Overriding the objection, Sally said, "So, we'll do our snooping without telling the police. Please, Gwen, we need to figure out who else wanted Frank dead. I'll extend my stay at the B&B so I can help you. We'll be sleuthing partners."

Sally – as Robin's mother – automatically believed her daughter innocent of wrongdoing. Having met Robin only two days earlier, Gwen had no clue about the woman's mindset, not to mention her physical ability to lift a man and drop him.

Worried about Sally's goal to prove her daughter innocent, Gwen was concerned that if she denied her cousin's plea, Sally might go off half-cocked and get herself into trouble.

The temptation to solve another mystery pulled at Gwen and she began to justify her involvement. Her private music students were on summer break. Ben was busy with police work. Replanting her flower beds would take no more than a few hours, her doctor's appointment a blip on the calendar.

But would Sally be more a hindrance than a help?

Several years earlier – when Gwen herself was considered the most likely suspect in a police investigation – Jenna's grandfather Hal had been her reluctant sleuthing partner. The following year, Gwen and her sister Tess had proved best friend Liz innocent of attacking the shopkeeper adjacent to her bookstore. And then Gwen had worked with Ben during the B&B case because of her membership in the Harbor Falls garden club.

And one final reason to help Sally prove her daughter innocent... what if Detective Warren was wrong about Robin's guilt? The person who'd placed Frank atop those cinder blocks would be roaming free while Robin sat in a jail cell. Gwen's sense of justice reared its head and finalized her decision.

She rested her hand on Sally's plump shoulder. "Why don't you stay with me while we sort this out? Jenna's in my guest room for the summer, but there's a comfortable daybed in my second-floor sitting room."

Sally again gripped Gwen in a tight hug. "You can't know how much I appreciate your generosity. I'll go pack my things at the B&B and be right back."

"Do your granddaughters know their mother's been arrested?"

"No," Sally answered, her expression crestfallen, "As Detective Warren was arresting Robin, she told me not to call the girls unless she couldn't convince the authorities that she was innocent. Robin hadn't alerted them about Frank's death either because she didn't want to ruin Allison's honeymoon or worry Ashley until it was unavoidable. I'll let both girls know when the time is right."

Sally trundled down the driveway and hefted herself into her white van.

Through the trees of the village green, Gwen watched her cousin's progress as she zoomed around Library Lane, through the North Street traffic light, and down Harbor Hill, disappearing behind the B&B.

Chapter Fourteen

… mid-day, Monday

When Gwen's cell phone vibrated, she pulled it from her jeans pocket and chatted briefly with the rental man.

The second she disconnected, it buzzed again. Groaning at the caller ID, she punched the green button.

"Hello, Detective Warren."

"Mrs. Andrews, I called to let you know I've arrested Frank Hennessey's wife for his murder."

Without admitting Sally had alerted her earlier but curious about his evidence, Gwen said, "So quickly, Detective?"

On the other end of the line, he cleared his throat. "I'm not obligated to explain, but his wife covered all the requirements… motive, opportunity, and means."

Unsatisfied, Gwen failed to disguise her disbelief. "I find it hard to swallow that Robin would do such a thing on the day her daughter was to be married."

He hesitated. "Crimes of passion are never planned, Mrs. Andrews. Think about how angry she must have been when her husband collapsed and ruined the march down the aisle. Excuse me, I have to go."

After the line went dead, Gwen stared at her phone. He hadn't shared any clues proving Robin was the guilty party.

Could it have been those impressions in the concrete floor? Gwen again racked her brain to recall Robin's footwear but came up empty. On Saturday, she'd never looked down at the woman's feet. Besides, who could match anyone's footwear to those overlapping imprints?

In case Detective Warren hadn't alerted Ben, Gwen dialed his cell phone and was passed to his voicemail. Damn. He was tangled in his Oakfield seminars. She left a message, thinking he'd call her later.

One second later, her cell phone vibrated. She pressed the answer button. "Ben, I didn't think I'd hear from you so soon."

"We're on a break. Anything wrong, Gwen?"

"Detective Warren arrested the stepfather's wife."

"Let me guess. You don't think she's guilty."

"I don't know Robin well enough to have an opinion one way or the other, but my cousin Sally – Robin's mother – is convinced her daughter's innocent."

"Not unexpected from a parent."

"Sally begged me to help her find his real attacker."

"And you couldn't resist the temptation?" Ben's tone was partially accusatory, partially admiring, partially amused.

Gwen wanted and needed Ben's support, so took care not to be argumentative. "If Sally's instincts are accurate, an innocent woman has been arrested, and the criminal is out there thinking he got off scot-free."

For a few long moments, Ben said nothing, and then, "I don't doubt your sleuthing abilities, Gwen. In the past, you've delved into sources the department doesn't consider relevant, each time flushing out the criminal."

"Thanks, Ben. Will Detective Warren object to me and Sally searching for someone else to arrest?"

Again, Ben hesitated. "From what I know of Warren's history, he won't like you questioning his judgement and he'll likely reject whatever you and your cousin uncover. When he arrested Sally's daughter, his investigation ended."

"I don't think he looked very hard for other suspects."

"Sorry, Gwen, I can't comment until I review Warren's case file and understand his reasoning. But I won't waste my breath asking you not to get involved. Have you formulated a plan with your cousin?"

"I'll suggest we visit the photographer Robin hired and view his photos without telling him why. If we're lucky, one of his images will show a guest with Frank on the chaise lounge. Hopefully, we can identify the other man."

"Or woman," Ben added.

Bolstered by Ben's encouraging reaction, Gwen continued. "The photographer's first name is Jeremy, but I know nothing else about him. Sally and I need his contact info from Robin. Would it be possible for us to visit her at the police station?"

"I'll text the chief and ask if he'll allow it." From the background, someone spoke to Ben. "Listen, Gwen, can you and Sally go no further than the photographer until I get back?"

"I'll try, Ben, but she's chomping at the bit."

"Understandable. Where's she staying?"

"She's checking out of the B&B and moving in with me."

"Good. Try to hold her enthusiasm in check." Noises behind Ben indicated the return of his audience. "Sorry, Gwen, I've got to go. I'll call you this evening."

"Break a leg, Ben." She missed the white-haired detective. The few minutes they'd carved out the previous evening – including his introduction to Parker's spirit – had only increased her yearning for Ben's male companionship.

She lowered herself to the edge of a planter box and contemplated the changes in her life over the past few years. First, Parker's unexpected death and her mourning until his spirit eased her misery. Enter Jenna and her grandfather Hal, who became Gwen's good buddy until she refused to move south, and he'd shattered their friendship.

And now Ben. Gwen had first met the white-haired detective while proving her best friend Liz innocent of attacking a nasty cigar bar owner. At first, Gwen had antagonized Ben with her unauthorized snooping. But when she exposed the culprit, she'd proven her worth as an amateur sleuth. Ben's respect inspired him to enlist her help last Christmas to resolve a death at the Harbor Falls B&B.

With their on-again, off-again dating habit, would they ever move beyond two people who shared an interest in solving mysteries?

She'd like nothing more than to carve out more time with Ben. Working on Frank's case would surely put them in the same place at the same time.

Chapter Fifteen

… early afternoon, Monday

"I'm back!" Sally's strident voice carried through the foyer all the way back to Gwen's kitchen.

Hurrying past the staircase, Gwen spotted Jenna struggling to drag an oversized suitcase across the threshold.

Behind her, Sally carried more luggage. "Jenna arrived the same time as me, so she's giving me a hand."

Snorting, Jenna said, "This is heavy, Sally. What's in here?"

Tapping her cheek, Sally answered, "Well, there's my wedding outfit plus dress shoes. Something more casual for the reception. A jacket and sweatshirt in case it gets chilly. Grub clothes for the ride back to the Cape. Assorted toiletries and my hairdryer. My second husband always complained I packed too much. That's one of the reasons I divorced him."

Gwen caught that there had been other reasons. How many husbands had Sally married and divorced? Her marital history would probably surface while the two of them searched for Frank's attacker. Diverting the discussion, Gwen tossed out, "Let's get your things upstairs."

Grabbing a smaller makeup bag, she led them up the staircase to the midway split, taking the righthand flight of steps toward the sitting room along the rear wall.

Sally stepped to the daybed fronting the bank of windows. On either side, two chairs with an end table between provided conversation areas. "What a delightful space. And the view of your gardens…" Sally's voice trailed off as she peeked outside.

"My husband Parker was a clever architect," Gwen said to explain the design.

"I didn't realize. Wish I'd met him." Sally gazed around. "I'll be quite comfortable here while we prove Robin has been wrongly arrested."

Jenna stepped between them. "You two are planning to find the guy who attacked Frank?"

"Right," Sally answered. "My Robin doesn't have the strength or the confidence to attempt such a heinous act." Sally waved toward Gwen. "Did you know our hostess has solved a few mysteries?"

Jenna's eyes widened. "There was more than one?"

Gwen's skin warmed. "Two more, actually. The nasty man who opened a cigar bar adjacent to my friend Liz's bookstore plus the garden club member who fell down the back stairs at the bed & breakfast."

Sally's turn to be surprised. "The B&B where my family was staying?"

"The very one," Gwen answered, wishing she hadn't phrased it in such a beguiling way.

Thankfully, Jenna and Sally didn't ask for details. Gwen had no desire to revisit the final moments of each case when her own life had been in peril. A touch of fear niggled at her belly. Would history repeat itself during their search for Frank's attacker? Would she regret her agreement to help Sally?

Ignoring the ominous prospect, Gwen pointed toward the mezzanine as it curved around the west end of the second floor. "Sally, you'll share my bathroom. When you're finished, unlock the opposite door. If you don't, I'll have to walk all the way around, through Jenna's room and this sitting room."

"Don't worry. I won't forget," Sally promised.

"Good," Gwen said, hoping her instructions stuck. "After you've unpacked, you can tuck your luggage under my craft bench down there." She indicated the opposite end of the sitting room before walking to a sideboard snugged against the mezzanine rail. "I'll empty these drawers for you and bring up a clothes rack for things that need hanging. If you need anything, say so. When you're done, meet me in the kitchen for a cup of tea and we'll make a plan."

When Jenna dropped onto the daybed, Amber jumped into her lap and began to purr. "I'll stay up here and keep Sally company while she unpacks."

Fifteen minutes later, Sally arrived at the island counter. "Jenna's still playing with your cat. She said she'll be down in a little while."

Before Gwen had a chance to suggest contacting the photographer, the rental truck rumbled to a stop out front. Both women hurried outside and directed the crew to the reception tables and folding chairs. Within minutes, the muscular men had hauled everything into their truck and driven away.

As they re-entered the kitchen, Sally said, "Thanks for contacting the rental company. I was going to call them myself until you found Frank's body and all hell broke loose."

"Making a phone call was no big deal, Sally."

"Well, still, I appreciate it."

Hugging Amber, Jenna ambled past them to the French door. "Gwen, when did you clean up your back yard? I was planning to help you."

"Early this morning," Gwen answered. "As soon as Detective Warren removed the crime scene tape, I picked up the litter. It wasn't as big a job as I thought it would be. With the tables and chairs gone, the backyard looks less cluttered, but I still need to replant quite a few flowers."

Shifting the cat into one arm, Jenna lifted her free hand and stared at her thumb. "You'd think after being raised on grandad's nursery I'd have a green thumb, but I swear it's black." She grinned. "Still, there must be something I can do."

"There is," Gwen confirmed. "You can climb my ladder and remove Ashley's lights. If they worked, I'd leave them up."

"Sounds like something I can handle." Jenna released the squirming Amber to nibble cat food beneath the island overhang, then rested her forearms on the counter, looking from Gwen to Sally and back again. "How do you plan to prove Robin didn't have anything to do with Frank's death?"

"First," Gwen answered, "I've asked Ben if we can visit Robin at the police station. She needs to tell us the full name of her photographer so we can contact him at his studio."

"Smart!" Sally commented. "Maybe his pictures captured someone walking Frank to the garage,".

Gwen instantly upgraded Sally's instincts as a sidekick. "We can only hope. But I was also wondering if there's a photo of Robin's shoes. There aren't any high-heeled imprints."

"That'll convince them it wasn't my girl," Sally insisted.

Gwen dreaded Sally's reaction if the pictures proved Robin was the guilty party.

Sally continued. "But I don't want to tell the photographer about Robin's arrest. What if Jeremy asks why she's not picking up his photographs? After all, she paid the deposit."

Jenna sat forward, her expression eager. "How about she caught a cold after getting sprayed by the firemen's hoses?"

Gwen cast an eye in Jenna's direction. "We might not want to mention the firehoses. His camera might have gotten wet. But a summer cold sounds reasonable. If we're allowed to visit Robin this afternoon, she can provide Jeremy's details and you can call him for an appointment tomorrow afternoon."

"Why not in the morning?" Sally asked.

"Because I have a doctor's appointment at ten,"

Jenna laid her hand on Gwen's arm. "You mentioned lightheadedness the other day. I'd feel better if you'd let me drive you to his office."

Gwen protested. "You're being overly cautious."

"But why take the chance?" Jenna challenged.

"All right, all right," Gwen acquiesced. "You can chauffer me. What are you doing with yourself this afternoon, Jenna?"

"I'm walking over to Baylies to double-check my summer classes. I can't believe I'll start on my master's day after tomorrow." Jenna pivoted back, her forehead wrinkling. "Now I'm worried about the two of you chasing a criminal."

Sally waved off Jenna's concern. "Don't you worry about us. With Gwen's experience solving mysteries, I'm sure she can keep us out of trouble."

Moving one hand behind her back, Gwen crossed her fingers that Sally's prediction would ring true.

***

Resting against the kitchen sink, Gwen recited Ben's text to Sally. "*I've spoken with Chief Brown. He'll allow only Robin's mother to visit. He'll call you with the time.*"

"That's progress," Sally commented.

"Have you found a lawyer for Robin?"

"I'm waiting for a call back from my divorce attorney."

"Can he handle a murder case?"

Sally shook her graying curls. "I doubt it, but he can recommend someone."

Gwen's cell phone buzzed.

The police chief spoke into her ear. "Sorry I can't let you tag along, Gwen, but murder suspects have different rules. Tell your cousin to be here within the hour. Her daughter's being transferred down to Plymouth by the end of the day."

"Thanks, Mike. I'll let her know."

"Listen to me," the police chief chided. "I know you well enough to sense you're not satisfied with Detective Warren's

102

arrest. I'd prefer you don't search for a different suspect. Not because I doubt your sleuthing abilities – we all know how successful you've been in the past – but I'd hate to see you land in another life-and-death situation."

Gwen glanced at Sally. "Not my plan either, Chief."

His stern words continued. "Please wait until Ben is back."

"He suggested the same thing. Sally and I are only gathering information."

"Well, you be careful, Gwen." The police chief disconnected.

"Well?" Sally asked. "When can I visit my girl?"

"Within the hour."

"Where's the police station?"

"Drive around the village green to the traffic light. Take a left onto North Street and drive about a mile. The station sits on the left. The visitor's parking lot is out front and well-marked. Our chief's name is Mike Brown. Tell the desk sergeant you have an appointment."

"Thanks, Gwen. Will you be here when I get back?'

"No idea. I'm driving to the garden shop to buy replacement flowers." Gwen opened a kitchen drawer and extended a spare key. "This unlocks my front door, which I've learned to lock whenever I leave."

"Thanks." Sally closed her hand around the key.

Standing at the front door, Gwen watched Sally's white van until it disappeared.

Chapter Sixteen

… mid-afternoon, Monday

As Gwen pulled into the dirt lane of Jenkins Garden Shop, she made a point of checking the name carved into the wooden sign. When she'd bought her initial batch of annuals a month ago, she hadn't noticed that the name remained unchanged. But that wouldn't have told her Hal hadn't sold the nursery. She'd have assumed the new owners kept the name for recognition.

No matter. Her mission was to buy enough plants to refill her flower beds. She parked and strolled toward the half-empty display tables.

"Gwen, is that you? Back again?"

Recognizing the voice, Gwen waved to the gray-haired woman behind the register. "Hi, Maggie. Afraid so. I have to replant many of the flowers in my gardens."

"Oh, dear," Maggie muttered. "I hope there wasn't a problem with our specimens you bought last month."

"No, no, not at all. An accident ruined mine."

Maggie nodded in understanding. "I've had the same problem myself. Usually from over fertilizing."

Without correcting Maggie's assumption, Gwen craned her neck to inspect the nearest plants. "I heard this morning the nursery hasn't been sold. I thought Hal had closed the deal."

Maggie's head wagged. "Nope. Oscar and his brother are battling the bank for their loan."

With no warning, Hal appeared around the back corner of the garden shop carrying a boxful of colorful New Guinea impatiens. He spotted Gwen and stopped dead in his tracks.

Shocked to see him and tongue-tied, Gwen stood frozen.

Hal stared. "I didn't expect to see you here."

Pushing aside the shock of seeing him, she regained her composure. "Ditto about you."

He placed the box of flowers near the register. "Maggie, can you put these out?"

"Sure." She lifted the flat and headed for the tables.

Hal focused his bright blue eyes on Gwen. "Haven't you bought and planted all the flowers you need for the summer?"

Though his words were accusatory, his tone was not. Gwen relied on her innate gentleness to keep their conversation civil. "It's a long story, and I won't bore you with it. How long have you been back in Harbor Falls?"

"I flew in late last night."

"Does Jenna know?"

His head shook. "Not yet. I'll call her as soon as I get a chance. Thanks again for inviting her to stay in your guestroom this summer. She's thrilled to be living with you. How's that working out?"

"She's a model house guest."

His laugh reminded Gwen of old times. No cliché applied to them more accurately than *'nothing stays the same'*.

Gwen decided to prompt their small talk. "Jenna mentioned you haven't sold the nursery."

Hal shuffled his feet, his boots caked with dried mud. "Yesterday my foreman Oscar called to say he and his brother finally secured their loan. We're signing papers this Friday."

"So that's why you flew back?"

"Partially. When I moved to Florida, I hired Oscar and his brother to take care of the place during the winter months while they tussled with the bank. When the selling season began, the demands overwhelmed them. I flew up early to lend a hand for a few days until the closing."

"For a second there, I thought you decided to be a snowbird." Her peripheral vision caught sight of a woman – her long tanned legs exposed below shorts – moving into the doorframe of Hal's old farmhouse situated behind the garden shop. The blonde surveyed them from a distance.

Gwen had no right to be jealous. She and Hal had been platonic friends, and she'd never allowed anything more serious. Still, she felt her skin warm. "Who's your lady friend?"

He glanced toward the porch and waved. "Her name is Joleen. She's a divorcee who lives around the corner from me, closer to the beach." When he looked back at Gwen, his face fell. "Don't misunderstand. She and I are only neighbors. When I mentioned I was visiting Harbor Falls, she said she'd always wanted to see New England and asked to tag along."

Gwen backed away. "You don't owe me any explanations. Your life is your own, Hal."

106

He gripped her arm to halt her retreat. "You know I'm still hoping you'll change your mind and move down to my Florida cottage. You'd love it, Gwen. The beach is only a block away, lots of parks for walking and restaurants for meals."

"Sounds perfect for you, but you know I don't want to leave Harbor Falls." His insults to her intelligence in December came to mind. She shook off his grasp and wiped at the dirt he'd deposited on her skin. "If you'll excuse me, I need to buy lots and lots of flowers."

He fell in step beside her. "Can I help you choose? Not that you need my opinion. You were always an excellent gardener."

"Thanks, but I'd rather check the tables by myself." She grabbed the handle of a nearby red wagon and placed it between them.

Still, Hal followed her into the retail area. "If you're purchasing a large quantity, how will you get them home? My delivery truck can hold more than your little four-door."

Gwen had given no thought to transporting the plants. Using her own car, she'd have to make several trips to cart them back home. This was not the time to dwell on their ruined friendship. "Sure. You'd allow me to drive your truck?"

"No, no. You'd need a special driver's license. I'll deliver your plants before the end of the day. And I can surprise Jenna at the same time."

Chapter Seventeen

… late afternoon, Monday

The moment Gwen unlocked her front door, an enticing aroma lured her to the kitchen.

"What are you cooking?" Gwen called out as she approached Sally standing at the stove.

Sally whirled around, her spoon clattering onto the stove's glass surface, her hand flying to her generous bosom. "Gwen! I didn't hear you come in. You shouldn't sneak up on a person."

"Sorry," Gwen apologized.

Ripping a paper towel from the roll, Sally wiped up the splatters. "What did you ask me?"

"I asked what you're cooking. It smells wonderful."

After rinsing off the spoon, Sally again stirred the contents. "My version of Tuscany soup. There's something soothing about cooking." She slipped the lid onto the pot.

"That's one of my favorites. What's your recipe?"

A glimmer of a smile lit up Sally's otherwise somber expression. "Sauté sweet Italian sausage along with slices of hot sausage, add beef broth and chunks of potato. Simmer for a half hour, add chopped fresh kale, and simmer for another ten minutes. Finish with a bit of cream. Serve with Italian bread and you've got a complete meal."

"Sounds easy enough," Gwen commented. "But you didn't have to make supper."

"Well, you opened your home to me during Robin's crisis. The least I can do is prepare a meal or two."

"If all your creations smell as good as that sausage soup, I won't refuse your bartering suggestion."

Sally rinsed her hands and placed her fists on her ample hips. "I know what you're thinking. I never refuse my cooking either. I have a plaque in my Falmouth kitchen: *'Skinny Cooks Can't Be Trusted'*."

Gwen chuckled. "I like *'Life is short, eat dessert first.'*"

"I've seen that one, too." Sally's face settled into a more serious expression. "Want to hear about my visit with Robin?"

Gwen perched on an island stool. "Of course. How's she holding up?"

Sally sat on the opposite stool and folded her hands on the granite surface. "She's scared, of course, and relieved to hear you and I are searching for the person who attacked Frank. She kept repeating she didn't do it, Gwen, and I believe her."

Gwen nodded, again worrying about Sally's reaction if they found evidence showing Robin as the attacker.

"Our visit was cut short when the officers arrived to transfer her to Plymouth. She'll be arraigned tomorrow morning."

"But you haven't hired a defense attorney yet," Gwen pointed out.

Sally made a face. "I'm waiting for my divorce attorney to recommend someone. In the meantime, your police chief told me the court will assign a public defender to lead Robin through the arraignment. When I hire a lawyer, he'll take over her defense. She's accused of murder, so my girl will stay in jail until the trial. I have no idea how long she'll be there." Sobs suddenly racked Sally's entire body.

Placing her hand on her cousin's shoulder, Gwen spoke in a quiet voice. "We'll get through this, Sally." The platitude was an attempt to give Sally hope. "Did you ask her for the photographer's name and address?"

Straightening, Sally pulled a tissue from her sleeve and wiped her eyes. "I did. Fortunately, she'd tucked Jeremy's info into her suitcase. We're lucky, too, that the detective didn't confiscate her luggage. I'd loaded her luggage, along with Frank's belongings, into my van this morning." Leaning sideways, she retrieved a manila folder from the other end of the counter and slid it across to Gwen. "I found her file in a zippered section. I've only glanced at the contents to make sure it was the right one."

Gwen pulled out the papers and flipped through the documents. "We'll delve into these details together." She removed the photographer's quote. "Huh. This is a surprise."

Sally leaned across the counter. "What is?"

"I assumed Jeremy's studio was located in a town on the Cape, but this quote shows a Plymouth address."

Sally rotated the paper, her forehead wrinkling. "What a relief. We won't have to deal with the bridge traffic. Should I call him now?"

"Might as well," Gwen answered. "Ask if we can stop by tomorrow afternoon. Tell him the kids eloped and you want to surprise them with a wedding album, even though the ceremony was abandoned. If he asks why Robin isn't calling him, use Jenna's reason that your daughter caught a cold. Order prints of all his photos. I have no idea how much he'll charge."

"Whatever it costs, I'll pay." Sally removed her phone from her apron pocket and punched in his phone number, giving Gwen a thumb's up when Jeremy answered:

"Jeremy, this is Robin's mother Sally."

She paused while he responded.

"Yes, it was a shame that their wedding ceremony was cut short. Allison and Cole eloped and are on their honeymoon. I want to surprise them with a wedding album, so I'd like to order prints of all your photos."

Again, she paused to let him speak.

"An online gallery? No, no, that won't be necessary. If you could please print every photo you snapped on Saturday."

When Sally made a face, Gwen assumed Jeremy was resisting her request.

"Oh, the size? I think 4x6 is all we need." She paused. "I'm aware this will cost more than your original quote. How soon can I stop by to pick up the prints?"

Jeremy answered.

"That's fine. I'll see you tomorrow afternoon."

Sally pressed the disconnect button. "Boy, that was like pulling teeth. But he'll do it."

"What time?" Gwen asked

"Two o'clock. That doesn't interfere with your doctor's appointment in the morning."

Sally's aggravated expression morphed into anticipation. "He didn't ask about Robin, so I didn't have to fib. He'll recalculate his quote." Sally waved aside the unknown amount. "Like I said, I'll pay whatever he charges."

Gwen pulled a legal pad from a kitchen drawer, flipped to a blank page, and noted the appointment.

Pursing her lips, Sally said, "Well, Gwen, I guess we're on our way to proving my girl didn't kill her husband."

"One step at a time, Sally," Gwen cautioned her cousin. "One step at a time."

Sally let out a breath of relief. "By the way, was your flower-buying mission a success?"

"Yes, but it came with a surprise," Gwen answered.

Sally raised one eyebrow. "Do tell."

Pleased to provide her cousin with a distraction, Gwen explained. "You wouldn't know this, but Jenna's grandfather used to own the Jenkins Nursery and Garden Shop south of town. He and I were good friends for a time. We came close to a romantic involvement, but I always resisted. Last December, we had a falling-out when he decided to move to Florida and insisted I should follow him like a puppy dog. When I refused, he said some hurtful words that ruined our friendship."

Gwen paused, deciding she'd shared enough of her personal history. "I thought he was in Florida until he appeared around the corner of the garden shop." She glanced at the kitchen clock. "He'll be here any time now to deliver my plants and surprise Jenna."

Her eyebrow still halfway up her forehead, Sally put her finger to her lips. "Mums the word."

Gwen glanced around. "Is she back from the college?"

Sally pointing her chin toward the staircase. "Upstairs."

***

The rumble of a truck alerted Gwen to Hal's arrival. She hurried outside and watched his nursery van back up the driveway, stopping several feet short of the garage entrance.

After he exited the vehicle, she joined him as he opened the rear door. "Thanks for delivering my flowers, Hal."

"No big deal, Gwen. Besides, it's a good opportunity to surprise Jenna. Is she here?"

"My cousin Sally is inside. She said your granddaughter is upstairs in the guest room. I don't know if she heard your truck pull in." She waved toward the cavity of the truck. "If you can unload the plants onto the driveway, I'll carry them back." She hefted a flat of New Guinea impatiens and strode toward her shed where a hose waited. Placing her first batch in the shade of the trees, Gwen swung around and nearly bumped into Hal, his arms filled with begonias in bright red, pink, and white. "Delivering these was enough, Hal. You don't have to haul them back here as well."

"Common courtesy, Gwen. I can't let you lug all these containers by yourself."

Wary he would again bring up the sore subject of her moving to Florida, she kept her response simple. "Thanks."

Though she'd expected Hal to nurse his resentment of her refusal to leave Harbor Falls, his attitude remained quite civil. She credited his lady friend Joleen as a calming influence.

After several more trips, he placed the final flat in the shade. "That's the last of them." He glanced around her back yard. "What happened here? Is this the long story you didn't want to share earlier?"

She took a deep breath and huffed. "No harm in telling you. On Saturday evening, a wedding ceremony for my cousin Sally's granddaughter was supposed to take place beneath my trellis, but it never happened. First, the bride's stepfather collapsed as he walked her down the aisle. Then the luminary bags hung in my red bark maples caught fire. They dropped onto the paper tablecloths and embers flew around the yard, landing on dried leaves and twigs. I called 911 before I grabbed my kitchen extinguisher. The wedding guests did their best to help. Luckily, the firemen arrived quickly, but the water from their hoses soaked everything and everybody. My flower beds were trampled in the process. As you might have guessed, the wedding was cancelled."

Gwen debated whether to mention finding the stepfather's impaled body but didn't know if Jenna would want her grandfather to know about the gruesome discovery. There was no point in continuing the story. If Jenna wanted to tell him, that was her decision.

"What a nightmare, Gwen. I'm so sorry." He lifted his arms toward her, quickly dropping them to his side. "It's a good thing Oscar and his brother raised enough flowers in the greenhouses to provide these replacements." He tore his eyes from her face and glanced toward the back of the old library. "Guess I need to let Jenna know I'm here."

As he spoke, Jenna exited through the French door, raced across the decks and the lawn, and threw her arms around his neck, nearly knocking him over. "Granddad, why didn't you tell me you were coming up?"

To give them privacy, Gwen began to water her new plants, close enough to overhear their conversation.

Hal led Jenna to a spot on the other side of the shed. "It was a sudden trip, sweetie. I flew in late last night and wasn't about to wake you up. I've been lending a hand at the nursery all day. Delivering Gwen's flowers gave me a chance to surprise you." He gripped her hands. "I have some good news."

Jenna's eyes widened. "What?"

"Oscar and his brother settled their financing. I flew up for the closing on Friday."

Pouting, Jenna said, "If you won't own the nursery and the old farmhouse anymore, you'll never live in Harbor Falls again."

He pushed her to arm's length. "That's been true since I moved to Florida. You're invited to visit me whenever you have a break from your classes. You let me know the dates, and I'll buy your plane ticket. You can stay as long as you like."

His dirty fingers flicked away the moisture on Jenna's check. Chuckling, he pulled a white handkerchief from his back pocket and swiped at the soil. "I haven't seen you since graduation a few weeks ago, so this trip is also a good excuse to catch up. Do you have time for dinner with me?"

Jenna's pout lingered, but she said, "Of course, Grandad, but you look tired. How about tomorrow night?"

He kissed her forehead. "You're not only observant, you're considerate. Tomorrow night it is. Decide where you want to eat, and I'll pick you up at five. But right now, I need a shower, a quick supper, and some sleep. See you tomorrow."

He stopped as he passed by Gwen, glancing down at the hose in her hand. "Don't you squirt me now." He grinned for a split second. "Let me know if any of those specimens aren't up to your standards." Without waiting for her response, he hurried to his delivery truck and sped away.

Jenna appeared at Gwen's side. "What a shock to see him. Why didn't you tell me he was in town?"

Because Gwen had finished her dousing, she began to roll up the hose. "He wanted to surprise you."

"Well, all right, you're off the hook. What can I do?"

Gwen answered, "Help me move these pots."

Handing red begonias to Jenna, Gwen grabbed pink ones and headed for the nearest flower bed.

When the last of the plants were positioned, Jenna asked, "Are you going to plant these now?"

Gwen shook her head. "No. It's been a long day. I'll get up

early tomorrow and put them in the ground. I'll need to shower and change before my doctor's appointment at ten."

"You'll let me drive you?"

"Of course. Sally and I are meeting Robin's photographer tomorrow afternoon. Do you want to come with us?"

"Sounds intriguing, but I'm going to pass. I have a lot of reading to do and need to buy a few more books."

"Do you need any money?" Gwen asked.

"No, but you're sweet to offer. Granddad transfers funds into my checking account every month."

Sally called out the French door, "Yoo hoo. Supper's ready if you can tear yourselves away from your gardening."

Gwen stretched her aching back. "We'll be right in, Sally."

***

That evening, long after Sally's sausage and kale soup had been ladled and devoured, Gwen settled into bed earlier than usual to read a few chapters of a new mystery before letting herself drift off to sleep.

In the middle of the fifth chapter, her cell phone buzzed.

"Sorry, Gwen, this is the first chance I've had to call. How was your day?"

Pleased Ben had remembered his promise, Gwen told him of Sally's visit with Robin at the police station, retrieving the photographer's file from Robin's luggage. and their appointment with Jeremy the next afternoon.

For good reason, Gwen didn't mention Hal being in town. More than a year earlier – when Gwen had first assisted the reluctant Ben during an investigation – Hal's jealousy of their semi-professional connection had nearly ended in a fist fight between the two men. Besides, with Hal flying south after Friday's closing, why open a closed book?

Chapter Eighteen

... early morning, Tuesday

Up with the first light of dawn, Gwen began the arduous task of installing her new annuals, perennials, and ornamental grasses. Hours later, she tamped the rich soil around the final plant and gave each a drink. Storing her tools in the potting shed, she stretched her aching back and decided to delay the top dressing of cedar mulch.

Though the freshly replenished beds restored the overall appearance of her back yard, weeks would pass before the flowers wiggled their roots into the soil and spurted new growth to fill-in each area.

Back inside, she found Jenna preparing their breakfast of oatmeal garnished with craisins.

"You were up early," her young houseguest commented.

"Since five," Gwen confirmed. "I wanted to put the replacement plants in the ground before the air warmed. Any sign of Sally?" Gwen poured herself a cup of decaf and took a seat at the island.

Jenna placed two bowls on the counter. "Not a peep."

They spoke in hushed tones as they ate until noises from the sitting room made their way to the first floor. Sally was up.

A rumbling truck sent Gwen to the front windows.

Matt's crew clambered out the doors, slamming them shut. In the blink of an eye, Sally appeared on the midway landing, her robe wrapped around her body. "Who's here?"

Gwen backtracked to the staircase and glanced up. "It's the construction crew."

A knock at the front door sent Sally flying up the staircase.

One of the men stood on the top step, baseball cap in hand. "Sorry to disturb you, Mrs. Andrews, but we need you to move the white van so we can back the truck up your driveway and unload the rest of our materials."

"I heard that," Sally called over the mezzanine rail. "I'll get dressed and be right out."

The crewman nodded and walked away.

Gwen closed the door and returned to the kitchen to finish her breakfast.

When Sally came back inside, Gwen poured her a cup of coffee and the three women sat in silent companionship.

Finishing her oatmeal, Jenna placed her bowl and spoon in the sink before planting an unexpected peck on Gwen's cheek. "I'm going upstairs to study, but I'll be back down in time to drive you to your doctor's office."

"See you later." Gwen and Sally relocated to the back deck to enjoy the cooler morning air and speculate about the clues they might find in Jeremy's photographs.

When Sally's cell phone buzzed, her eyebrows shot up at the caller ID and she quickly punched the green button. "Fred, I'm so glad you called. I've been trying to reach you for days."

Retreating inside to give Sally privacy, Gwen went upstairs and tidied her own bedroom before entering the shared bathroom. She stopped dead in her tracks. Mouth tight, she picked up the wet bath towel heaped in a pile and hung it on the shower doorframe to dry. She wrung out the washcloth dripping from the lip of the sink and draped it from a side towel rack. Retrieving a sponge, she soaked up the excess water from the tiles and tossed multiple soiled tissues into the trash basket. Pushing Sally's vast array of bottles and jars to the left side of the vanity, Gwen gathered her own toiletries – plunked atop the toilet seat – and positioned them on the right.

Finding an equally chaotic condition in the sitting room didn't come as a surprise. Sheets, pillows, and coverlet tumbled in haphazard fashion from the daybed to the hardwood floor plus clothing concealed nearly every surface.

Re-hanging the blouses and slacks on the portable laundry rack and tucking other garments into the drawers she'd cleared for Sally's use, Gwen restored the sitting room to a presentable condition. As she smoothed the coverlet into place, she heard Sally huffing and puffing up the staircase. Gwen swallowed her irritation and planted a smile on her face.

"Whew, that was uncomfortable," Sally said.

Gwen didn't know if her cousin was referring to the phone call or the climb up the staircase.

And then Sally noticed Gwen's activity. "Oh, I'm so sorry about the mess. I rushed out to move my van and forgot all about straightening up. You must think I'm a slob."

121

Willing to give Sally a second chance, Gwen fibbed, "No, I don't. You were simply distracted." Giving the coverlet a final pat, Gwen looked over at her cousin. "When you said, *'that was uncomfortable', w*ere you referring to your phone call?"

Sally plopped into the nearest chair. "Yes. That was Frank's brother Fred. He's been in Europe. As soon as he landed in Boston, he called to apologize for missing the wedding."

"Did you tell him about Frank's death?"

"I did. Hated to break the news over the phone, but it couldn't be helped. When he asked if he could drive down here later this afternoon to hear all the details in person, I gave him directions. I hope you don't mind."

Despite Gwen's wariness about the brother of alcoholic Frank, she empathized with his loss. Besides, it was too late to withdraw Sally's permission. "Under similar circumstances, Sally, I'd make the same request, so I have no problem with his visit. We need to be back from Jeremy's studio before Fred arrives. Our day is shaping up to be a busy one."

As they entered the kitchen, Jenna raced down the staircase. "We should leave right now, or you'll be late."

Gwen glanced at the wall clock. "I'm glad you're paying attention to the time. Let me grab my shoulder bag and I'll be right with you."

Ten minutes later, Jenna walked beside Gwen into the medical building and stayed with Gwen until they reached the door of her general practitioner's office, then turned to leave. "I'll wait for you in the car."

122

Before Gwen could ask why, Jenna bolted to the outside. "That's strange," she murmured. She'd ask Jenna later why she didn't want to sit in the waiting room.

After more than a half hour wait, Gwen followed an assistant into an exam room and was handed a not-so-flattering gown. Her favorite physician's assistant entered and recorded Gwen's blood pressure, temperature, and EKG results. Gwen waited again. Ten minutes later, both the PA and her doctor entered, his tablet open, ready to add their chat to her file.

He peered at Gwen over his glasses. "How've you been feeling lately?"

"Other than a few dizzy spells, fine."

He tapped his screen. "Your blood pressure is elevated. I want you to reduce your salt intake, walk thirty minutes a day, and avoid stress."

"Avoid stress?" Gwen glanced at the PA then back to the doctor. "Ha! That's not going to happen anytime soon!" It occurred to Gwen that she was beginning to sound like Sally.

He placed his hand on her shoulder. "Take a deep breath and tell me what's been going on."

Gwen relayed the recent tragedies, mildly satisfied at raised eyebrows from both medical professionals.

"Those circumstances certainly explain your elevated blood pressure," he said. "I'm going to prescribe a mild diuretic to bring it down to an acceptable level."

Gwen had been healthy for nearly seven decades. She wasn't old enough – in her opinion – to be falling apart.

His voice droned on. "The pill will remove excess water from your veins. We'll see you again in three months to check your levels."

Nearly denying the medical issue, Gwen stopped at the front desk and registered the date of the follow-up appointment in her phone calendar, mumbling the entire time.

The instant Gwen settled into the passenger seat, Jenna asked, "What did your doctor have to say?"

"He claims my blood pressure is high," Gwen grumbled.

"Hmmm. What did he recommend to bring it down?"

"Cut down on salt, exercise every day, and take a diuretic."

"Sounds do-able." Jenna narrowed her eyes. "You don't seem very pleased with his diagnosis."

"His findings serve to remind me that I'm getting old and that's not what I expected."

"I don't consider you old, Gwen. How about we walk together every day? That should keep your doctor happy."

"Thanks. That won't seem like exercise at all." Despite the hindrance of the steering wheel, Gwen half-hugged Jenna before clicking the buckle of her seatbelt.

Sliding the gear shift into drive, Jenna exited the parking lot. A half a mile up the road, she pointed to a fork. "Highway or backroad?"

"Definitely back road," Gwen answered.

As leafy overhead branches cast shadows upon the pavement, Gwen asked an impulsive question. "Why did you rush out of the medical building like it was on fire?"

"The smell." Jenna swerved onto the shoulder, switched off the engine, and stared straight ahead. "Are you aware that both my parents died when I was four?"

Sensing an uncomfortable sojourn into the past, Gwen unbuckled and turned sideways to face Jenna. "I'm sorry to say I attended their funerals."

Jenna's knuckles on the steering wheel turned white. "After their car accident, Granddad took me to the emergency room. My mom and dad were both heavily sedated and never woke up. I was too young to understand the concept of saying goodbye. The smell of antiseptic brings it all back. That's why I rushed out of that medical building." Jenna glanced over, her eyes glistening. "Did you know my grandfather back then?"

"Not really. He and I talked about flowers at his garden shop each season. I didn't get to really know him until he asked me to prepare you for the music competition."

Jenna swiped at her cheek. "Those tutoring sessions with you and your sister were very special to me."

"To me and Tess, too. You worked so hard to improve your technique. When you won the competition, we couldn't have been prouder." Because Jenna seemed lost in her memories, Gwen voiced a memory of her own. "I've never told you this, but your mother was one of my most promising students. I was saddened when she died. Then years later you arrived on my doorstep and played your flute as beautifully as she had."

Jenna's eyes widened. "No one's ever told me that. Thank you. Granddad didn't talk much about my mom. Now I

125

understand he was grieving his only daughter. Don't get me wrong, he was great when I was growing up, but I missed out on having a mother." Jenna choked out her next words. "I can't bear the thought of losing you like I lost my parents."

Gwen pried Jenna's hands from the steering wheel and enclosed them in her own. "I don't plan to die any time soon."

"I want you to live at least a few more decades."

Lifting one hand, Gwen let her fingers drift along Jenna's cheek. "I'm too old to take on the role of your mother, but I'd be honored if you'd think of me as your sort-of grandmother."

"Really?"

"Yes, really. I've never said this out loud, but I think of you as the granddaughter I'll never have."

Jenna squeezed Gwen's hand, "Yes, yes! You can't know how happy you've made me."

"Oh, I think I have some idea." Gwen grinned as she shook out her crushed fingers.

"Now I love living with you even more."

"And I love having you under my roof. Just don't call me Grandma."

Jenna laughed. "Deal. And our first *family* project is to lower your blood pressure."

"Deal," Gwen repeated. "Let's swing by the pharmacy to pick up my prescription plus a home blood pressure monitor."

"You've got it, *Grandma*," Jenna teased.

Chapter Nineteen

… early afternoon, Tuesday

When Jenna mentioned the results of Gwen's checkup, Sally frowned. "Have you always had high blood pressure?"

Lowering herself onto a stool, Gwen rested her chin in one palm. "No. This is something new."

Sally leaned on the opposite side of the island counter. "Allison's wedding disaster and Frank's death must have been the cause. I'm so sorry."

"There's no way you could have predicted what was going to happen, Sally. And I was having dizzy spells before you arrived. But I'll reduce my salt intake and exercise." Gwen pulled a prescription bottle from her shoulder bag. "Plus take this little diuretic pill." She hoped the combination would eliminate her dizziness but didn't expect the stress to dissipate until Frank's attacker was apprehended.

"I offered to walk with Gwen every day," Jenna pointed out. "You're welcome to join us, Sally."

"Thanks. I'll let you know." Sally's expression remained serious. "I want to do my part. I'm taking charge of all our meals while I'm staying here. And I'll drive us to Jeremy's."

"Thanks," Gwen responded, "but I don't think my medical condition is all that dire."

"Not so, Gwen," Jenna piped up. "While you were picking up your prescription, I researched high blood pressure on my phone. You need to follow doctor's orders."

"I will, I will," Gwen promised.

Sally opened the fridge door and removed a container of her special soup. "We have time for a bite of lunch. Consider this our last high sodium meal."

***

During the drive to Plymouth, Sally glanced over. "What are our chances that Jeremy photo'd a guest with Frank?"

"I can't predict, Sally. Cross your fingers."

Ten minutes later, Jeremy waved them into his studio. Framed wedding photos covered the left wall.

Sally indicated the somber war pictures obscuring the right wall. "Are those also your work?"

"They are. I was a war photographer for more than two decades until I injured my knee." He waved down his left leg.

Sally gazed around. "That's when you set up this studio?"

"Yes, ma'am," Jeremy answered. "I couldn't live on the disability compensation. Taking pictures is my only skill, so a photography studio made sense. Besides, photographing weddings and family events beats war images any day."

"How did my daughter find you?"

"Yellow pages. You can imagine my surprise when Robin walked in. I didn't realize who she was at first."

Sally's expression revealed her confusion. "What do you mean, who she was?"

128

"She didn't tell you?"

"Tell me what?"

"Have a seat." He waved them both to a couch facing happy brides and grooms. "I'll be right back."

As he disappeared through a curtain, Gwen noticed his slight limp, but it didn't seem to slow him down. The sound of drawers opening continued until he reentered, sat on the opposite couch, and extended several prints to Sally.

Gwen peered over her cousin's shoulder at a handsome man in military fatigues.

Sally concentrated on the photos. "Oh, my God! This was Robin's first husband, Kyle."

"One and the same." Jeremy beamed. "Kyle and I were stationed at the same base and became friends between deployments. He showed me a picture of his wife when she was four months pregnant with twins. A few weeks ago, when Robin hired me, she used her second husband's last name for the contract. I didn't make the connection until she mentioned one of her twin daughters was getting married. That's when I recognized her auburn hair and the shape of her jawline. Fate had brought us together all these years later."

To Gwen, Jeremy's analysis of Robin's identity made perfect sense, given his photographer's eye.

When Sally offered the photos to Jeremy, he waved her off. "You give those to Robin. I promised I'd locate them for her."

Sally placed the prints near her purse. "I'm sure she'll be touched by these pictures of Kyle. As will her girls. Thanks."

Jeremy sat forward. "I'm bummed she didn't come with you. I was hoping to see her again."

When Sally didn't answer, Gwen noticed her deer-in-the-headlights expression and rushed to the rescue. "Robin came down with a terrible head cold. She can hardly breathe."

"What a shame." Jeremy reached beneath the low table between them and handed an oversized envelope to Sally. "These are the prints for your surprise album."

Sliding the contents onto the table's surface, Sally gave them a cursory review. "Is this all of them?"

Jeremy seemed taken aback. "Well, except for the out of focus shots. You don't want those."

"I'd like them, too, Jeremy. What you consider out of focus, I might find charming." Sally batted her eyelids.

"I'm afraid it would take me a while to sort through all the photos to find just those blurry images for printing. You'll have to come back tomorrow."

Sitting forward. Gwen asked, "Will your entire file fit on a thumb drive?"

Jeremy looked at her with interest. "Yes, it will. Saving it will take a few minutes. I'll do that right now."

He disappeared through the curtain, and they listened to the whir of a computer. He soon rejoined them and placed a thumb drive in Gwen's outstretched hand. She tucked it in her pocket.

While Sally wrote a check for the balance due, Gwen ventured an observation. "I noticed you and Robin having words as she was leaving on Saturday evening."

For an instant, confusion muddled Jeremy's expression. "Oh. You mean when she was running away from her unconscious husband?"

A perfect description of Robin's hasty exit.

"Yes, that was it," Gwen confirmed. "Your conversation appeared to be intense."

"Well, I guess it was. I was trying to arrange a day and time for her to pick up those pictures of Kyle. I figured she'd want them right away." He waved at the small stack beside Sally's purse. "But Robin totally lost her cool. She was yelling that her drunken husband had ruined her daughter's wedding and she was in no mood to make any plans." Jeremy hesitated. "Piece of work, her second husband. I can't help but wonder why she married the guy."

As Sally handed her check to Jeremy, she said, "As you can imagine, Robin was devastated when Kyle was killed overseas. Raising their twin daughters without him nearly did her in. When she met Frank, she married him without knowing about his love affair with the bottle. She tolerated his drinking but always hoped he'd stop."

Jeremy snorted. "Too bad she was dead wrong."

Chapter Twenty

... mid-afternoon, Tuesday

Jeremy's prints obscured Gwen's dining room table as she and Sally poured over each image, deflated when they found no evidence of a person approaching Frank on the lounge chair.

"How disappointing," Sally huffed. "Whoever moved Frank must have waited until Jeremy left."

Gwen leaned over the prints. "There wasn't much reason for Jeremy to continue taking pictures after the fires started, but let's not give up yet. We need to take a look at the blurry shots that Jeremy didn't print. Follow me."

In the upstairs guest room, where a laptop computer sat on a corner desk next to a printer, Gwen inserted Jeremy's thumb drive and waited for the large file to download. One by one, they picked out the blurry images and printed them.

Back at the dining room table, Gwen divided the pictures into two piles. Pushing the majority to the middle of the table, she arranged six pictures side by side. "Do you notice anything in these, Sally?"

After a few minutes, Sally tossed Gwen a baffled look. "I have no idea what you're seeing."

Gwen tapped on each. "These guests were taking pictures."

Sally squeezed Gwen's arm. "You're a genius!"

"Do you recognize any of them?"

Sally carried the six prints to the window for a closer inspection, shaking her head. "Sorry, they're too blurry."

"I have an idea." Without waiting for a reply, Gwen pulled open a drawer in the oversized hutch and removed a silver-handled magnifying glass.

After repeated scrutiny, Sally made negative clucking noises. "Too fuzzy. I'm afraid I'm no help at all." She flung the photos to land atop the others.

Gwen held up a finger. "Wait a minute. When you searched Robin's luggage for Jeremy's file, did you see a guest list?"

"I wasn't looking for one. Let's go check."

They hurried to Sally's van parked at the front curb and pulled a piece of luggage to the rear edge. Flipping open the latches, Sally rummaged through the contents and removed a sheath of papers. "Here it is."

Sure enough, the list of names appeared to be those of the wedding guests. Beside each were phone numbers, some checked off, others crossed out.

"Great," Gwen said, feeling a surge of progress. "All we need to do is call and ask if they'll email their digital pictures. You start at the top and I'll work from the bottom up."

Retreating to the kitchen island, they slid the list back and forth as they dialed one phone number after another.

Many of Gwen's calls went to voicemail. Of those who answered, three had left their cell phones at home. Two agreed to forward their photos and asked for Gwen's email address.

A ping on Gwen's cell phone announced the arrival of an email. She read the subject line, her shoulders slumping. "False alarm. A reminder of the next garden club meeting."

Sally frowned. "Let's be patient. How many of the guests did you actually talk to?"

"Only a few," Gwen answered. "One brought her SLR camera without realizing her batteries were dead. The two who are emailing digital photos sounded younger. I'm guessing they were friends of either Allison or Cole, but I don't know if they're included in Jeremy's blurry photos. I left lots of messages asking people to call me."

Sally peered once more at the six photos of the unidentifiable picture-takers. "I think you're right. Even out of focus, these guests all impress me as middle-aged or older."

"How did you make out with your calls, Sally?"

"About the same as you. One man is emailing his digital pictures. Several didn't bring either cell phone or camera, so are no help at all. I also left lots of messages to get back to me, but it's tough to predict how many will actually call."

"Let's cross our fingers," Gwen reassured her cousin. "Oh, one elderly fellow said he doesn't own a cell phone but already dropped off his disposable camera at the local CVS." Gwen ran her finger down the legal pad and found her notation. "His name is Peter Edgecombe."

Sally chuckled. "That's Uncle Peter, my first husband's uncle on his mother's side. He's a sweet old guy and I've stayed in touch with him over the years."

This would have been the perfect time for Gwen to delve into Sally's marital history but decided against it. "Your Uncle Peter said if we want the prints, we'll have to pick them up."

Sally tapped her temple. "That's right. When he turned ninety, he gave up his driver's license. He must have hitched a ride with another wedding guest on Saturday. With all the activity, I didn't get a chance to say hello."

"Do you have his address? He hung up before I could ask."

Sally opened her cell phone contacts and scrolled to his name. "Yep, here he is." She tapped the Google map link and studied his location.

Gazing over Sally's shoulder, Gwen recognized street names in East Sandwich. "You know, Sally, when the others call us back, we should arrange face to face meetings. They might have noticed someone hanging around Frank but didn't take a picture."

"Hindsight is always twenty-twenty," Sally preached. "Too late for the few we already talked to. Maybe the others when they return our calls. Did Uncle Peter say what day his pictures will be ready?"

"No, but I can't imagine it'll be much later than Thursday or Friday. He promised to call when he has them in hand."

Sally made a face. "We'll have to deal with the traffic on and off the Cape. But the bridge bottleneck will be worth the hassle if any of Uncle Peter's snapshots caught a man moving Frank. I can't wait to prove to Detective Warren that the villain isn't my Robin."

A disturbing thought popped into Gwen's head, but she kept the warning to herself. What if the picture-taking guest was the one who approached the drunken Frank? He or she could not have photographed themselves.

And how would Sally react if a guest's snapshot revealed Robin as the last person at Frank's side? Though when would she have snuck back? Last time Gwen had seen Robin, she'd been fleeing around the corner and down the driveway.

***

While she was upstairs in her bedroom, one of the guests called back. Gwen sat on her bed to finalize a second Cape Cod visit. Downstairs, the doorbell announced a visitor. Assuming it was Frank's brother Fred, she covered the mouthpiece and yelled down, "Sally, can you get that?"

"Sure," Sally called back.

Gwen finalized the arrangements and scurried to the mezzanine rail, unashamed to eavesdrop on her cousin's conversation below.

A familiar male voice said, "Oh, hi. I was expecting Gwen." Not Fred.

"I'm her cousin Sally. Who are you?"

"My name's Hal Jenkins."

Gwen froze. She didn't want to appear enthusiastic about Hal stopping by. At the same time, it would be unfair to give him reason to think she might change her mind about moving to Florida. She leaned over the rail and continued to listen.

136

Hal's voice echoed up the staircase. "I'm taking my granddaughter to dinner this evening."

"Of course, Mr. Jenkins," Sally's voice cooed. "I'll let Jenna know you're here."

The guestroom door flew open and Jenna sped along the mezzanine rail, whizzing past Gwen. "I saw Grandad drive up. I'll see you later."

She hopped down the staircase, yelling, "I'm coming!"

Chapter Twenty-One

… early evening, Tuesday

Sipping iced tea on the rear deck in the waning light, Sally regaled Gwen with stories about her life in California, bummed none of her friends came to the wedding. "I can't blame them," Sally defended. "Plane tickets are so expensive these days."

From the driveway, a man's deep voice rumbled, "Hello."

Sally leaned around Gwen. "Fred. You were supposed to text me when you got close to Harbor Falls so I could flag you down. Visitors don't realize this old library is a home."

Gwen shifted her position to see a healthier version of Frank Hennessey. No sagging eyebags, no sad-sack expression or red nose, no belly straining against his shirt. Energetic as he hopped up the end steps, Fred was obviously a younger brother.

"I did text you, Sally," Fred replied. "I typed this address into my GPS, but when I knocked on the front door, nobody answered. I heard voices back here, so I took a chance."

Sally whipped out her cell phone and grunted. "Damn phone is dead. I need to charge my battery." She stood up and waved toward Gwen. "This is my cousin Gwen Andrews. She'll keep you company while I go plug it in."

Getting used to Fred's vigorous appearance, Gwen extended her hand. "I'm sorry about your brother's death."

"Thanks. I always knew Frank's lifestyle would do him in, but to hear the way he died was quite a shock. Like I told Sally on the phone, I need to hear all the details and see where he met his end."

Gwen indicated an empty deck chair. "While we wait for Sally, would you like a glass of iced tea?"

"Thanks, I would."

Gwen rose and went inside. As she moved around the kitchen, she glanced out the bay window. Fred had stepped off the decks to pace her back yard. Was he inspecting her newly planted flowers or ignoring them altogether?

Sally came up beside her. "Quite a shock, isn't he?"

Gwen nodded, keeping watch on Fred's meandering. "How many years between the brothers?"

Sally's eyebrows flew up. "None. They were twins."

"You only said they were brothers. As a twin, Fred must be doubly upset."

"I expect he is. You're probably wondering why Robin didn't marry Fred."

"The thought crossed my mind. Are you willing to share why she didn't?"

Sally leaned against the stove. "Fred travels for his work, so Robin didn't meet him until months after her marriage to Frank. She married Frank *because* he was a twin. She thought he'd understand her twin daughters more than most men. Like I told Jeremy, she wasn't aware of Frank's drinking problem until much later. Apparently, my girl thought she could reform her second husband, but she failed like most women who think they can alter a man's habits. She's never mentioned divorce."

"What does Fred do for a living?"

"Some sort of engineering consultant," Sally answered. "I don't know his job description, but Frank used to complain about his brother never being around much."

Gwen opened the fridge door, brought out the pitcher of mint iced tea, and filled a glass.

By the time she and Sally rejoined Fred, he had suspended his wandering and returned to the deck. He grasped the offered glass, downing half the contents. "Thanks. I didn't realize how thirsty I was." He swiped his hand across his lips. "Okay, Sally, I'm ready to hear what happened to Frank."

Sally began to speak. "First of all, you didn't miss Allison's wedding. The ceremony in Gwen's gardens never took place."

As Fred glanced toward the back yard, she rushed to add, "It looked much prettier before the disasters on Saturday. If you'll be patient, we'll explain." She waved him to sit before she continued, her voice gentle. "It all started when your brother collapsed as he walked Allison down the aisle toward the justice of the peace."

"God damn it!" Fred exploded to his feet, knocking his chair sideways. "He was drunk at the wedding? I tried to get him into AA. Stubborn fool." Fred's eyebrows scrunched together as he peered down at Sally.

She pulled on his jacket with one hand while righting his deck chair with the other. "Don't you want to hear the details?"

Sitting down, Fred mumbled, "I do. Sorry for my outburst."

Undaunted, Sally continued. "We were fortunate he didn't take Allison down with him. She could have lost the baby."

"What baby?"

Sally's face ripened to a shade of pink. "With you being out of town, you wouldn't know my granddaughter's pregnant."

Fred waved off the update. "Doesn't matter these days. I'm glad she and the baby are okay. And after Frank fell?"

Sally began again. "The bridegroom Cole and his best man Brodie carried him up here and placed him on that chaise lounge." She pointed to the opposite end of the deck.

Resting his forearms on his thighs, Fred leaned forward. "I don't understand why the ceremony was cancelled just because Frank collapsed. Couldn't a guest have taken his place?"

Sally shrugged both shoulders. "I'm sure one of the men would have gladly walked her to her groom and given her hand in marriage, but something else happened before any of them had the chance. Ashley had lit real wax candles inside paper luminarias. They caught fire and dropped onto the paper tablecloths. The breeze blowing up from the harbor swirled live embers all over Gwen's back yard, creating multiple small fires. She called 911 and grabbed her kitchen extinguisher. Some guests tried to put out the flames with their feet or their jackets. The hose trucks and firefighters showed up and prevented any major damage, but everything was soaking wet, including the bridal party and many of the guests. Robin called off the wedding and sent everyone home."

Fred shook his head. "Before you explain how those events connect to Frank's death, where *is* Robin? She hasn't been answering her cell phone either."

"Be patient, Fred." Sally promised. "Gwen, tell Fred what happened after everyone left Saturday evening."

Although rattled by Sally's unexpected command, Gwen sat forward. "I needed to separate myself from the disaster in my gardens, so I wandered to the boundary of my property on North Street." Gwen swiveled and pointed to the distant row of birch trees. "I stayed down there for about a half hour watching the guests cross the village green to their cars parked behind the bank. When I thought the coast was clear, I took my time walking back up here. As I approached this upper deck, I found the lounge chair empty, so I figured Frank had woken up and made his way over to the B&B."

Fred's gaze didn't shift. "But he hadn't?"

"Unfortunately, my assumption was wrong," Gwen admitted. "On Sunday morning, my summer houseguest joined me to inspect the damage to my gardens. As we were passing the bushes near my new garage, we noticed what turned out to be a black shoe. When we moved closer, we discovered your brother's body impaled on the cinder block half wall."

Fred gripped the arms of the deck chair, his color fading. "Sally mentioned that. But you said his *body*. You were so sure he was dead?"

Challenged, Gwen stuttered, "I'm no EMT, so I called 911."

"How long did it take them to get here?"

"A few minutes."

Fred clenched his fists. "And they pronounced him dead?"

"They did. The police chief also sent a detective."

Fred's tone sharpened. "Why?" He swirled his ice cubes.

"Well, I don't know about other states, but in Massachusetts, if someone dies without a doctor present, the police investigate."

Fred stood up and paced the deck boards. "And what did the police decide?"

Sally reentered the conversation. "Detective Warren arrested Robin yesterday for suspected murder. That's why she's not answering her cell phone."

Halting his restless movement, Fred stared at Sally, his eyes moist. "Robin? I suspected Frank wasn't the easiest drunk to live with, but don't you think she went a little too far?"

Gwen watched her cousin's reaction.

The darts in Sally's eyes could have killed a mouse at ten feet. "I can't believe you think Robin did it."

Fred held out both palms. "And you don't? The detective must have had some pretty damning evidence to arrest her."

Getting to her feet, Sally stomped to stand in front of him. "I don't think Robin attacked Frank, and I intend to prove it."

"How? Are you going to hire a private eye?"

"Not exactly," Sally answered.

"Okay. Exactly what *are* you planning?"

"I don't think you really care, Fred, but I'm going to tell you anyway."

As if Detective Warren was listening around the corner, Sally lowered her voice. "Gwen agreed to help me investigate. This afternoon, I bought the prints from the wedding photographer. Unfortunately, none of them showed someone leading Frank to the garage."

Content to let Sally explain their plan, Gwen eased back in her deck chair.

"So, the photos were a dead end?" Fred blushed. "Sorry, poor choice of words."

Sally ignored his remark. "Not quite. Gwen noticed guests in the background taking pictures."

"What's so special about that?"

"Think about it, Fred. What if one of them took a snapshot of a man with Frank? We've been calling the people on Robin's guest list to locate the picture takers."

"Are you telling them my brother died?"

A mirthless laugh escaped Sally. "Of course not."

"So, these people don't know you're looking for a killer among them?"

Sally's gray curls quivered. "No."

Fred tilted his head. "Why would they agree to give you their pictures?"

"Simple," Sally explained. "We're saying their snapshots will be placed in a memory album for Allison & Cole."

"I don't know, Sally. I think you're on a fool's errand, but you're brave to buck the detective who arrested Robin. If you find an incriminating snapshot, will he pursue it?"

"No idea," Sally said, her tone flustered. "Gwen has a little clout with the local police department. If we spot an image with potential, we'll pass along the snapshot."

"Well, good luck," Fred commented. "Me, I only want my brother to have a decent burial. By the way, where *is* his body?"

Gwen raised her hand, feeling like a first grader. "Probably with the medical examiner. He would normally notify next of kin, but with Robin in jail, you'd be the contact person."

"I guess I would," Fred conceded. "I'll stick around while I handle the details. Where's the nearest lodging?"

"Across the village green," Gwen answered, pointing. "That oversized white colonial is the Harbor Falls Bed & Breakfast."

"Seems convenient enough," Fred said.

Gwen's landscape lights blinked on.

Fred handed his empty glass to her. "It's getting too dark to inspect the spot where you found Frank. I'll come back in the morning. Good night, ladies." He sprinted along the deck boards, quickly out of sight. The retreating sound of a car engine confirmed he had driven away.

Sally stared at Gwen. "I can't believe Fred could think Robin is guilty. He's assuming the detective has a valid reason for arresting her. I don't know why I thought he'd help us find the real killer, but Fred's not going to lift a finger."

Gwen placed her arm across her cousin's shoulders and led her inside. "We don't need him, Sally."

***

Reading more chapters in bed an hour later, Gwen answered Ben's phone call. "Hi. Are your sessions proceeding as planned?"

"Yep. Same as last week. Don't get me wrong, Gwen, it's gratifying to share my experience with other officers, but the repetition is wearing on me. I'm more interested in your day. Was your meeting with the photographer productive?"

His voice sounded like honey to her ears "Not at first. His photos hadn't captured anyone approaching Frank in the longue chair. But then I noticed a half dozen guests in the background taking their own pictures."

"Your eagle eye, Gwen. Let me guess. You and Sally called those six guests?"

"I wish it had been that easy. The focus was fuzzy. Sally couldn't identify any of them. We had to contact every invitee from Robin's list to locate the ones who took snapshots."

Gwen repeated the responses before telling Ben about their plan to schedule visits with the picture-takers.

"Listen, Gwen, when you meet with them, don't say you're looking for someone who was angry with Frank."

"Sally and I are only collecting their snapshots."

"Try to limit your conversation to that purpose. Can you keep your cousin's enthusiasm in check until I return tomorrow? I have no idea what time."

"I'll try to steer our visits into Thursday or even Friday."

"Good. I'll worry less about you if I'm in Harbor Falls instead of out in the western part of the state."

146

Gwen couldn't quite read his tone and wondered if his concern was personal or professional. To keep the conversation moving, she said, "I'm not expecting any trouble. What did you do with yourself during your off hours in Oakfield?"

Ben described the restaurants and shops until his yawn traveled through the handset. "Sorry, Gwen, I need to get some shuteye. My final session ends after lunch tomorrow, and then I'll drive back to Harbor Falls."

After Ben disconnected, Gwen pictured the white-haired detective. What were the chances they'd move beyond sleuthing partners and occasional dinner dates?

Chapter Twenty-Two

… early morning, Wednesday

After pausing to admire the sun's rays as they shimmed across the waters of Massachusetts Bay, Gwen and Jenna surrendered the view and hiked back up Harbor Hill to complete their early morning walk.

They were about to cross North Street when a man's voice called out, "Gwen Andrews, is that you?"

Fred Hennessey hopped down the wide steps of the Harbor Falls Bed & Breakfast and sprinted toward them. "I thought that was you. Thanks for recommending this B&B."

"I've never known anyone to be disappointed," Gwen commented. "How are you holding up, Fred?"

In a somber tone, he answered, "I'm doing okay."

"If you're on your way to my place, you're welcome to walk with us." Gwen indicated Jenna. "This is my summer houseguest Jenna Jenkins. She was Allison's bridesmaid until the wedding fell apart."

Fred nodded toward Jenna. "Nice to meet you."

Not sure how to react, Jenna stared at him. "You look really familiar."

"Probably because I'm Allison's step-uncle, Frank's twin brother Fred."

"Oh." Jenna murmured. "I'm sorry for your loss."

"Thanks. I'm still coming to grips with the way he died." Fred waved toward North Street. "Shall we cross?"

They were soon striding through the village green, silent as they made their way toward Gwen's home.

***

They found Sally busy at the kitchen stove. Despite her polite greeting, the unspoken tension between her and Fred charged the air. She slid crisp-edged crepes onto plates. "Jenna, are you eating with us this morning?"

"Thanks, Sally, but no. I have to scoot over to Baylies for my first class. I have a protein bar in my bookbag. See you both later." Jenna rushed up the staircase. A minute later, the front door slammed.

Adding fresh fruit, Sally handed one plate to Gwen. "Have you eaten, Fred?"

"Not yet," he answered. "When I spotted Gwen, I rushed out of the B&B before breakfast was served. But your crepes smell delicious. I'll have one if there's enough."

"Coffee?" Gwen asked, lifting the carafe.

"Sure. I'd love a cup."

While they ate, the three struggled to make small talk. Swallowing his last bite, Fred pushed his plate aside. "That was delicious Sally." He turned to Gwen. "Can you show me where you found Frank?"

"Of course." Gwen peered over at Sally. "Do you want to come with us? You haven't asked."

149

Sally patted her mouth with a napkin. "I've been avoiding that spot, but it's time."

Gwen waved them outside, leading both to the front edge of the garage's concrete slab.

Fred's gaze roamed the rudimentary structure. "Where?"

Moving along the cinder block wall, Gwen stopped and pointed. "Those dark drips are where I found him."

Sally took in a sharp breath. "Fred, do you really think Robin is strong enough to heft Frank on top of that wall?"

Fred stared at the telling stains. "Sally, you must have read about people hoisting a two-ton car to free a man trapped by a defective car jack. A rush of adrenaline could have given Robin the strength. He was drunk, so wouldn't have had the energy to fight her off."

Sally's back visibly stiffened. "You're letting your imagination run wild. Robin had no reason to do such a thing. Did you ever see Frank strike my girl?"

"No, I haven't," Fred admitted.

"Well, there you go," Sally blustered.

Gwen knew Sally was grasping at straws. Hadn't she noticed Frank's sharp tongue and the way he bent back Robin's wrist on wedding day? Robin's bruised cheek beneath her makeup? Her outfit covering every square inch of her skin, possibly hiding additional bruises? Sally was defending Robin as any mother would, but was she in denial?

"But then," Fred countered, "I only saw the two of them during short visits between my business trips. Frank would have been on his best behavior. If my brother abused Robin, I don't excuse him, but I wish to hell she'd filed for divorce before it came to this." He waved at the blood-stained blocks.

"My daughter didn't do it," Sally insisted. "With Gwen's help, we'll find the guy who did and get my girl out of jail."

"You may not believe me, Sally, but I hope you're right." Fred's gaze moved to the concrete slab. "What are those indentations?" He squatted down for a closer inspection.

"Shoe impressions," Gwen said. "The crime lab tech made castings, but I don't know how they'll match them to anyone's shoes or boots. The imprints overlap. For all I know, they were left by my construction crew."

Fred glanced at Sally. "How are my step-nieces handling the death of their stepfather?"

"Neither of the girls were at the B&B when the detective arrived with the news of Frank's death," Sally answered. "Allison and Cole eloped early Sunday morning. And Ashley had already returned to the Cape with Brodie."

Beginning to pace the garage floor, Fred said, "Did Robin tell anyone that Frank hadn't returned on Saturday night?"

"She didn't mention his absence to me," Sally replied. "That's why I rushed over here after I listened to Gwen's voicemail about finding Frank in her garage. I didn't want to panic until I had more information."

"And then Robin was arrested the next day." Fred stated as he paced a few more steps before turning back "You haven't said how my nieces are handling both tragedies."

Sally's head dropped, along with her volume. "Both girls were long gone by the time their mother was arrested."

Fred's eyes flashed. "You said that. Have you told them?"

Sally's head moved side to side.

"Why not?" Fred pursued.

Her expression turned combative. "I have my reasons."

"And what are they?" Fred demanded.

Sally huffed. "Robin made me promise not to say anything until we could convince the police that they arrested the wrong person. I agreed that we shouldn't ruin Allison's honeymoon."

Fred stepped within a foot of her, his face contorting. "If one of my parents died, and the other one was arrested, I'd want to know right away, honeymoon or not. Why not tell Ashley?"

Fluttering her hands, Sally said, "I've been waiting until Gwen and I find evidence to release Robin from jail."

"Doesn't Ashley realize her mother hasn't returned home from the wedding?"

"Probably not. This is her last summer as a camp counselor, so she never moved back in with Robin after graduation."

Fred shook his head, glaring at Sally. "I'm sorry, but my nieces need to be told. They're both adults now. I'll call them if you won't. I'll need their phone numbers."

Sally crossed her arms. "No. Robin will be upset that I've gone against her wishes, but I'll call my granddaughters."

Fred's cell phone buzzed, and he moved a short distance down the driveway to take the call. After a minute, he disconnected and rejoined them. "Business. It can wait until after Frank's funeral." Pulling out a handkerchief, Fred wiped his eyes and focused on Sally. "Did Frank and Robin purchase a prepaid funeral plan?"

"No idea. She's never mentioned it."

"Then I need to talk to her. Where is she?"

"She was at the Harbor Falls jail until they transferred her to Plymouth late Monday. She was arraigned yesterday."

Fred half-turned, anxious to leave. "I'll be in touch."

"If the Plymouth jailkeepers let you see my girl," Sally called after him, "remind her I'm searching for a criminal attorney and I'll come see her again as soon as I'm allowed."

"I will." Fred sprinted down the driveway and across the village green toward the B&B.

"Sally," Gwen began. "At least Fred is handling Frank's funeral. That's one less thing for you to worry about."

"And I'm thankful he's stepping up. But he's wound tight about his twin's death. If he's not allowed to see Robin, he might explode."

"We'll hear what happened eventually." Gwen stepped away. "I'll give you some privacy while you call Allison and Ashley."

"Thanks. I'll be tongue-tied if I have an audience."

Chapter Twenty-Three

... late morning, Wednesday

While Sally called her granddaughters, Gwen dragged the garden hose to each flower bed and watered the newly installed plants. Despite the rising temperature, she hauled bags of cedar mulch from the potting shed and spread the contents to conserve the moisture soaking into the soil.

"Wow, the new flowers make a big difference."

Gwen whirled to see Jenna standing five feet away. "Goodness, you startled me."

"Sorry." Jenna squatted down to admire a pink blossom.

Glancing from one floral patch to the next, Gwen nodded. "A distinct improvement, though the leaves and petals need a few weeks to fill in the spaces."

Jenna inhaled. "I love the smell of fresh mulch."

Gwen stared at Jenna. "Hey, why are you home so early? I didn't expect to see you until supper time."

"My first class was shorter than I expected, mostly an overview. My next class doesn't begin until two this afternoon, so I came back to check up on you."

Gwen couldn't hold back a smile. "You didn't need to. Sally's here to keep an eye on me." She pointed to the upper deck, where Sally spoke into her cell phone.

"Who's she talking to?" Jenna asked.

"Probably Ashley. Could be Allison. She's telling the girls about Frank's death and their mother's arrest."

Jenna walked beside Gwen toward the potting shed. "They weren't told?"

As Gwen disposed of the mulch bags, she explained Robin and Sally's good intentions to not ruin Allison's honeymoon or upset Ashley until Robin had been released from jail.

Jenna said nothing as she absorbed their reasoning.

Gwen removed her gardening gloves and washed her hands in the shed sink, her concerns switching to Ben. Had he been put off their friendship by his Sunday evening encounter with Parker's spirit? Next time she saw the detective, she'd pay close attention to his demeanor. If he returned to Harbor Falls early enough today, would he stop by?

Jenna's voice broke into Gwen's contemplation. "By the way, mulching doesn't replace our evening walk."

Locking the potting shed door, Gwen paused and glanced at Jenna. "Don't my gardening efforts count as exercise? We *did* walk this morning."

A resigned expression appeared on Jenna's unlined face. "Oh, all right. But this is a one-time only pass."

"Thank you, drill sergeant," Gwen mocked. "Did you have a nice dinner with your grandfather last evening?"

"Sure did. He treated me to dinner at The Wharf."

"Their chef is exceptionally creative," Gwen commented as they crossed the lawn. "What did you order?"

"The shrimp casserole and crème brûlée for dessert." Jenna's eyes sparkled. "We talked about my master's degree classes, his cottage projects, his new neighbors..." Jenna's voice trailed off.

As they passed through the jinxed wedding trellis, Gwen placed her hand on Jenna's arm. "If you're trying to be tactful about your grandfather's lady friend, you don't need to be."

Jenna pursed her lips as if debating what to share and what to keep to herself.

Gwen perched on the edge of a planter box, indicating Jenna should do the same. "Let's have a chat."

After Jenna settled on the opposite planter, Gwen began. "After I got over the shock of seeing your grandfather at the garden shop, Joleen appeared in the door of the old farmhouse, so he told me who she was."

Lifting her chin, Jenna murmured, "He said there's no romance between them."

Though baffled Hal had confided this fact to his granddaughter, Gwen followed his lead. "There was no romance between him and me either. We had some fun times until I refused to move south with him. We've both moved on."

Jenna raised her eyes, a cautious expression on her young face. "So, your feelings won't be bruised if I meet this Joleen before they fly home?"

Surprised and relieved by her question, Gwen answered, "Not at all. You should get acquainted with her while she's up here just in case they get serious."

Jenna pushed herself from the planter's edge. "Granddad mentioned one more thing."

"What?"

"The police log of the Harbor Falls Gazette listed an ambulance called here on Sunday morning."

Now on her feet, Gwen stopped short. "What did you say?"

Jenna flapped her hand. "Oh, don't worry. I didn't mention I was with you when we found Frank's body or that you're helping Sally find the real attacker. I told Granddad none of what happened last weekend was your fault and he shouldn't worry about me. The last thing I want him to do is demand I move out."

Crossing the lower deck, Gwen glanced over at Jenna. "I don't want him to force you out either."

As they approached the upper deck, Sally appeared in the French door. "Great timing, you two. Lunch in ten minutes."

***

A few hours later, in the community room of the Oakfield Police Department, Ben brought up the final visual on the white wall. During the sessions, the officers had been attentive to his presentations. One of them with spousal abuse experience shared his encounter with battling families. Ben hadn't minded. He preferred audience participation.

Soon, he'd pack up his materials and drive east to Harbor Falls. Although he'd called Gwen both evenings, he preferred to be sitting next to the lady. Even if the ghost of her husband showed up again.

Chapter Twenty-Four

… early evening, Wednesday

Gwen loaded the dishwasher with soiled supper dishes as Sally passed them over. Behind them, Jenna perched on an island stool and asked, "How do you come up with your recipes, Sally? So far, all your meals have been winners."

Sally slapped her hips. "I love to cook. Can't you tell?"

Without agreeing or disagreeing, Jenna said, "I'm curious about Fred. All I know is he's Frank's twin."

Sally handed Gwen the final glass then turned and rested one hand on the island. "I've only seen him twice since I moved to the Cape. He travels quite a bit for work, so he didn't visit Frank very often." Sally glanced at the kitchen clock. "I should call him." She retreated up the staircase.

Jenna waited until Sally was out of earshot. "How's your cousin handling the tragedies of the past few days?"

Sliding a capsule of dishwashing detergent into the door, Gwen set the machine to squirt and splash before facing her houseguest. "Sally's hard to read. On the outside, she's all bluster and snarky remarks, but I suspect she's terrified we won't find evidence to prove Robin wasn't the last person with Frank after the wedding was cancelled."

More suddenly than Gwen expected, Sally rejoined them.

"The Plymouth jail allowed Fred to visit Robin. She gave him the name of the funeral home on the Cape and provided some details for the obituary. He said she's putting on a brave face but is anxious to be released. He decided not to upset her so didn't mention that I'm calling the twins."

"That's good. What's he doing next?" Gwen asked.

Seeming to have run out of steam, Sally plopped onto the stool next to Jenna. "The medical examiner's office was closed by the time Fred found it this afternoon, so he's going back tomorrow morning. He'll stop here beforehand to pick up a copy of the guest list. After he meets with the funeral director on the Cape tomorrow, he'll share the details with the friends and relatives invited to the wedding. He's staying at the B&B again tonight."

"It sounds like Fred's making all the arrangements by himself," Jenna commented. "No other brothers or sisters?"

"I'm not aware of any," Sally answered.

"Have you caught up with Ashley or Allison?"

Sally seemed to deflate. "I'm waiting for Ashley to call me back before I interrupt Allison's honeymoon. I don't know why that girl is ignoring my messages."

"Do you want me to try?" Jenna offered.

"No, no, dear," Sally said. "I'm sure she'll call soon."

As if on cue, Sally's cell phone buzzed. She squinted at the caller ID. "Hello?" When the person on the other end responded, she barked, "Well, it's about time." Sliding off the stool, Sally barreled toward the music studio.

Jenna lowered her volume. "She'd have answered differently if she's talking to Ashley, don't you think?"

"You'd think so," Gwen agreed without predicting whether Sally would tell them later. "Do you want to see the photographer's pictures?"

"Sure." Jenna hopped off the stool. "Where are they?"

"On the dining room table. Follow me."

Five minutes later, a shadow fell across the wedding day images, causing both Gwen and Jenna to jump.

Sally seemed unaware she'd startled them. "My divorce attorney finally got back to me. I didn't want to pick any ole criminal lawyer from the yellow pages, so I asked him for a recommendation. He gave me the name of a good attorney down in Plymouth. I spoke with the receptionist. If I don't get a call today, definitely tomorrow."

Sally tapped Jenna on the shoulder. "Did Gwen and I miss anything in those prints?"

"Don't think so," Jenna answered as her eyes roamed across the display of photographs. "Gwen pointed out the guests taking pics in the background. Too bad you haven't heard from all of them."

"Too bad is right," Sally blustered. "I'm antsy to get my hands on their snapshots and spot someone approaching Frank. I'm bothered that the others haven't called back."

Gwen's cell phone vibrated on the countertop near the stove, and she rushed to the kitchen to grab it. After a quick conversation, she returned to the dining room. "Sally, that was your Uncle Peter. He'll be picking up his prints tomorrow morning. I said we'd drive down after lunch."

"Great. The sooner the better," Sally said. "Jenna, do you want to come with us?"

"Can't, Sally. I have classes, reading, or papers every day. You two won't be seeing much of me."

As the evening progressed, two calls came in from guests who hadn't taken any pictures. "You know, Sally," Gwen said, "we should be cross-referencing who took pictures and who didn't. Where's Robin's guest list?"

After Sally retrieved it, Gwen reread her scribbles on the legal pad, drawing lines through two names before noting Uncle Peter in Sandwich for a pick-up and their second stop in Yarmouth Port.

Chapter Twenty-Five

… mid-evening, Wednesday

An hour later, after Jenna retreated to the guestroom to read her textbook and Sally headed up to her temporary quarters in the sitting room, Gwen went outside and strolled past the circles of glow cast by the landscape lights.

When she was halfway to the swing, a man's voice called from the driveway. "Gwen?"

Ben was back!

Without intending to, she compared him to Hal Jenkins, who'd been her buddy, her pal, her companion. At that time in her life, she'd wanted nothing deeper, and definitely not a physical relationship. But with Ben, a romantic entanglement seemed more than possible.

"Yes, it's me," she answered, skirting her flower beds, and meeting him near the fishpond. She greeted him with a more-than-friendly hug.

The previous summer, during a ride in Ben's Corvette, she felt the tingle of attraction. But was Ben interested in her on a personal level? She'd wait until she sensed that his sentiments matched hers. "I didn't know if you'd stop over tonight."

His grey eyes searched her face. "Your windows weren't dark, so I figured you weren't sleeping yet."

"Don't forget Jenna and Sally are living here. They could have been awake, and I could have been in dreamland."

He laughed. "I'll keep them in mind. I'm glad I noticed your silhouette walking back here. No prying eyes."

Encouraged by his implication of naughtiness, she said, "Let's sit on the swing."

After they'd settled, Ben reached for her hand. "I missed you while I was in Oakfield. Phone calls don't do it for me."

Relief flooded her. Ben meeting Parker's ghost on Sunday evening hadn't put him off their friendship. And would a man who wasn't interested hold her hand?

Gwen squeezed back. For a split second, she worried she'd been too suggestive, then decided questioning her reactions at her stage of life squandered precious time.

Rocking gently back and forth, they chatted amiably until Ben crushed their easy comradery. "If you don't mind, I'd like to see those photographer's pictures. Plus, anything else you've learned and your plans with Sally."

Had she misread his handholding? Was Ben only interested in Frank's murder? Though Gwen hated to abandon the romantic potential of the swing, she admitted that his trained eye could shed new light on their sleuthing. Swallowing her disappointment, she said, "Sure."

They crossed the lawn and the lower deck before stepping onto the upper deck. When Gwen reached for the handle of the French door, Ben swirled her around, leaned down, and kissed her with such intensity she could hardly catch her breath.

When he released her, his eyes sparkled with mischief. "I've been wanting to kiss you since you hugged me earlier. Hope you didn't mind."

Gwen touched her fingers to her lips. "I've been wondering if you'd ever kiss me." She threw her arms around his waist and laid her head on his broad chest.

He spoke into her hair. "To be honest, Gwen, I've wanted to kiss you since we went dancing last December, but I resisted in case you weren't interested." He placed his forefinger beneath her chin and lifted her face for a second kiss.

Breaking apart, they stared at each other.

"I'm definitely interested, Ben."

He chuckled. "Show me those photos so we can get back to your swing."

They snuck inside to the dining room table where the prints were still spread out. Whispering so she didn't disturb Jenna or Sally, Gwen showed Ben the six pictures revealing guests in the background with their cell phones held near their faces.

Ben whistled under his breath. "This was a great catch on your part. Any callbacks today?"

"A few." Gwen stood close. If Ben moved the slightest bit, he'd bump into her. "Sally's Uncle Peter is picking up his prints tomorrow. We'll visit him in the afternoon."

Ben tapped one of the photos. "This must be him."

Gwen squinted at the blurry image. The tall man with a full white beard was barely discernable. "Hadn't tried to pick him out. But you're right. The other five appear to be women. Two guests called who didn't take any snapshots, so at least we're narrowing down the list of amateur photographers at the wedding."

"I'll stop by tomorrow morning to chat with you and Sally before you drive down to the Cape."

"Good idea. Sally will listen to your advice if it gets her closer to freeing Robin. Come early enough to have breakfast with us. She's a great cook."

"I never turn down a free meal. What time?"

"Eight o'clock should work."

Ben yawned and glanced at his watch. "Sorry, Gwen, I know I promised snuggling on your swing, but I'm beat. How about dinner tomorrow evening?"

"I never turn down a free meal either," she echoed.

"Great, it's a date. Why don't you walk me to my car?"

Settled in his leather seat, Ben rolled down the window, reached for Gwen's hand, and kissed it. "See you at eight."

***

Zooming around the village green, Ben felt like he was flying rather than driving. Gwen's energetic welcome-back hug signaled all the encouragement he needed to kiss the lady. How could she have wondered if he'd ever work up his nerve? And how was he going to concentrate on police work?

Again, he toyed with the idea of retiring from the police force. Then he'd have all the time in the world to explore new possibilities with Gwen.

***

Gwen floated back to the swing; her thoughts filled with Ben. Again, she touched her lips. His kisses had been deep and passionate. She chuckled out loud at the silliness of encouraging an intimate relationship at her age. But why not?

"Gwen, it's good to hear you laugh."

Directly ahead of her, Parker's spirit began to take shape. Ben had not mentioned meeting her husband's ghost. She had taken that as a favorable omen and such a relief.

"Parker! So much has happened since Sunday evening."

He lowered his faded body beside her, hardly denting the cushion. "Tell me."

Gwen dove in. "On Monday, Sally's daughter Robin was arrested, and Sally begged me to help her uncover the real attacker, so I invited her to move in while we check around."

"Sounds like something you'd do." Parker smirked. "Tell me your plans."

She explained the photographer's photos revealing no one near Frank, but other guests taking snapshots. She mentioned retrieving Uncle Peter's prints the next afternoon, and their frustration that more guests weren't calling back.

"Do I need to caution you to be careful?"

"No, you don't. You sound like Ben."

"If I recall, he was quite confident in your abilities when he enlisted you last December." Parker's pale eyebrows lifted. "Are you getting enough sleep?"

"Sleep is not the issue, Parker. You know me. As soon as my head hits the pillow, I'm sound asleep. But my doctor did warn me about my high blood pressure. I'm taking a diuretic and walking twice a day with Jenna."

"I'm glad you're following doctor's orders. Now tell me more about your white-haired detective. Is he the reason you were laughing a minute ago?"

"Oh, Parker, I feel strange talking to you about Ben."

"You shouldn't," he admonished in his whispery voice. "I've told you more than once I don't want you to live a celibate life. Sorry things didn't work out with Hal. But this Ben seems to be a better match for you. When he met me a few nights ago, he didn't even flinch."

Still getting accustomed to her husband's spirit encouraging her to develop male companionship, Gwen squirmed. "Hal was my buddy, but I never even told him about you, Parker. Ben is different. You're not his first ghost. Plus, as a detective, he understands my fascination with mysteries. We at least have that in common."

Even with Parker's permission to date, sharing her glee about Ben's kisses would border on meanness.

"And your Ben seems to have no problem with my visits." Parker began to fade. "Sorry, Gwen, I have to go. At least I can warn you now." And he was gone.

Chapter Twenty-Six

... early morning, Thursday

As Gwen emerged from her bedroom, she spied Jenna slipping on Skechers outside the guest room and called, "Ready?"

Jenna straightened. "Sure am. Let's go."

In the kitchen, Sally filled Amber's food and water bowls. Gwen called, "Looks like my cat likes you more than me."

"She'll like whoever's feeding her," Sally retorted. "Don't worry, Gwen. When I leave, she'll come back to you."

"I can only hope," Gwen said as Amber ignored her. "Jenna and I are going out for our morning walk. We should be back for breakfast before Detective Snowcrest joins us at eight."

Sally glanced over. "Don't you worry about the detective. I'll make extra so he can have his fill. See you in a bit."

For their morning walk, Gwen suggested the sidewalk bordering her side lawn. Halfway along, she pointed. "See those ruts? Wedding guests ignored my no parking signs. I need to add soil and plant grass seed."

"What a shame," Jenna said. "Will the lawn recover?"

"Only if I drag my hose down here every day until the seeds sprout." Gwen immediately regretted her snappishness. "Forgive my whining, Jenna."

"You're forgiven."

When they reached the birch trees, they turned left. Further up, Gwen waved toward the opposite side of North Street. "Let's cross over and walk through the Baylies campus. Since I retired, I rarely venture over there. You can point out the building where you're taking your classes."

After dodging a blue car and a delivery truck, they stepped onto the college grounds, walking quietly beside each other. Gwen admired the open spaces dotted with revered old oaks and maples, the building foundations camouflaged by low-growing evergreens, paths edged with rhododendrons, plus rose gardens and flower beds alight with Mother Nature's reds, pinks, and yellows.

As they passed the central pond, water splashed from the fountain, creating ripples. Waterlilies floated and purple iris hugged the banks.

Drinking in the picturesque surroundings, Gwen breathed deep. "I'd forgotten the beauty of this campus."

Jenna pointed at the oldest brick building. "This is where my morning class is meeting."

"How many students?"

Jenna hesitated as if counting heads. "Eight. Yesterday's session was mostly an overview. Afterwards, the professor helped me compare the academic calendars with the courses required for my master's degree. After these summer classes, I'll take a full load for the fall and spring semesters plus a few next summer. Combined, they should give me the credits I need for the degree. Then I begin my search for a position."

"Can you handle another long stretch of bookwork?"

Jenna laughed. "After years of college for my bachelor's degree, I think I can endure the additional education."

They strolled along until Gwen said, "When I was still in bed this morning, an idea came to me. Would you like to stay with me beyond this summer until you earn your master's?"

"Like to? I'd love to! Thank you." Jenna threw her arms around Gwen and hugged tight for several long moments.

"You could show a little more enthusiasm."

Jenna laughed. "You won't get tired of me underfoot?"

"Not at all. You've been a model houseguest, and I don't expect you to go downhill any time soon. Besides, who better to share the old library than my sort-of granddaughter?"

They entered the brick building. As their footfalls echoed down the hallway, neither one spoke. Jenna came to a stop at a specific door and turned the knob.

A curly-haired woman looked up from the podium. "Jenna? You're a little early."

"Good morning, Professor. This is my hostess and dear friend Gwen Andrews."

The woman stared. "Professor Andrews? I don't know if you remember me, but I loved your music history class. You brought the composers to life. Real people instead of mere names and dates in a book."

Gwen moved closer, struggling to remember this woman's name. Her mind blanking, she relied on social niceties. "So good to see you after all these years. Do you enjoy teaching?"

"I do. Especially when I'm blessed with students like Jenna." The professor smiled brightly as she placed her hand on her notes. "I'm so sorry, but I need to finalize my plan. Good to see you, Professor Andrews. And Jenna, I'll see you for class in a little while."

Leading the way down the hallway and back to the entrance, Jenna asked, "What's your favorite building?"

"Hands down the library at the top of The Dimple."

They maneuvered the various pathways and soon stood below the long run of steps.

Jenna glanced over at Gwen. "Want to go inside?"

"Sure." Gwen rushed to the top step. When the world swirled around her, she plopped down and dropped her head in her hands.

Jenna hustled to her side. "What's wrong?"

"My head is spinning. I've always had a bad habit of holding my breath when I run up steps."

"Did you take your medication this morning?"

"I did. I think this wooziness is more a gift of my age than my blood pressure."

Jenna frowned. "I'm pressing you too hard. From now on, we won't be so ambitious with our walks."

Gwen pushed herself to a standing position. "See, I'm fine. My fault. I'm the one who decided to run up those steps."

"We'll share the blame. Let's head back."

Minutes later, as they approached Gwen's library home, Matt's truck pulled up and three men jumped out. A muscular workman met her halfway. "Sorry, Mrs. Andrews, but we're all you get this morning. The rest of the guys are working another job. We'll get started on the framing for your garage walls."

Gwen squinted up at him. "Whatever progress you make is fine. The crime scene delay wasn't your fault."

Ben's red Corvette pulled to the front curb.

Picking up her pace, Gwen hurried ahead of Jenna and gripped his door handle. "Good morning, Ben." Warming at the memory of his kisses the night before, she winked at him before introducing Jenna.

***

Entering ahead of the chattering Jenna and Ben – apparently fast friends – Gwen found Fred sitting at the island scrolling through his cell phone. She'd forgotten he was stopping by for a copy of the guest list. There was no extra car out front, so he must have walked over from the B&B.

Near the sink, Sally stirred something in a bowl, a total absence of small talk between them. Had they argued again about Robin's purported innocence?

Gwen attempted to break the tension. "Good morning, Fred. Didn't know you'd be here so early."

Not bothering to hide her irritation, Sally spoke over her shoulder. "He arrived right after you and Jenna headed out for your walk. I invited him to breakfast, but he's not interested."

Had Fred's refusal to eat Sally's cooking annoyed her?

"Oh, all right, Sally, I'll stay." He swiveled in Gwen's direction. "I stopped over for a copy of Robin's guest list."

"Sally's busy, so I'll get that for you." On her way to the copy machine in the guest room, Gwen passed Ben and Jenna. She tilted her head toward the kitchen, hoping they would get the hint that intervention was required.

Nodding his understanding, Ben positioned Jenna ahead of him before urging her forward.

By the time Gwen returned with Fred's copy, the four were discussing a logical format for Frank's obituary.

Because the island countertop was too crowded to handle extra diners, Gwen grabbed some plates to set the table in the dining room.

Fred lifted them from her hands and followed her, noticing the photographs before she had a chance to move them. "What are these?"

"The wedding day pictures from the photographer Robin hired. Sally and I are creating a memory album for the kids."

"Oh, that's right. She mentioned these yesterday."

Fred set down the plates, picked up the smaller stack of six pictures, and squinted at the images. "Are the guests in the background taking snapshots?"

"They are. We're hoping one of them captured someone approaching Frank on the upper deck or near the garage."

Fred dropped the photos and sifted through the larger stack. "I still think you and Sally are on a fool's errand."

Gwen seethed. Fred still believed Robin had attacked Frank. She snatched the prints from his hands. "Let's finish setting the table."

***

Ben wiped his lips. "Those were the best blueberry pancakes I've ever eaten."

Sally beamed. "Well, I researched the best foods for people dealing with high blood pressure. Berries, oatmeal, bananas. I'm working them into our meals while I'm playing chef."

"I have to admit, Sally," Fred added from his place at the far end of the table, "I'm impressed."

"Don't know how Gwen and I will survive after you leave." Jenna complained.

The words lightened Gwen's outlook. One day – hopefully soon – she and Sally would uncover the perfect clue that proved Robin innocent. Sally and her freed daughter would drive back to Cape Cod, leaving Gwen to the idyllic peace of summer with only Jenna and Amber – and hopefully Ben – to share the serenity.

She glanced over at him, startled to find him gazing back at her. Uninterrupted evenings with the detective would certainly be a welcome bonus.

Chapter Twenty-Seven

… mid-morning, Thursday

After breakfast, Ben changed his seat to linger beside Gwen at the dining room table. Jenna cleared the dishes before heading out to her class. Fred departed to deal with the grim duty of claiming his brother's body. When the defense attorney phoned, Sally disappeared upstairs.

"You know, Gwen," Ben began when they were alone. "I won't be scared off if you're the one with high blood pressure."

Gwen shot him a sideways glance. "How'd you guess?"

"Process of elimination. Jenna's too young. I doubt Sally knows Fred's medical status. And I don't think she'd announce her menu adjustments if she were the one. That leaves you."

"I should have known you'd figure out it's me."

Sally hurried down the staircase, her palm covering the microphone end of her cell phone. "Gwen, the criminal lawyer can drive up now from Plymouth to discuss Frank and Robin with both of us."

"Sure," Gwen agreed. "We're not due at your Uncle Peter's until after lunch."

Sally settled the timing with the lawyer, ended the call, and took a chair opposite Gwen and Ben. "She'll be here within the half hour, depending on traffic."

Abandoning his plan to steal another kiss, Ben instructed his brain to concentrate. "Why don't we discuss your tactics for this afternoon? Where are those six photographer's prints?"

"Right here," Gwen answered as she swiveled to snatch them from the sideboard behind her.

Ben spread them on the table in no particular order. "Before we go any further, let me make myself clear. I don't usually go behind the back of another detective, but Detective Warren didn't request photos from the photographer or the guests."

"So, you think we're on the right track?" Gwen asked.

Ben shrugged one shoulder. "Only time will tell."

Sally tented her fingers. "Why is he so convinced of Robin's guilt?"

"His evidence appears to be circumstantial." Ben ticked off the elements. "Robin's bruises, her abandonment of Frank while he was passed out, and her opportunity to sneak back to his side while Gwen was at the other end of her property. He must think Robin is strong enough to lift Frank. Motive, method, and opportunity... all he needed to make the arrest."

Sally hissed, "Well, he's wrong."

Ben shifted his gaze away from Sally.

She leaned into his face. "You don't think my Robin's innocent?"

"I haven't met your daughter," Ben said, his tone a bit testy. "Even if I had, my gut instinct about her guilt or innocence is irrelevant. I need solid proof that someone else moved Frank into Gwen's garage before I can challenge Detective Warren."

"Hold on, Ben," Gwen said, raising her hand. "You didn't mention if Detective Warren spoke to any of the guests before he arrested Robin. I'm wondering if any of them even know Frank's dead."

Pushing back his chair, Ben said, "I'll call Warren right now and ask." Cell phone in hand, he retired to the music studio.

***

At first, the two women sat in silence.

Too far away to decipher Ben's murmured conversation, Gwen leaned closer to Sally. "Any idea when Fred will publish Frank's obituary in the papers?"

Sally's gray curls jiggled. "Fred didn't say. He probably won't stop at the newspaper offices until he meets with the funeral director and settles the details of the service."

"Makes sense," Gwen said, tapping her chin. "If the guests aren't aware of Frank's death, they could find out from his funeral announcement."

"What does that matter?"

"Could be nothing, Sally. I'm just thinking out loud."

***

Ben returned to the dining room table. "Perry didn't have a copy of the guest list, so he didn't call any of the guests."

"So," Sally grumbled, "he arrested my girl without turning a critical eye on anyone else who was at the wedding."

Rather than encourage Sally's bitterness, Ben placed the six photos of the background picture-takers side by side. "Which guests are you visiting this afternoon?"

177

Distracted from her resentment, Sally tapped the blurry photo of the white-bearded man. "My Uncle Peter in Sandwich. He requested prints from his disposable camera."

Ben picked up Uncle Peter's hazy likeness and studied it as he had with Gwen the night before. "What's the likelihood he snuck back to Frank and led him into the garage?"

Sally snorted. "Slim to none. Uncle Peter's in his late eighties or even early nineties. He walks with a cane, so he would lose his balance if he struggled with Frank. Besides, he doesn't drive. If he hitched a ride with another guest, he couldn't have hung around after Robin cancelled the wedding."

Waving his hand over the remaining prints, Ben asked, "Who's next?"

Gwen referred to the legal pad. "Kelly in Yarmouth Port."

"Any idea which woman in which photo?" Ben asked.

Sally sorted through the other five, her head shaking. "I'd be guessing. She must be a friend of Robin's, but I've never met her."

"That covers two of the six who took snapshots on wedding day," Ben commented.

"Two of the six that Jeremy captured with his camera," Gwen amended.

Nodding his concession, Ben said, "You might get lucky and discover others. I'd like to keep tabs on your whereabouts."

"I appreciate your vigilance," Gwen said, smiling at him.

Ben's heart dissolved into an embarrassing puddle until he collected his wits. "Write down the name and address of Uncle

Peter and this Kelly in Yarmouth Port. If you arrange to meet anyone else while you're on the Cape, text me their details."

Gwen tore a sheet from the legal pad and passed it to Sally. "We can do that."

Sally referred to Robin's guest list, wrote down the two names and addresses, and slid the paper to Ben, saying, "Gwen and I can make more follow-up calls while we wait for the defense attorney to arrive."

Gwen held up her forefinger. "The alternatives to a guest attacker would be someone who followed Frank to the wedding or even a deranged stranger."

"Your first option is unlikely, but possible," Ben conceded, "and I doubt Harbor Falls is sheltering a random maniac. At least let's hope not."

He straightened, glancing from Gwen to Sally. "A word of caution. All the guests are potential suspects, even if you don't come across a photographic record."

"If we don't," Sally said, "I don't know how we'll prove Robin is innocent."

"And another thing," Ben continued without acknowledging Sally's worry. "Keep in mind that the guests were not told that Frank is dead."

At this point, he glanced over at Sally. "If you let that detail slip and that your daughter's been arrested for her husband's death, the savvier guests might figure out your real purpose for requesting their snapshots is to find an ill-tempered attacker among them. They could refuse to share their photos."

"I'll do my best not to blurt." Sally's snarky tone exposed her irritation at his implication that she was a blabber mouth. "I guess we shouldn't ask if they noticed anyone near Frank after he collapsed even if they didn't take a picture?"

Ben pushed back his chair. "No, you shouldn't. That'll blow your cover story. Stick with your memory album for the bride and groom, which I assume you're doing."

"You assume right," Sally confirmed. "I like the idea of preserving the wedding day images for the kids, even if the planned ceremony never took place."

"Oh, one more thing," Ben added. "I've been thinking about those shoe impressions on Gwen's garage floor. Sally, do you have Robin's luggage?"

Her forehead wrinkled. "Yes. Her suitcase and Franks are in my van."

Ben stepped toward Gwen's foyer. "Let's go have a look."

Chapter Twenty-Eight

… late morning, Thursday

As Ben dragged Robin's luggage to the back edge of Sally's van, the three workmen from Matt's construction crew sauntered down the driveway. "Mrs. Andrews, we're heading out for an early lunch, but we'll be back."

"Thanks for letting me know," Gwen called.

As their truck rumbled off, Ben searched through the suitcase, pulling out several pairs of women's shoes. "Which ones did Robin wear for the wedding?"

Sally pointed to navy blue low-heeled pumps.

Ben inspected every inch. "I don't see any concrete. What shoes was she wearing at the police station?"

"I didn't notice," Sally admitted.

"That's okay. I can find out." He closed the lid, rezipped the suitcase, and latched the van's back door. "I'd prefer to go with you both this afternoon, but I think you'll have more success without me."

"We'll be careful," Gwen promised.

"Thanks for the tips," Sally added and headed inside.

Gwen walked Ben to his Corvette. As they stood beside his driver's door, he leaned down and stole the kiss he'd been denied since breakfast.

Pulling back, Gwen glanced at her front windows. "You're naughty. Sally might be watching."

Recovering from the taste of her lips on his, Ben slid his brain into gear. "I don't know about you, Gwen, but I don't care who sees us."

She slapped his arm in jest. "After Frank's attacker is caught, we'll carve out more time for smooching."

"I'm going to hold you to that promise. Don't forget, I'm taking you to dinner tonight. How about I pick you up at six?"

"Sally and I should be back from the Cape long before that. See you later."

***

During the halt of the noisy garage construction, Gwen and Sally found quiet spots at opposite ends of the back yard. Gwen in the arbor swing and Sally on the upper deck. They set about re-dialing the unresponsive guests.

Heeding Ben's warning, Gwen resisted the temptation to ask each guest if they had noticed activity near Frank. One woman – who'd taken no photos – expressed her disgust at the stepfather's drunken collapse and regret that the fires had damaged the beautiful gardens.

Gwen's final call was more fruitful. When she told the guest that she and Sally could stop by to download her snapshots, the woman said to come around three-thirty because she walked her dog at four. Gwen asked for her address and disconnected.

Sally ambled over from the upper deck and scooted Gwen to the other end of the swing cushion. "Any luck?"

"Yep." Gwen pulled her legal pad onto her lap and jotted a note. "Erica near Mashpee Commons by three-thirty today. Remind me to grab my thumb drive and the special cable before we head out."

"I didn't speak with any of them," Sally moaned. "Only more messages to call me."

Patting her cousin's knee, Gwen said, "Let's cross our fingers they call. We have to remember to control our impulse to gain sympathy by mentioning Robin's arrest."

Sally snorted. "By we, you mean me, Gwen. Like I told your white-haired detective, I'll keep my mouth shut. We'd be up the old creek if the culprit among them guesses the real reason we want their snapshots."

When Sally reached for her buzzing phone, it fell from her hands and slid across the arbor platform, skittering down the step and landing in the dry grass before she caught up with it.

Watching Sally's comical chase, Gwen repressed a grin.

Finishing her conversation, Sally pushed the disconnect button and shouted "Bingo! That was Travis in Cotuit. I guess Jeremy didn't catch him in a background photo because the others appear to be females. He's working from home and said we should stop by any time this afternoon." She commandeered the legal pad from Gwen's lap, quickly adding his name and address to their list of visits.

"We're making progress, Sally."

"Let's hope it continues." Sally tilted her head. "Do you happen to have a road atlas of the Cape?"

"Sure do. It's on a shelf in my music studio."

"Great. The map on my phone is way too little. Let's go inside and plan our route."

After locating each town, they determined the sequence of their stops, Sally's finger tracing the various roadways. "First, Uncle Peter in East Sandwich. Second, a scenic drive along 6A to Kelly's in Yarmouth Port. Third, Travis in Cotuit. Fourth, your dog walker in Mashpee." Sally looked up from the atlas. "We seem to be on a roll, Gwen. You know what?"

Suspicious of the gleam in her cousin's eye, Gwen couldn't avoid delivering the obvious response, "What?"

"Let's assume we'll hear from the last three picture-takers by the end of the day, but it'll be too late to visit them. Rather than battle the bridge traffic twice, why don't you pack a bag and stay overnight at my house in Falmouth?"

Always a sucker for a house tour, Gwen said, "Great plan."

Sally bubbled with enthusiam. "Falmouth is a perfect ending point for this afternoon's loop. Tomorrow morning, we'll be in the area to retrieve any other snapshots before we head back here to Harbor Falls."

It occurred to Gwen she'd be spending more time on Cape Cod than she had for years. After Frank's case was closed, she and Ben could drive down for lunch at a quaint cafe with an afternoon stroll along a sandy beach. If they planned their day trip during the week, they'd avoid the weekend crowds.

Gwen winced. Ben was supposed to pick her up at six for dinner. She hated to cancel, but if Sally collected those additional snapshots on her own, she might forget herself and blurt out the news of Frank's death and Robin's arrest.

The danger was not worth the risk.

***

When Gwen's name popped up in Ben's caller ID, he wasted no time hitting the answer button. "You missing me so soon?" he teased. When she hesitated, he sensed her reason for calling was not going to make him happy.

"I'm so sorry, Ben, but I need to postpone our dinner."

"Can you tell me why?"

"Of course." She explained Sally's suggestion to stay overnight on the Cape so they'd be in the area to collect potential photographs the next morning.

"I'm disappointed, Gwen, but I understand you wanting to keep Sally out of harm's way. Let's hope one of the guest's snapshots reveal someone besides Robin with Frank so you'll be done with this merry chase."

"My fingers are crossed," she said. "Ben, if this trip doesn't provide damning evidence, I don't know where else to look."

"Don't predict defeat, Gwen. You can't know what you and Sally will uncover."

"You're in an encouraging mood," Gwen commented. "Can I have a raincheck for dinner?"

"You bet. Let's loosely plan for tomorrow night."

"Deal."

"And, Gwen, don't forget to text me if you arrange any additional guest visits."

"I will."

In the background, Ben heard Sally calling Gwen's name.

"Sorry, Ben, I have to go. The defense attorney is here."

In the detective suite, Ben placed his cell phone on his desk blotter. Gwen was a clever lady, but she'd gotten herself into dicey situations more than once while chasing clues to uncover a criminal. She'd had several sidekicks along the way. Hal Jenkins, her sister Tess, and Ben himself. For this case, her cousin Sally assumed that role. But she was a loose cannon.

Ben's concern ratcheted upward. Would they collect a potentially incriminating snapshot without incident?

***

Vexed she wouldn't see Ben that evening, Gwen descended the staircase. At the sound of voices, she paused at the mid-point landing and peeked through the open balusters. In the living room below, Sally handed a check to a suited woman with blonde hair captured in a chignon style. Gwen realized that she had failed to pick up on Sally's earlier statement that '*she*' was driving up from Plymouth.

Deep in conversation, neither attorney nor client noticed Gwen until she paused beside them.

"Oh, Gwen, you startled me," Sally blurted. "Let me introduce you to Ursula Evans. I've hired her to defend Robin."

After a cordial greeting, Ursula asked. "Can you walk me through the scene?"

Gwen nodded, saying, "Right this way." Out the front door, she led Sally and the lawyer up the driveway.

In the garage, Gwen skirted the constructed walls lying flat on the concrete floor to the spot where Frank had drawn his last breath. Ursula snapped digital photos and jotted notes as she confirmed details.

Sooner than expected, the construction crew returned and resumed their clamor. The three women retreated inside.

The thick walls of the old library did little to dull the noise of drills and hammers, causing Gwen and Sally to raise their volume as they provided Ursula with a timeline: Robin's arrival with the drunk Frank; the bruises Gwen had noticed; his collapse during the ceremony; the luminary bag fires; the wedding cancellation; Gwen's retreat to the end of her property; returning to find the chaise empty; discovering Frank's body; Detective Warren's hasty arrest; the search for a photo showing a different culprit.

Satisfied she had a good grasp of the events; Ursula drove off to conduct her interview with Robin.

Sally closed the front door behind the lawyer. "What do you think, Gwen? Does Ursula seem sharp enough to run circles around Detective Warren's circumstantial evidence?"

"Hard to say. She encouraged our hunt for an incriminating snapshot to implicate someone besides Robin."

Sally's shoulders slumped before straightening. "She did say she'll try to arrange a visit for me. Let's eat a quick lunch. I can't wait to get my hands on Uncle Peter's prints."

While Sally toasted flatbread sandwiches, Gwen hurried to the garage to alert the men about her trip to the Cape. Their progress was remarkable. The walls that earlier had been lying flat on the concrete floor were now bolted to each other and to the twice-as-high cinder block wall, concealing Frank's rebar spike. The blood stains on the sides of the cinder blocks remained in full view for anyone who knew to look.

Gwen hailed the crewman who'd spoken to her earlier.

He hustled to her side. "Mrs. Andrews, glad you came out to check on us. Want a quick tour?"

At her nod, he detailed the raising of the roof, the installation of the automatic door, and the estimated timing of the finish work, which was at least a week away.

"It's looking great. Thanks for the update." Turning to go back inside, Gwen remembered why she'd gone out in the first place and pivoted back, calling, "I'm driving to the Cape this afternoon and won't be back until sometime tomorrow."

He ambled back to her and she handed him a slip of paper.

"Here's my cell phone number in case something comes up while I'm out of town."

Returning to the kitchen, she gobbled Sally's flatbread topped with chicken salad, pineapple, and shredded carrot.

When Gwen started to pick up her dishes, Sally said, "I'll clean up. You go upstairs and pack an overnight bag. Don't forget your thumb drive and the transfer cable."

Chapter Twenty-Nine

… after lunch, Thursday

Gwen gritted her teeth as Sally maneuvered through the traffic clogging the Sagamore Bridge onto Cape Cod. Preferring the accelerator over the brake, Sally tended to tailgate.

Searching for a distraction, Gwen said, "Did the guests you spoke to ask if Allison rescheduled the wedding?"

"A few," Sally answered. "I simply told them that the kids eloped and are on their honeymoon."

"And you still haven't heard from Ashley?"

"Not a peep. I don't know why that girl is ignoring me."

"Maybe there's a perfectly logical explanation," Gwen suggested, hoping her words were true.

"Maybe," Sally echoed, merging with the Route 6 traffic and crossing the bridge without incident. "Gwen, can you navigate us to Uncle Peter's house? I haven't been to his place for decades."

Gwen pulled up the map app on her phone, registered Uncle Peter's address, and instructed Sally to take the next exit. They soon turned onto the less busy and more scenic Route 6A, aptly named Old King's Highway.

Slapping the steering wheel, Sally said, "I hate the idea that someone invited to the wedding attacked Frank."

Being two miles from their next turn, Gwen looked up from her phone's GPS. "That *is* disturbing. But one of them could be the person we're hoping to uncover. Ben doubts the culprit crashed the wedding. I didn't know any of the guests, so I'd be useless to identify the crasher… if there was one."

"You're not alone. Other than my immediate family, I only knew a few of them, like Uncle Peter. Robin and Frank invited their friends, Allison and Cole the twenty-somethings."

Having no other input about the guest list, Gwen turned to her navigator duties. "Take a left, then a quick right."

Sally drove along a dirt lane until they spotted a farmhouse and outbuildings among several acres of flat land segregated by trenches. "Here we are. Now I remember this place."

"Your Uncle Peter lives on a cranberry bog?" Gwen exclaimed, stating the obvious.

The white-bearded man from the blurry photo appeared at the oversized entrance and waved.

Sally hurried up the pathway, stretching high to hug him.

He pushed her to arm's length and studied her face. "So good to see you, Sally. I missed you and Isaac when you moved to California all those years ago. He was my favorite nephew." Uncle Peter's eyes misted. "I was so sorry to hear about his accident. How have you been holding up?"

"I'm feeling more grounded since I moved back to New England." She turned him in Gwen's direction. "This is my cousin Gwen Andrews. She owns the home and back yard where the wedding was supposed to take place."

Uncle Peter grasped Gwen's hands. "A happy event turned sour." He clicked his tongue. "Are your beautiful gardens salvageable?"

Gwen found herself wishing this gentle old man were her own uncle as she concentrated on his question. "I've already replanted the annuals and perennials. With a bit of TLC, Mother Nature will take care of the rest."

He stroked his white beard. "Mother Nature's a good woman." Moving to stand between her and Sally, he said, "Can you both stay for a glass of iced tea?"

"I wish we could," Sally answered, "but we're picking up snapshots from a few other guests this afternoon, so we're on a tight schedule."

"In that case, come with me and I'll locate the photo envelope." He led them into the house and through a central hallway to a huge old-fashioned kitchen at the rear.

"I tried to sell this place years ago," Uncle Peter explained as he searched one surface after another, "but I never found a buyer. Not too many folks are interested in working a cranberry bog these days. After a while, I took it off the market and hired a foreman plus a crew to handle the day to day chores. Even with their expense, I still turn a tidy profit." He circled the kitchen once again, muttering, "Just as well. Lots of memories of me and Maude in this old house. I don't see that envelope in here. Let's check in the den," he murmured, waving them into the adjacent wood-paneled room.

"Ah, here it is." He handed the packet to Sally.

She tucked it into her handbag. "Thank you, Uncle Peter."

"Mind you, I only looked through those briefly. Don't know if any of them will be good enough for your memory album."

"I'm sure we'll choose a few," Sally promised.

"After the shock of their ruined wedding wears off, the kids will appreciate your efforts. You said they eloped?"

"They did. Probably for the best, with the baby coming."

Without comment, Uncle Peter circled around to a wide staircase and waved up the steep steps. "The upstairs is completely closed off. With my walking difficulties, it's easier to live on the ground floor."

On impulse, Gwen glanced down at his feet to see a pair of well-worn slippers. Of course, he wouldn't be wearing the dress shoes he'd worn to the wedding. If Uncle Peter weren't as frail as he pretended, and he was the guy who attacked Frank, the soles of his dress shoes would bear the evidence of concrete residue. Looking up at him, Gwen shook her head. What was she thinking to suspect this kindly old man?

When they paused at the front door, Uncle Peter said, "You know, Sally, I've loved your Christmas cards and letters over the years, but I'd much rather spend time with you in person."

"Me, too, Uncle Peter," Sally agreed. "As soon as I return to my home in Falmouth, we'll do lunch."

His bushy white eyebrows lifted, wrinkling his forehead. "You haven't returned to your home on the Cape?"

Once again, Gwen rushed to the rescue. "I invited Sally to spend a few days with me in Harbor Falls so we could catch up

192

on our lives while she was living in California. And now we're working on this memory album together."

"So you are," the old man mumbled without challenging the explanation. "Well, off with you both. You've got places to go and people to see." Uncle Peter smiled sadly as he waved goodbye from his doorway.

Chapter Thirty

…early afternoon, Thursday

Back in the car, Sally blew out a breath. "Gwen, I nearly spilled the beans about Robin's arrest because I haven't returned to my Falmouth house. Thanks for saving my bacon."

"You'd do the same for me," Gwen said as she buckled her seatbelt. "Should we have a look at Uncle Peter's snapshots?"

Sally backed down his driveway and drove along his dirt lane before coming to a stop when they reached the paved road. She slammed the gearshift into park. "Can you reach my handbag on the back seat?"

Stretching through the opening, Gwen looped her finger through the strap and pulled it forward.

Sally located the envelope. "Cross your fingers."

They studied each snapshot. Most of the people were blurry because the subject was in motion. Other images focused on the wedding trellis, the set-up of rented chairs, Gwen's flower beds, the potting shed, the swing, the woods bordering her property. There were a few snaps of the firemen and their truck. None of Frank passed out or anyone near him.

"Rats," Sally huffed, nudging the prints back into the packet. "None of these will help Robin, though we can use a few in the album as location shots." She glanced at the dashboard clock, slammed the van into drive, and skittered onto the pavement. "I wish we had time to stop at Grey's Beach. I love that boardwalk."

"Parker and I strolled it many times," Gwen said, "but that was more than a decade ago."

"A great reason for you to come back for a real visit." When Sally's phone buzzed, she pushed the steering wheel answer button to send the call to the Bluetooth system. "Hello."

"Grandma, this is Ashley. I lost my phone and the replacement was just now delivered. I listened to your messages. What do you want to tell me?"

Sally glanced at Gwen. "You know, sweetie, I'm driving right now, and I don't want to be distracted. Can you come to my house tonight?"

Ashley didn't answer right away, drowned out by whoops and shouts in the background. Her voice returned. "Sure, grandma. What time?"

"How about seven?"

"Fine. See you later." The line went dead.

"Sounds like she's in a noisy area," Gwen ventured.

"She is. Did I mention this is her last summer as a camp counselor down in Brewster? She graduated with a degree in child psychology. I'm just grateful that Ashley's willing to spend time with me."

"Have you decided how to tell her about Frank and Robin?"

"That's been keeping me awake at night, but I think I've settled on the best approach. We'll see how it goes when my granddaughter is sitting across from me this evening. I didn't want to tell her over the phone."

Having no opinion of the potential fireworks, Gwen guided Sally a few more miles along Route 6A to a condominium complex on their left. "Here we are."

As they cruised the various streets of the development, they spotted a golf course running behind the buildings.

"Very posh," Sally commented.

When they located the correct unit number, Sally parked.

A sun-bronzed woman in a golf cart sped from the opposite direction and up the driveway, screeching to a halt. She hopped out and sprinted to Sally's window. "I'm Kelly. Your timing is perfect. Glad you found me. Lots of people get confused with the streets winding around the fairways. Give me a sec to store my clubs. I'll be right with you."

Unstrapping the golf bag heavy with clubs, Kelly carried it with little effort to a storage cabinet at the rear of her garage. She hurried back as Sally and Gwen exited the van. "My husband has an early tee time tomorrow, so I was instructed to remove my clubs from our cart after today's nine holes with the girls." Kelly snickered and rolled her eyes. "Men."

Sally dove into the reason for their visit. "We've never met, but Robin speaks fondly of you."

Kelly's face dropped. "Robin? You're not the woman who called to view Unit 313?"

Paling, Sally forged ahead. "No, I'm Robin's mother Sally. You spoke to Gwen here on the phone about the digital snapshots you took at Saturday's wedding. We're making a memory album for the bride and groom."

Kelly's hand flew to her chest. "I'm so sorry. I'm expecting a potential buyer to view the unit next door. Forgive me for making assumptions. Please come in. After I wash my hands, we can download my pics."

As Gwen entered the home, she admired the soothing decor. Every nook boasted a tasteful adornment. As a real estate agent, Kelly seemed to maintain her home as an always-staged unit to entice new owners.

After detouring into a powder room for less than a minute, Kelly emerged and pulled out her phone, scrolling through her pictures. "Here they are. I'm sorry I don't have more to contribute to the memory book."

Gwen held out her thumb drive and cable.

Kelly connected it to the side of her phone. Tapping the keys in quick succession, she soon handed it back. "There you go. I haven't had a chance to look at them. I hope there's something you can use. I almost deleted them after the wedding was cancelled. Is Robin's daughter making new plans?"

Sally kept her tone light. "The kids eloped."

"Good for them. Much less fuss." Kelly paused. "I wasn't surprised when Frank collapsed. With all his drinking, it was only a matter of time. Robin's life would be so much better without him. I hope she leaves him this time."

Sally's lips twitched, possibly resisting a snide remark. "Well, Gwen and I need to scoot. Nice to meet you, Kelly."

Gwen glanced down at the photo that showed Robin's feet, not surprised to see soft-cleated golf shoes. There was no way to know if her wedding day footwear carried the residue of concrete.

Seemingly unaware of Sally's reserved response, Kelly said, "You, too, Sally. Tell Robin we'll do lunch soon," and she shut the door behind them.

Seated in the van, Gwen said, "You know, Sally, like Ben said, we shouldn't assume the attacker was a man. Kelly had no problem schlepping that heavy golf bag."

Pulling away from the curb, Sally drove in silence for a block. "You're right. And she was no fan of Frank's. Do you think she did away with him like any good friend would do?"

"Hard to say. I try not to jump to conclusions. Any idea if she came to the wedding by herself?"

Sally's head wagged. "Nope, and I don't know who we'd ask without arousing suspicion."

"If we don't come across a snapshot of her with Frank, we have nothing to report to Ben except our reaction to her."

"You're right," Sally admitted.

When they reached the exit, Sally pulled the van over. "Let's have a look at Kelly's snapshots."

Gwen plugged the cable with attached thumb drive into her phone and brought up only nine pictures. None gave the evidence they'd hoped to find.

"This is so frustrating," Sally fretted. "But it'll be all right. We just need to keep going. Which direction, Gwen?"

"Hold on." Gwen tapped her cell phone map and read the

directions. "We're going to turn right, then straight for a few miles, left onto the Hyannis/Barnstable Road, which becomes Bliney Lane. After it crosses Route 6, a few more miles before we merge onto Route 28."

"One instruction at a time," Sally griped. "I'm too preoccupied to remember all those turns."

Chapter Thirty-One

… mid-afternoon, Thursday

Cotuit's Main Street boasted an array of shops, private homes, the public library, and historic society, all surrounded by neatly trimmed bushes, well-established trees, and colorful flowers. The quaint town had not changed since Gwen and Parker strolled its streets many years before.

Glancing down at her screen, Gwen gasped, "Hold it, Sally, we missed a turn."

"That's no biggie. What's the name of the next street?"

"Left onto Cross, then another on Oceanview Avenue."

Several turns later, Sally propelled the van along Bluff Point Drive. Gwen gaped at the elegant oceanside structures. "These homes must cost millions."

"Good guess," Sally agreed. "I wonder how Robin knows someone in this neighborhood."

Circling the cul-de-sac, Sally pulled into the driveway of a mini mansion. Through the shady lane that extended beyond the house, a dock stretched into Cotuit Bay.

Sally peered in awe. "Do we have the right place?"

Gwen doublechecked the legal pad. "This is the address you wrote down."

"Hello there," a male voice shouted.

They looked up to see a casually dressed man with a neatly trimmed beard exiting the double-door entrance and striding toward them.

His mouth widened in a cordial smile. "I'm Travis. You must be Sally." He opened her door and extended his hand to assist her from the driver's seat. "I'm glad you called and offered to stop by. Working from home can get lonely."

"Nice to meet you, Travis. This is my cousin Gwen." Sally's face took on a confused expression. "I…I'm sorry, but how does my Robin know you?"

"She never mentioned working for me?" His grin implied a mischievous streak. "I think I'm insulted. Robin was my assistant for several years until she re-married. She was a crackerjack. I've never found her equal. Please come in."

They followed him through a high-ceilinged foyer into an expansive room with a view of Cotuit Bay through arched windows topped by stained glass transoms. The water beyond sparkled in the afternoon sun.

Travis glanced down at Sally. "Robin told me all about her mother living in California. I wish we'd had a chance to get acquainted at last Saturday's wedding." He shook his head. "Sad business. And her husband's spectacle. I never understood…" Travis caught himself and changed the topic. "You said Robin's daughter and her bridegroom eloped?"

Sally nodded. "They did and are on their honeymoon."

In sleuthing mode, Gwen checked his footwear. Loafers in need of a spit shine. Definitely not the shoes this elegant man would have worn to a wedding. Her eyes swept the generous space and noticed a drafting board in one corner of the great room. "You're an architect, Travis?"

"Guilty as charged. Do you know any?"

Moving closer to peek at the plans in progress, Gwen resisted touching the blueprint. "My husband. He designed the conversion of the old village library into the home where the wedding was supposed to take place."

"A remarkable achievement," Travis affirmed. "I was admiring the clever modifications last Saturday. Any chance I could sit down with him and trade design ideas?"

Gwen's face warmed. "Unfortunately, my Parker died several years ago."

Travis's jovial expression wilted. "I'm so sorry."

"Thank you. In many ways, he's still with me," Gwen hoped her words revealed sentiment, not a secret ghost.

Sally gazed out the windows. "I hate to rush you, Travis, but could we look at your snapshots? Gwen and I are due in Mashpee by three-thirty."

"Of course, of course. Let me find my cell phone. I'm forever misplacing it." He ambled from the great room into the adjacent dining room, reappearing with cell phone in hand. "Not sure there's any for your memory album, but I'll let you decide." They scrolled from one picture to the next.

"Do you mind if I download these?" Gwen asked.

"Be my guest."

After transferring his snapshots, she returned his phone.

Travis massaged his forehead. "Do you think Robin might be interested in resuming her old job with me? My most recent assistant resigned last week because she's moving to Boston."

Sally stared at him. "I have no idea, but I'll pass along your offer." She indicated the entire property. "I can't imagine she wouldn't want to work in these picturesque surroundings."

"Great. My phone number hasn't changed. I'll wait to hear from her." Travis waved them toward his foyer. "Let me walk you ladies out."

Chapter Thirty-Two

… mid-afternoon, Thursday

The dashboard clock read quarter to four by the time Sally parked in front of a Cape Cod style cottage within a mile of the Mashpee Commons shopping center.

When a trim woman in patterned tights answered their knock, Sally said, "Sorry we're late, Erica. I think we crammed too many stops into the afternoon."

Erica waved her hand in a dismissive manner. "Don't worry about it. Rosco will just have to wait for his afternoon walk."

With no barking, an oversized shaggy dog appeared at Erica's side, a leash gripped in his teeth.

She leaned down and pushed unruly hair from the canine's face. "Heard your name, did you, Rosco? I know…you're ready to go. As soon as I transfer some snapshots from my phone, we'll head out."

As if the dog understood her words, he dropped the leash to the floor and sat down, his now-exposed eyes inspecting Gwen then Sally as if suggesting, *Well, get on with it.*

"What's his breed?" Sally asked.

"Old English sheepdog."

"He's sweet," Gwen commented. Although she was a cat person, she warmed to dogs who didn't bark, jump on visitors, or drool. Rosco exhibited none of those off-putting habits. One day, she might consider owning a dog like Rosco.

Erica reached behind the door. "My cell phone's right here. Did you bring a transfer cable?"

"Sure did." Gwen held out her connected devices.

"Great. This will only take a few seconds."

When Erica handed them back to Gwen, Sally snapped her fingers. "Gwen and I have been so intent on collecting candid photos that we haven't bought the memory album. Can you recommend any stores in Mashpee Commons?"

"Lady Luck is smiling on you today," Erica answered. "I happen to own a bridal shop over there. Why don't you stop in and my assistant will show you our assortment of albums?"

"Perfect," Sally said. "We'll let you two go for your walk."

As Erica and Rosco escorted them out, Gwen tried to look inconspicuous as she checked Erica's feet. Walking shoes. Totally inappropriate with a wedding outfit. Another strike-out.

With Erica already around the corner with Rosco, Gwen and Sally climbed into the van and viewed the dog owner's snapshots. When they came to a photo of Frank with several people, Gwen nearly bounced in the van's seat like a little kid until she realized the people were her and Sally with Robin as they stared down at the passed-out Frank.

***

After an extended comparison of the wedding albums in Erica's shop, Sally hemmed and hawed, finally buying the first one that had caught her eye.

As they exited the bridal shop and were walking toward the van, Gwen said, "Sally, you've been doing all the driving. Why don't I take a turn and you can navigate?"

"Thanks, Gwen, I could use the break. On our way to my house, we'll stop at the grocery store and buy a rotisserie chicken for dinner. There's a Shaw's on this road before we enter Falmouth proper."

Following Sally's instructions, Gwen steered the van out onto Route 28, identified as the Teaticket Highway. If she remembered, she'd google the history of the unusual name.

"I don't know if you noticed, Sally, but I've been checking the shoes of each guest we visited this afternoon."

"Why?"

"The shoe impressions in the concrete floor of my garage."

Sally slapped her forehead. "Say no more. The person involved in the struggle with Frank would have a bit of concrete on his or her shoes. Did you spot any?"

"Unfortunately, no, but only because none of them were wearing the shoes they would've worn to the wedding."

Before Sally could comment, her phone buzzed, and a voice came through the van's speaker. "Sally? This is Robin's friend Nicole. You left a message to call."

"Thanks for getting back to me," Sally said. "I'm collecting guest snapshots for a memory album. We've been downloading images onto a thumb drive so we can resize, etc."

"What a delightful idea," Nicole gushed. "I'd love some of mine to be chosen. How about early tomorrow morning?"

Wiggling one eyebrow in Gwen's direction, Sally said, "I'm in Falmouth right now. I can pick them up this afternoon."

"No, no, that won't work," Nicole countered. "I'm heading out and won't be home until the wee hours. How about this idea? I manage the Dunkin at the rotary near the Bourne Bridge. The drive time crowd eases up around ten. I can hand you my phone and you can download my snapshots. Does that work for you?"

Sally grinned. "Sure does. See you in the morning and thanks." She disconnected. "How perfect is that? Her donut shop is on our route to Harbor Falls. Where's your legal pad?"

Gwen tilted her head toward the back seat. "Under my shoulder bag behind me. Can you reach it?"

Unbuckling her seat belt, Sally twisted to her knees and squeezed through the opening. She grasped the pad and plopped back into her seat, emitting a loud grunt from the effort. After checking off Nicole's name on Robin's guest list, she made of note on the legal pad about their meeting.

Gwen glanced over from the driver's seat. "We can't know for sure if Nicole was one of our six picture-takers. There could be others who weren't caught in the background of Jeremy's photographs. We should try to catch up with the guests who haven't gotten back to us. How many are left?"

Sally ran her finger down Robin's list. "Eight. We'll call them one final time this evening."

"You know what, Sally?" Gwen didn't wait for an answer. "Since Ben warned us against asking if they noticed activity around Frank, we probably shouldn't bother arranging face-to-face meetings with the rest of them."

"Good point. If any of them happen to be close by, we'll stop by in the morning for their pictures. Otherwise, we'll ask them to email."

"And hope they know how," Gwen added, spotting the big sign for the Shaw's supermarket, and pulling into the lot. She maneuvered the van into a pull-through parking space.

Sally opened her door. "You stay here and keep the A/C running. I won't be long."

While Gwen waited for Sally, she pulled up the snapshots they'd collected over the past few hours. After taking a second look, she realized they hadn't missed any incriminating candids of Frank with another guest. Isolating the photo of her and Sally and Robin hovering over the unconscious Frank, Gwen studied the details.

The angle provided a clear view of Robin and her outfit. She'd chosen a plain navy pantsuit. The cut of the pants and jacket camouflaged her plumpness. On the shoulder, a silver broach contrasted with the dark fabric. She wore the low-heeled navy shoes Ben had inspected for residue.

While there was no incriminating photo, Gwen was encouraged that if she and Sally managed to come across a snapshot of a woman with Frank in the waning light of evening, they'd be able to eliminate Robin by her outfit.

But wait. Robin could have changed her clothes at the B&B before hurrying back to Gwen's upper deck and Frank. The shoes remaining in Robin's suitcase appeared to be clean. That meant the shoes she was wearing the next day when arrested would possibly reveal concrete residue. If so, those shoes could be the incriminating evidence that proved Detective Warren's arrest had been valid.

How could Gwen tactfully ask Sally to sneak a peek at her daughter's footwear when she visited Robin at the jailhouse?

Chapter Thirty-Three

... late afternoon, Thursday

Sally exited the supermarket lugging two bags overflowing with groceries. A loaf of bread poked from the top of one.

Gwen hopped out and hurried around to open the back door. "I see you bought more than the rotisserie chicken," she teased, her nose sniffing the warm bag. "Which smells scrumptious by the way. These supermarkets have quite a set-up for slow roasting a dozen birds at the same time."

"You can't buy an uncooked chicken for the price," Sally disclosed, leaning the bags against one another so they wouldn't spill during the ride. "I don't remember what's in my pantry, so I bought a few russet potatoes, a zucchini, and a few things for breakfast."

Resettled in the driver's seat, Gwen followed Sally's directions and soon entered the center of Falmouth.

Sally pointed. "Pull into the driveway of that weathered-shingle saltbox."

"You live on the Falmouth Green?" Gwen struggled to maintain control of the steering wheel. "I've toured many of these historic homes over the years. I don't recall yours."

Sally chortled. "That's because no one famous ever lived in my house."

As Gwen exited the van, she gazed at the homestead. Flower boxes graced each windowsill, overflowing with purple petunias in need of a drink. Manicured evergreens camouflaged the foundation and a central chimney jutted through the roof. "Sally, your home is so historic."

"I was fortunate this one went on the market when I was house hunting last fall. And the price was right." Hoisting the grocery bags, Sally tilted her head toward the rear of the house. "We'll go in through the kitchen. Spread out the keys in your hand and I'll point out the one that unlocks the back door."

Gwen took the lead up the stepping-stone path through the pachysandra. Crossing the open porch, she thrust the key into the lock and pushed it to swing noiselessly on its hinges.

Plunking the groceries onto the kitchen table, Sally plucked out two potatoes. "I'll get these going before I give you the nickel tour." Setting her oven to 350 degrees, she scrubbed the potatoes, punctured both with a fork, and set the microwave on high for six minutes. As it counted down, Sally stored the groceries, placing the hot chicken on the stovetop. When the timer dinged, she rinsed the potatoes and without drying them placed them in her preheated oven, setting the stove timer to fifteen minutes.

Gwen observed her cousin's routine with interest. "That's an interesting way to bake potatoes."

"I've used this method for years," Sally confided. "Quicker than the traditional hour in the oven without losing that incomparable baked potato taste."

Gwen murmured, "I'll have to remember that."

Sally crooked her finger. "This way, Gwen. The tour won't take long. This is a small saltbox for its time."

They entered the adjacent living room, sprinkled with blue and white upholstered furniture, stained wooden tables, shell-filled lamps, and glass-fronted bookshelves. Framed Cape Cod scenes graced the walls. Wide pine floors peeked out between scatter rugs. A tiled fireplace at the central corner added a hint of cozy, though no fire was blazing.

Spotting a photo of a younger Sally gazing into the camera while a be-speckled man smiled down at her, Gwen pointed and asked, "Sally, is this you and Isaac?"

Sally lifted the framed picture from the carved mantelpiece and touched the man's face, her expression wistful. "Yes, this is us. Do you recall the collapse of the Nimitz Freeway?"

Gwen paused to bring the event forward. "The one caused by an earthquake where the upper level of the highway fell into the lower one?"

"Yes." Sally's eyes misted. "Isaac drove that overpass twice every day. I had found out that morning I was pregnant with Robin." Sally stopped talking, the rest of the calamitous tale unspoken.

"I'm so sorry," Gwen said, knowing the words were of little comfort. She'd shared thirty-seven years of marriage with Parker before his tragic death. Sally had enjoyed far fewer with her Isaac. Not wanting to dwell on their common sadness, Gwen sidestepped. "You stayed in California for a long time."

Sally returned the photo to the mantel. "That's right. After I lost my sweet Isaac, I married a younger co-worker to provide Robin with a father figure. After two years of making each other miserable, we admitted we were a bad match and divorced. I settled into life as a single parent. Years ago, Robin moved to New England with her twins. Last fall, I decided it was time to reconnect with my family." A shy smile touched her lips. "Let's finish my meager tour, Gwen. Watch your step."

Sally mounted a run of steep steps. Arriving on the second floor, she identified her master bedroom, then her home office in a second room. Entering the third with a single bed, Sally opened a closet door and waved upward.

Gwen peeked in to see a run of steps to the dark attic.

"Newer houses don't have this luxury, Gwen. Makes it easier to retrieve decorations as each holiday comes and goes."

"No doubt," Gwen agreed. "My only storage areas are the third-level lofts with pull-down ladders and the basement."

Returning to the first floor, Sally led Gwen into a parlor with a twin corner fireplace fronted by a cluster of stuffed chairs, a continuation of the Cape Cod décor on every surface.

Through an archway, they entered a small dining room with four chairs surrounding a square maple table. Along one wall sat a cherry sideboard. On the opposite, a hutch filled with blue and white Delft dishes.

From the kitchen, Sally exited to a tiny back yard, fenced-in to mark the boundary with the neighbors.

"You've done a wonderful job with a small space, Sally."

Glancing around, Sally commented, "Most of this landscaping was here when I bought the house. I replaced the patio blocks and added the café table and chairs. Not all that comfortable, but the set adds an air of charm."

Gwen ran her fingers along the curve of the metal chair. "Charm is the perfect word."

"My yard can't compare to yours, Gwen, and there's no way I could have fit the number of people invited to Allison's wedding. I'm so glad you were willing to let me borrow your gardens. Who knew it would turn into such a disaster?" Sally inhaled and released the air with an exasperated whoosh.

Gwen rested her arm across her cousin's shoulders. "Don't fret. There was no major damage. My gardens will bounce back. And we'll find evidence to prove someone besides Robin attacked Frank."

"You're such a Pollyanna, Gwen, but that's better than being a negative Nellie."

When the oven timer dinged, Sally turned. "Let's go in. I need to sauté the squash."

As they entered the kitchen, Gwen sniffed the air. "Love the smell of those quick-baked potatoes."

Thirty minutes later, between bites, the two women once again viewed the collected snapshots on Gwen's cell phone, once again disappointed that none exonerated Robin.

Gwen glanced at Sally. "Do you think Travis has potential as Frank's attacker?"

"That's crazy, Gwen. Why would you suspect him?"

214

"Well, he didn't quite say anything negative about Frank, but he was thrilled that Robin might come work for him again."

"So, he did away with Frank to free Robin from a possibly abusive marriage?"

"Oh, I don't know, Sally. My imagination is panicking."

Sally slumped in her chair. "I'm beginning to think we'll never get my poor Robin out of jail."

"Don't give up," Gwen soothed, though she wasn't feeling all that positive herself. "Nicole will provide a few more snapshots tomorrow morning and we still have a chance to strike it rich with the remaining guests."

Sally carried their plates to the sink, washed and dried them, then opened a small door on the side wall and tossed the towel through an opening.

"What's that?" Gwen asked, fascinated by Sally's action.

"A laundry chute. There's one on the second floor as well. It drops dirty laundry on a table near my washer and dryer in the basement."

"Your house is full of surprises."

"One of the reasons I bought it." Sally tilted her head for Gwen to follow her into the living room. Once there, she retrieved the guest list from the coffee table. "Let's divide the list and call the rest. I hope they're home."

They separated to dial their half. When they met up, Sally had spoken to two who lived near Provincetown at the tip of the Cape. Too far to drive in the morning, so Sally asked them to email their snapshots, which they agreed to do.

Gwen had talked to three who didn't bother taking pictures and left a second message for the last guy. She'd packed her tablet for the Cape sleepover, so when the emails arrived from Sally's efforts, Gwen opened the attachments.

Sally hovered, snorting when they saw no snapshots of Frank with another man. "The old saying applies to us, Gwen. *If we didn't have bad luck, we'd have no luck at all.*"

"Let's keep a positive attitude." Gwen ached to find proof of the person who'd led Frank to his death so she could explore life with Ben.

A knock sounded at the front door.

Both women raised their heads like dogs on point.

"Must be Ashley." Sally hurried to let her in.

Then Gwen heard, "Oh, Brodie, you came too."

Chapter Thirty-Four

... early evening, Thursday

While Sally broke the news to Ashley of Frank's death and Robin's arrest, Gwen made herself scarce by watering the petunias in the outdoor window boxes. Then she dallied in Sally's back yard until the mosquitos sent her inside, easing the door closed behind her as quietly as she could.

In the kitchen, Ashley pried herself from Sally's embrace and dabbed her swollen eyes with a tissue.

Brodie shifted from one foot to the other, seemingly at a loss of what to do or say.

Gwen gestured for him to follow her into the living room. As he came closer, she whispered, "Best to let Ashley absorb the news of Frank's death and her mother's arrest without us hovering."

A confused expression clouded his face. "What arrest?"

Gwen froze. She'd assumed Sally had revealed both misfortunes, but Ashley was reacting only to Frank's death. Had the man been a decent stepfather despite his addiction?

Touching Brodie's sleeve, Gwen said, "I spoke out of turn. Let's wait for Ashley's grandmother to fill in the blanks."

His face contorted as he shouted, "I don't want to wait. Tell me the rest of it now."

Brodie's outburst drew Sally from the kitchen. "What's going on here?"

Gwen rushed to speak before Brodie could say a word. "Sorry, I'm afraid I mentioned Robin's situation."

"What situation?" Ashley demanded as she came up behind Sally. "Is there more bad news, Grandma?"

Sally grasped her granddaughter's elbow and guided her to the couch, forcing her to sit down. "I'm afraid so, sweetie. The police detective decided your mother was the one who attacked your stepfather. She was arrested a few days ago."

"A few days ago!" Ashley threw off Sally's hand and jumped to her feet, glaring down at her grandmother. "Why didn't you call me?"

"I did, sweetie," Sally answered without admitting she'd delayed until Fred shamed her into it. "I left several messages, but I didn't hear from you until this afternoon when Gwen and I were driving."

"And that's another thing." Ashley swiped at new tears creating a river through her makeup. "What's Gwen doing here? And why were the two of you driving around together?"

Sally leapt up and gripped Ashley's shoulders. The young woman's struggle to free herself appeared useless. "If you will please calm down, I'll explain."

Deflated, Ashley plopped into a chair with Brodie settling on the arm, his hand resting on her shoulder.

Sally began with Gwen and Jenna's discovery of Frank's body on Sunday morning, guiding Ashley and Brodie through the events of the past few days, ending with the collection of the guest snapshots.

Ashley turned an earnest gaze on Sally. "I'm sorry I yelled at you, Grandma. It wasn't your fault I lost my phone. As soon as I listened to your messages, I called."

"Let's not play the blame game," Sally soothed. "What matters now is identifying the person who attacked your stepfather so we can convince the authorities to release your mother."

"I should have done something." Ashley grumbled. "Or at least said something. I noticed bruises on my mother's arms and cheeks." She lifted red-rimmed eyes to Sally. "Grandma, do you think my mother killed Frank?"

Sally brushed strands of auburn hair from Ashley's wet cheeks. "I firmly believe your mother didn't do it. That's why Gwen and I are going to all this trouble to prove someone else led your stepfather into the garage."

Ashley sat back on her heels. "I need to see my mom. Do you think they'll let me visit her?"

Sally pulled Ashley to a standing position. "I'll ask the attorney I hired."

"Please make that call now, Grandma." Ashley turned to Brodie. "Can you drive me back to the camp so I can pick up my car?"

"That's too far. How about I drive you to Plymouth tomorrow?" Brodie's expression revealed his deep feelings. "I've built up sick time. I'll take the day off."

"Thanks, Brodie. You're the best. I'll call and find another counselor to take over my outings with the kids for the next few days." Ashley grasped Sally's hand. "Do you have room for me and Brodie to stay here tonight?"

"Of course." Sally enfolded her granddaughter.

As Sally dialed the attorney, Gwen signaled to Ashley and Brody. "Why don't we go outside and give your grandmother some privacy?"

"That's a good idea," Ashley said. "I need to make my own phone call anyway."

After Ashley hung up, Gwen steered her and Brody around the perimeter of Sally's tiny yard, hoping the distraction would offset some of their anxiety. Gwen identified the flowers, bushes, and trees, though she sensed neither Ashley nor Brody were paying any attention.

From inside the house, Sally yelled, "Hey! Where did you guys go?"

"Out back," Gwen shouted.

Sally gathered them around her patio table. "My lawyer said she should be able to arrange a visit with your mom. We'll call her in the morning before you drive up to Plymouth."

Ashley rounded the table and threw her arms around Sally. "Thank you, Grandma. I'm so sorry I yelled at you earlier."

Patting Ashley's arm, Sally said, "It's already forgotten. But listen, have you heard from your sister?"

"No, and I didn't expect to. Before she and Cole snuck away from the B&B Sunday morning, Allison said they were turning off their cell phones until they get back. They were afraid Mom would give them a hard time about eloping."

Sally shifted in her chair and supported her chin in her hand. "In that case, there's no point in my leaving another message on her cell phone. If you hear from her before I do, do you feel comfortable sharing the news about Frank and your mother?"

Ashley scrunched up her nose. "Not sure. I'll decide when I'm talking to her."

"Well, if she talks to you first, ask her to come and see me at Gwen's house. We're driving back there tomorrow."

Ashley's facial expression clouded. "You're returning to Harbor Falls?"

"Yes, Ashley," Sally confirmed in no uncertain terms. "When permission comes through that's it's my turn to visit your mother, I don't want to fight the bridge traffic. Besides, Gwen and I can't investigate if we aren't together."

Sally heaved herself upright. "Well, I'm going in. It's been a long day and my bed is calling me. Ashley, you'll sleep with me. Gwen, you can have the single bed in the guest room. Brodie, you'll be comfortable on the parlor couch. I'll bring down some pillows and blankets."

Gwen stood up. "I'll get my overnight bag from your van."

***

Settled in Sally's guest room, Gwen dialed Ben.

"You sound tired," he commented.

"I guess I am. I'll have no trouble falling asleep tonight."

"Any problems retrieving those snapshots today?"

"None at all," she said, then described Uncle Peter's cranberry bog, golfer Kelly's mistaking them for house hunters, Travis's mini mansion on Cotuit Bay, and Erica's shaggy dog Rosco.

"Were any of their pictures helpful?"

Gwen's mood plummeted. "Only one showed people near Frank. But when I looked closer, it was me and Sally with Robin before she stomped off and argued with Jeremy."

"He's the wedding photographer? Didn't he explain their confrontation?"

"He said he was trying to arrange a time for her to pick up the Army pictures of her first husband Kyle."

"Has Robin confirmed their conversation?"

"I didn't mention their encounter to Detective Warren. When Sally is allowed to visit the jail, she can check with Robin for her version. Jeremy sounded truthful. I guess he's off the hook as a possible attacker."

"Like I said before, Gwen, if Robin didn't do it, one of the guests orchestrated Frank's death. So, none of the people in your back yard last Saturday are off the hook… yet."

Gwen yawned. "Sorry, Ben, but I'm beat. Sally and I will be back in Harbor Falls sometime tomorrow. I'll text you when I walk in my front door."

Chapter Thirty-Five
... early morning, Friday

When Gwen entered Sally's kitchen the next morning, her cousin glanced over from the table and shook a note in the air. "Ashley and Brodie took off before I woke up. She wants to be waiting at the jailhouse door when permission comes through to visit her mother. I need to call Ursula."

"Is Ashley still debating if her mother attacked Frank?"

Sally let the note flutter to the tabletop. "I couldn't say. One second, she seemed ready to defend her mother. The next she panicked Robin might have done it."

Gwen sat next to Sally. "All you can do is keep searching for proof." Once again, Gwen mentally crossed her fingers, hoping whatever evidence they uncovered pointed to someone besides Robin.

Folding the note, Sally tucked it in her pocket. "Are you okay eating English muffins with P&J for breakfast?"

"One of my favorites."

***

After washing the few dishes and cups they'd dirtied, Sally opened the pantry door and removed an insulated bag. She added the container of leftover rotisserie chicken from the fridge plus two ice packs from the freezer before zipping it closed. "This will make a delicious chicken soup for our next lunch at your place."

Gwen hadn't sensed her face falling, but her expression must have slumped.

Sally turned fretful. "I'm sorry, Gwen. I'm inviting myself to stay with you even longer. I'll move back to the B&B."

Gwen had given no thought to Sally's continued habitation of the second floor sitting room. When she'd suggested her cousin move in until Robin was released from jail, she hadn't considered how many days it might take to unmask the real culprit. Too late now. The precedent had been established.

Forcing her face into an agreeable arrangement, Gwen said, "No, no, Sally, you don't need to do that. Stay with me until we wrap this up. I have to confess, though, if we don't come across an incriminating snapshot soon, I'm at a loss about where else to look for clues."

"Don't try to discourage me," Sally urged. "I'm adopting your positive attitude. You go upstairs and pack your bag while I call Ursula about Ashley's visit with Robin."

Because Gwen's stay had been only the one night, her belongings hadn't wandered far. A few toiletries in the small guest bathroom, and her pajamas tossed at the foot of the bed.

On her way to the steps, Gwen met up with Sally lugging another suitcase. "I need a change of clothes for your place. Should have brought my wedding outfit back here."

Sally's statement required no response so Gwen asked, "Were you able to catch up with Ursula?"

"Yep. Caught her as she was leaving her office. She hasn't arranged family visits yet, but I sense she can be quite persuasive. Let's head out." Sally lifted the extra suitcase and managed to descend the narrow stairs without falling.

The drive from Falmouth to the rotary didn't take long and was fortunately uneventful. Lots of cars crowded the Dunkin parking lot, so Sally drove around back and parked.

Inside the shop, every table was filled with young women. The chatter among them implied they knew each other.

Always curious, Gwen sidled up to the nearest one. "If you don't mind me asking, what's the occasion?"

"Oh, we're all from the same neighborhood and we're picking up our kids from camp this afternoon. We decided to meet here for a cup of coffee before we tackle the weekend."

Gwen wished the young mother well and resumed her position in line near Sally.

When they reached the cashier, Sally leaned close. "Is Nicole available?"

The young lady looked left and right. "I saw her a second ago. Let me check the bakery. Who are you?"

"My name's Sally."

"Okay. I'll be right back."

Seconds later, a middle-aged woman with wild hair escaping a net barreled through the swinging door, holding her phone aloft. "Sorry, Sally. As you can see, we're quite busy. I didn't know all these moms were planning to stop by. My snapshots from last Saturday are on the first screen." Nicole placed her phone in Gwen's outstretched hand. "Let me treat you both to a coffee. What would you like?"

"Thanks. Large black for me," Sally answered.

Gwen glanced up from connecting Nicole's phone to the thumb drive to peruse the menu. "Thanks from me, too. I'd like a medium vanilla chai with almond milk."

***

Scrambling into the van's seats, they placed their drinks in the cup holders.

Gwen pulled up Nicole's snapshots and held her cell phone screen at an angle. "Here we go, Sally. Cross your fingers."

One by one, they sorted through the images. One by one, they were again disappointed.

Gwen huffed. "So much for my brilliant idea to chase down the background picture takers."

"Don't give up yet," Sally encouraged. "We still have one more guest who hasn't called back."

Gwen glanced over. "You've become an optimist."

"Right now, it's my only option."

A call came in on Sally's phone, Ursula's voice clear on the Bluetooth system. "Sally, I've arranged visitation, but only one relative at a time and I have to accompany the visitor. Who's first? You or your granddaughter?"

Though Sally seemed to deflate, her voice strengthened as she answered. "Definitely my granddaughter Ashley. A friend drove her to Plymouth early this morning. If you'll give me the details, I'll pass them along."

Through the speaker, Ursula said, "Why don't you give me her cell number and I'll contact her directly?"

Sally repeated Ashley's number twice for clarity then said, "I'm heading back to Harbor Falls now. Do you have any idea when I'll be allowed to see Robin?"

"I'll let you know, Sally."

Because they were still sitting in the Dunkin parking lot, Sally texted Ashley that the lawyer would be in touch. Then she barked, "Let's go, Gwen," and surged forward, circled the building, and merged into traffic.

There was little congestion on the Bourne Bridge. The weekend visitors heading toward the Cape far outweighed the few cars vacating it.

Sally pointed at the opposing lane. "I love it when everyone else is headed in the other direction."

On the mainland side of the Bourne Bridge, Sally veered the van onto Route 6, and soon merged into Route 3 traffic heading north. They sped up the highway, entering Harbor Falls in record time.

Approaching the converted library, Gwen saw no construction truck and no crew. She figured the men were either taking another early lunch break or playing hooky. But she wouldn't bother Matt unless the men didn't show up.

Chapter Thirty-Six

… late morning, Friday

Gwen carried her overnight bag and Sally's suitcase upstairs while Sally stored the rotisserie chicken in Gwen's fridge.

When Gwen rejoined her cousin, Sally announced, "I'm going to pop over to your grocery store and pick up what I need to make chicken soup. We'll eat a late lunch,"

"It'll be delicious, I'm sure," Gwen said, holding up her cell phone. "I'll let Ben know we're back."

As Sally's van zoomed away, Gwen texted Ben. *Sally and I are back in Harbor Falls, so stop over when you're free.*

His text reply arrived immediately. *Heading into a meeting with the chief. Will stop over after.*

Gwen slid her cell phone in her pocket only to remove it a second later when it buzzed. Although she didn't recognize the number, she answered, thinking it might be one of the construction crew explaining why they weren't working on her garage.

"Is this Gwen?" the caller asked.

"Yes, who is this?"

"Gabriel Taylor."

Gwen racked her tired brain to recall the name.

The man kept talking. "You left a message two days ago and another last night to call you about wedding photos."

The name from the guest list fell into place.

"Of course, Gabriel," she said. "Thanks for getting back to me. Sally and I were down on Cape Cod yesterday and early this morning. We could have retrieved your snapshots, but we're back in Harbor Falls now."

He laughed deep and hearty. "Doesn't matter where you are because I'm out of town. Your message suggested emailing everything. But my girlfriend snapped quite a few stills, and I was playing with my new video camera, so I shot a lot of footage. The files are too large to email, so I downloaded everything to a thumb drive for mailing to the address on the wedding invitation."

"That's wonderful. Thank you," Gwen said, downplaying her excitement at this last chance to save Robin. "When are you planning to mail it?"

"Already on its way. I requested Priority Mail, so it should arrive in your mailbox tomorrow."

Gwen could barely contain her elation. A large batch of prints *plus* a video. "I appreciate your extra efforts, Gabriel. I can't wait to see your images."

After they said their goodbyes, Gwen exited through the French door to find Jenna sitting on a deck chair. "Hey, I thought you'd be in class this time of day."

Jenna squinted up at her. "The professor received an urgent text and had to leave. But before she rushed out, she assigned us to write a summary of the next two chapters." From her lap, Jenna hefted a thick tome with both hands.

"Let me know if you'd like me to review your paper," Gwen offered.

"Thanks. A second pair of eyes never hurts." Jenna raised one eyebrow. "Was your snapshot gathering a success?"

"We didn't find a photo to exonerate Robin if that's what you're asking."

"I never spent a lot of time with Robin," Jenna recalled. "When she came to visit Allison at Baylies, the two of them always went off by themselves. Do you think it's possible Robin killed Frank?"

Gwen dropped into the adjacent deck chair. "I met Robin for the first-time on wedding day, so I can't speculate about her mindset where her husband is concerned. I hope Sally hasn't misplaced her conviction that Robin's innocent."

Jenna laid her hand on Gwen's arm. "Don't over-exert yourself while we're trying to bring your blood pressure down. Did you and Sally walk around Falmouth last night?"

"More of a stroll, but we were moving throughout the day."

"In that case, we'll resume our routine this evening."

At the sound of an engine out front, Gwen hurried along the deck and down the driveway, hoping it was the construction crew returning to work on her garage.

To her displeasure, it wasn't the burly men. Instead she saw Hal holding the door open for his lady friend Joleen. As Gwen watched, the last of her resentment for his insulting words last December drained away. Seeing him now evoked no emotion, either good or bad.

She raised her hand in greeting. "Hello."

Beside him, Joleen stared up at Gwen's library home, her mouth partially agape.

Hal stepped toward Gwen, his intense blue eyes focusing on hers. "The closing is a done deal. The nursery is now owned by Oscar and his brother. I brought Joleen to meet Jenna before we drive to the airport."

Gwen waved toward the back yard. "Your granddaughter is on the rear deck reading a very thick textbook."

"Thanks. We won't be long." Hal tucked his hand under Joleen's arm and escorted her up the driveway.

Chapter Thirty-Seven

... early afternoon, Friday

In Chief Brown's office, two Harbor Falls detectives sat on Ben's right with Detective Warren on his left. Ben glanced at his watch.

"Going somewhere, Ben?" the chief asked, sliding his glasses down his nose.

Not wanting to appear disinterested in the meeting, Ben said, "No, sir. Only distracted by the details of a case."

Detective Warren raised his head from his notes. "I hope you're not referring to the homicide at the old library on the village green. I heard the rumor. Gwen Andrews is helping her cousin search for evidence to prove her daughter's innocent. The case is closed, Ben. I arrested Robin Hennessey. Her fate is in the hands of the DA. Don't waste your time."

"Ease off, Warren," the chief warned. "You're not familiar with our town or its residents. Are you worried Gwen will uncover proof you've arrested the wrong person?"

Detective Warren sneered. "You let amateurs interfere in police affairs?"

"Not interference," the chief made plain. "Gwen Andrews has more than once unearthed evidence we missed. She's an invaluable asset, and I don't think of her as an amateur."

232

Warren shot back. "So, you approve of Ben reopening a case I've wrapped up?"

"I approve of uncovering the truth," Chief Brown said, his tone dangerously even.

"If you recall, I'm on loan to your department at your request."

"That's true," the chief confirmed. "I deemed it prudent to bring in another detective while Ben was out of town."

With an angry shove, Warren crammed papers into the folders on his lap. "Well, he's back. If you doubt my competence, I should stop wasting my time and yours."

"An excellent suggestion," the chief retorted. "You're free to return to your precinct whenever you want."

"In that case, I'll be on my way." Detective Warren jumped to his feet and tossed his folders onto the chief's desk, his outrage obvious as papers escaped and flew in all directions.

When the door slammed behind the insulted Warren, one of the detectives spoke up. "I'm glad to see him go. Perry Warren thinks he's the reincarnation of TV detective Columbo."

Ben picked up documents and handed them to the chief.

The second detective chimed in. "I hate to trash talk another officer, but he rushed to judgement before he gathered enough evidence to support that arrest. Plus, he acted like he was in charge while Ben was in Oakfield."

Chief Brown tapped his desk blotter to get their attention. "You should have mentioned this to me. I thought you were getting along fine with Warren."

"We didn't want to sound petty, Chief," the first detective offered. "But he's gone now. Why don't we divide the cases he's been working on?"

"Good idea," Chief Brown agreed, sorting through Warren's folders, and handing one to Ben. "Here's the file for the Hennessey homicide. Study the evidence and let me know what you think."

"Thanks, Chief. To bring you up to speed, Gwen's cousin Sally bought all the prints from the wedding photographer, hoping to find visual evidence of an alternate attacker."

The chief scowled. "Warren didn't ask for those photographs?"

"No, sir. It seems Warren set his sights on Mrs. Hennessey as an abused wife who snuck back after the wedding was cancelled and lured her husband to Gwen's new garage. As far as I know, there's no direct evidence to support Warren's theory. He didn't speak with anyone on the guest list or even the victim's twin stepdaughters. The best evidence we have is those overlapping shoe impressions in the concrete, but from what I can surmise, it would be difficult to match those up to whoever was involved in the scuffle."

Leaning closer, the chief scowled. "Is there more?"

"Unfortunately," Ben confirmed. "In the background of the wedding prints, Gwen noticed guests taking pictures. She and Sally drove to the Cape yesterday to collect those snapshots. Gwen texted a few minutes ago. They're back in Harbor Falls, so I'm going to go over to see what they brought with them."

234

"No wonder you've been preoccupied with the time," the chief blustered. "Get yourself over to Gwen's and have a look at those snapshots."

In a flash, Ben exited the chief's office. Hustling to his desk in the detective suite, he spread out the meager contents of Warren's file. A cover sheet with basic details and a case number plus Dr. Otis' report verifying that the death was not accidental, and Warren's meager wire bound notebook.

But there was no report from the lab about those shoe impressions and no interview sheet for Robin Hennessey, so no admitted abuse at the hands of her husband, and no explanation of her whereabouts on Saturday evening.

There was no real evidence at all.

***

In no hurry to go inside, Gwen inspected her rose bushes on the front fence, all the while worrying about Hal's introduction of Joleen to Jenna. After Hal and Joleen headed for the airport, Gwen would check on Jenna's reaction. Meeting her grandfather's new female friend could be stressful.

When Gwen's cell phone vibrated, she was glad for the distraction. It was Matt stating he was sorry but had assigned his crew to another job for the rest of the day. He promised they'd tackle the unsightly pile of leftover lumber in the corner of the garage first thing Monday morning.

As Gwen finished her call with Matt, a car pulled to the curb and a door slammed. Before she had a chance to pivot away from her roses, someone came up behind her and enveloped her in strong arms, nuzzling her neck where the sun had kissed it. "I'm glad you're back, Gwen."

Speechless, but not panicked, she spun around and lifted her face to gaze into Ben's pale gray eyes.

He put his finger to her lips. "We'll talk about the snapshots in a little bit, but not until I ask you an important question."

She grasped his finger and pulled it away so she could speak. "And your question is…?"

"Wanna redeem your raincheck for dinner tonight?"

Interlocking her fingers at the back of his neck, Gwen teased, "No one else has invited me, so sure."

Before Ben had time to react, Hal, Joleen, and Jenna strolled down the driveway from the back yard.

Hal stopped short and stared. "I knew it!" he shouted. "You refused to move to Florida because you were hooking up with that white-haired detective!"

Gwen disengaged from Ben's embrace and stepped in front of Hal, trying desperately to control her volume. "Listen, Hal. You and I were friends until you dictated that I should move south and live with you. I'm sorry if this bruises your ego, but I never envisioned a physical relationship between us. You may have exchanged New England winters for Florida sunshine, but I'll never leave Harbor Falls."

Not done, Gwen waved toward Joleen. "You have now met this nice lady. Go fulfill your romantic fantasies with her. You need to fly back to Florida and let me live the life I choose up here in New England."

236

Seemingly dumbstruck at Gwen's uncharacteristic outburst, Hal's mouth opened and closed like a hungry fish.

Joleen backed away, her expression dazed.

Jenna covered her mouth, obviously unsettled.

Ben moved to insert himself between Gwen and Hal, then changed his mind and let their drama play out.

Sally's white van screeched to a halt at the curb and she exited in a burst of energy. "Is everything okay? What's going on here?"

Hal's skin flushing, he answered, "Nothing now." He glanced at Gwen. "All I can say is I'm sorry."

Stepping toward Jenna, he placed his calloused hand on her shoulder. "I'm serious about you flying down for a visit. Let me know the dates of your college breaks and I'll buy your plane tickets."

Jenna threw her arms around his neck and kissed his whiskery cheek. "You'll be the first one I call."

Tossing daggers in Ben's direction, Hal shooed Joleen toward his rental, hopped in, and sped away.

Chapter Thirty-Eight

... early afternoon, Friday

With a mixture of regret and relief, Gwen observed Hal's car as it circled the village green.

She glanced over at Jenna. "I'm sorry. I don't usually lose my temper."

With a look of resignation, Sally marched toward her van. "I have groceries to put away." She whipped open the back door. "Jenna, why don't you give me a hand?"

Tossing a confused expression toward Gwen, Jenna hefted a handled bag and followed Sally toward the front door.

Behind her, Ben whispered, "I've never seen you lash out. Was Hal aware of Parker's ghost?"

"What?" Gwen turned to face him, wondering why he was asking such a question. Would Ben be insulted if he hadn't been the first to be introduced to Parker?

Ben placed his hands on her shoulders and stared into her eyes, his voice mellow as he spoke. "I didn't mean to startle you. Just curious if Hal knew about your husband's spirit."

Still wondering his reason for asking, Gwen shook her head. "No, I never told Hal about Parker's visits."

"Any idea why not?" Ben slid his palms down her arms and grasped both her hands, his touch not restraining, but gentle.

When she didn't say anything, Ben continued. "I'm just thinking out loud, Gwen. If Hal had known about Parker, he might have understood why you didn't want to move from Harbor Falls. He might have stayed in New England to pursue a more intimate relationship with you."

Startled by Ben's interpretation, Gwen stared down at her sneakers. She'd never thought to excuse Hal's behavior because of her secretiveness about Parker's return. Why *hadn't* she confided in Hal? She'd never analyzed her omission.

"Don't misunderstand me," Ben added. "I'm thrilled Hal's flying back to Florida." He squeezed her hands. "You said you want to live the life you choose. Does your life include me?"

Once again, another question from Ben brought Gwen up short. She'd been content to let her relationship with the white-haired detective evolve one day at a time. But Ben was questioning their future. She couldn't imagine her days without a phone chat or him stopping by. Ben's surprise kisses the other night had been an unexpected and exciting bonus.

Rather than a verbal response, Gwen stretched up on her tiptoes and kissed him squarely on the lips. "Does that answer your question?"

Before Ben had a chance to speak, his cell phone buzzed. "Sorry, Gwen. Unfortunately, I'm still on the clock."

Reading the message, his shoulders drooped. "Damn. The chief needs me at a crime scene. A raincheck for my response to your kiss?"

"One raincheck deserves another," she teased.

He cupped her cheek. "You can show me those snapshots from the guests later."

Gwen gave him a harmless shove. "Off with you, then. I'll see you at six."

As Ben dropped into the driver's seat of his unmarked sedan, he glanced back at her, a huge grin on his face. As he pulled away, she wiggled her fingers in his direction and turned to go inside, nearly taking a nosedive over the front yard fence. Catching herself before she tumbled into the thorny rose bushes, she crossed her fingers that Ben hadn't been glancing in his rearview mirror.

***

Entering the kitchen, Gwen found Sally busy at the sink.

Jenna sat at the island, her fingertips racing across her cell phone keyboard. Without looking up, she said, "One of the other students in my master's class is organizing a study group. I'm heading over there to join them."

"Lunch before you go, Jenna?" Sally asked. "I'm making spinach salad."

Jenna responded with a tight smile. "Thanks, Sally, but I don't have time. See you later."

After the front door closed, Sally raised an eyebrow at Gwen. "She seems tense. Did something happen between you and her grandfather?"

Settling on an island stool, Gwen relayed the gist of her charged words with Hal. She almost added Ben's notion that Hal might have reacted differently if he'd been aware of

Parker's spirit but caught herself. Now was not the time to scare Sally with a ghost story.

"Hmmm," Sally commented. "Sorry I missed the drama."

"Jenna had been hoping Hal and I would marry so I'd be her official grandmother," Gwen began. "I adore that girl, so the other day I explained that he and I would never marry and offered to be her unofficial grandmother. Still, I'm guessing she's disturbed by my angry words with her grandfather. I suspect she rushed off just now to avoid me."

Snapping off the spinach stems, Sally added artichoke hearts and raw mushrooms to the bowl. "Finding out life doesn't always go the way you planned is a hard lesson." She whisked a balsamic dressing, poured it over the salad, and placed a serving in front of Gwen. "By the way, tonight's dinner is roast pork with apple cranberry compote, which can double as a pancake topping in the morning."

"Sounds delicious, Sally, but Ben is taking me to dinner tonight. Any possibility of leftovers?"

"Of course." Sally sat on a stool opposite Gwen. "How serious are you and Ben?"

Gwen hesitated, blaming Sally's interest on her self-assumed role as chef and caretaker.

Sally raised one hand. "No, no, don't answer. Forgive my nosiness. You and Ben seem to be a good fit." Sally swallowed a forkful of salad. "Any idea what time Jenna will return?"

"None, but you could text her. If you'll give me your cell phone, I'll register her number in your contacts."

When Gwen handed the phone back, Sally said, "Can I impose on you to help me choose the best guest snapshots for Allison's memory album?" Sally hefted a bag from the floor to the counter and removed photo paper. "Before grocery shopping, I bought this at Staples. Can we print our favorites on your Hewlett Packard upstairs?"

"Of course." Gwen noticed the Harbor Falls Gazette on the counter behind Sally. "Did you buy the newspaper?"

Sally grabbed it and passed it over. "Nope. Spied it in your home delivery mailbox. I haven't looked at the obituaries."

Checking the front-page index, Gwen rifled through the sections. "Here we go." Her finger traveled down the notices. "I don't see anything here for Frank."

"Might be too soon. Besides, Fred may have decided not to publish his brother's obituary in your local paper. After all, Frank lived on the Cape, not here."

"You're probably right." Gwen refolded the paper and placed it atop an empty stool. "I'll read the rest later."

***

Returning to the laptop in the guest room, Gwen plugged the thumb drive into the USB port. She and Sally reviewed each image with an eye to clarity and content. Gwen cropped and resized as needed before printing. On the guest bed, they alternated the casual snapshots with Jeremy's professional photos.

Crossing her arms, Sally surveyed the layout and switched several photos.

Approving of the new sequence, Gwen asked, "Have you heard from Ashley?"

"Not yet. I hope she calls me soon. I'm anxious to hear about her visit with her mother." As an afterthought, Sally added, "I also need a call from Ursula about my visit."

When Sally's cell phone buzzed, she snapped it up from the guest bed. As she studied the caller ID, her face fell and she mouthed, *Not Ashley.* "Hello, Jeremy."

Gwen missed the Bluetooth in Sally's van that allowed access to the other side of a conversation. Sally's pitch rose as she spoke, "You did? That's wonderful. Do you want me to drive to your studio to pick them up? Or Gwen and I are both at her place if you want to drop them off."

After an instant, she said, "Oh. How about tomorrow?"

Another response from Jeremy.

"Great. We'll see you in the morning."

Disconnecting, Sally met Gwen's eyes. "Good news. Jeremy found a few of our wedding day pictures mixed with another job. He's on his way to a photo shoot, so he'll drop them off here in the morning."

"He could have left them in his studio mailbox," Gwen complained, eager to see the additional prints.

"Nope. He wants to point out a few details in person."

"Hmmm," Gwen murmured. "We didn't tell Jeremy that Frank died or that Robin was arrested and that we're searching for an alternate attacker. I wonder what he thinks is so important in his photos?"

"No idea, but cross your fingers, Gwen. His bonus pictures may be our last chance to clear Robin."

"Not quite our last," Gwen corrected. "I forgot to mention that the last guest Gabriel called to say he overnighted a thumb drive with his video footage from wedding day plus prints of the snapshots his girlfriend took. My mail carrier should deliver his package tomorrow."

"We're going to find the real killer soon," Sally predicted. "I can feel it."

Gwen wished her own confidence matched her cousin's optimistic hunch.

Chapter Thirty-Nine

… early evening, Friday

At six-twenty, Ben parked his Corvette at Gwen's curb, jumped out, and raced to her front entrance. When she answered the door, he said, "Sorry I'm late."

"I'll let you off the hook," she promised. "I thought you might have gotten stuck at that other crime scene and would have to cancel our dinner date."

"Nope. Finished up there, returned to the station, then back to my apartment for a shower and a change of clothes."

"You clean up good," she commented, glancing from his white hair to his shiny shoes.

A laugh escaped him. "Thanks."

"I do believe you're blushing, Ben Snowcrest. Do you want to come inside and look at those snapshots Sally and I collected on the Cape?"

He shook his head. "No time if we're going to make our dinner reservation. Maybe when we get back. Are you ready?"

"Give me a sec."

Through the open door, he watched her hurry to the dining room table and grab a small purse. "I'm leaving now," she called to Sally and Jenna, the two clearly visible as they sat at the kitchen island, their forks poised in midair.

245

Sally waved. "Hope your dinner is as good as ours."

The aroma of roast pork wafted to Ben's nose, taunting his taste buds.

Gwen rejoined him. "Okay, let's go."

He escorted her to the Corvette and opened the passenger door, impressed that Gwen recalled how to drop into the low-slung sports car. She aimed her rear end at the leather seat and sat down backwards before swinging her legs inside.

"Where are we going for dinner?" she asked as she buckled her seat belt.

"Back to the scene of the crime."

"Your crime this afternoon took place at a restaurant?"

Her alarmed expression gave him pause. "No, no," he hurried to correct. "I didn't mean crime as in wrongdoing. I meant the restaurant where I took you for our first real date."

Her eyes widened. "The Lazy Lobster?"

"Bingo. I didn't have a chance to check if they booked entertainment tonight, but if they did, are you up for some music and dancing after we eat?"

***

As they drove north from Harbor Falls, Gwen studied Ben's profile. Strong jawline. Clean-shaven cheeks. Bushy white eyebrows. And that distinctive crop of white hair. When he caught her looking, he reached for her hand and squeezed. "Let's talk about the case and then drop the topic."

She squeezed back. "Fine with me."

"You first."

Gwen began to recap her day. "Well, none of the snapshots proved helpful. But the wedding photographer called Sally this afternoon. He found more photos from the wedding day and is dropping them off tomorrow morning. Plus, the last guest overnighted some prints and a video, also due tomorrow."

"You're gambling one of those will reveal an alternate attacker?"

"These are probably our last hope to prove Robin innocent. If these are a bust, I have no idea where Sally and I can look next for clues. Has anything developed on the police investigation side of Frank's death?"

Ben concentrated on the road as he spoke. "This afternoon's meeting was unusual. Detective Warren complained to the chief that we'd allow you and your cousin to usurp his closed investigation. He didn't appreciate the possibility of being one-upped by an – and these are his words – amateur sleuth. He left in a rage and went back to his old precinct. My other detectives were glad to see him go."

"Warren may have reacted too soon," Gwen countered. "I'm not sure Sally and I are going to uncover a different suspect. I hate to say this, Ben, but I'm beginning to wonder if Robin *is* the one who did away with her husband."

***

Though the Lazy Lobster was teeming with diners, the maître d' led Ben and Gwen to their window table with no fuss. As they finished their seafood dinners and wine, the sultry voice of a singer floated in from the adjacent lounge.

"Are you ready for some dancing, Gwen?"

At her nod, he informed the passing waiter and asked for the bill. After paying, he escorted Gwen to the next room where they spotted an empty table along the rear wall. Alternating their dance moves between fast tunes and slow ballads, they were soon giddy with exhaustion. As Ben guided her from the floor, he leaned down and whispered, "How about a detour before I take you home?"

"I'd love it. It's too early to call it a night." After she retrieved her purse, they made their way to the parking lot and secured their seatbelts before Ben slid the gearshift into drive.

***

The Corvette hugged the curvy back roads. Eventually Ben pulled into the remote parking lot for Duxbury Beach. As dusk settled, only a few cars remained. They chatted nonstop as they strolled across the Powder Point Bridge and were soon walking barefoot in the cooling sand. Ben tied his laces together and slung his shoes over his shoulder. Gwen simply looped her fingers through her sandals and let them dangle. The moon struggled with a bank of haze to provide a sporadic path in the golden sand.

Coming to a section of shoreline free of seaweed and broken shells, Ben whipped out a thin blanket he'd tucked into his back waistband. With a flick of his wrist, he spread it on the sand. "Care to join me?"

Lying on their backs, they waited patiently for stars to peek out between darkening clouds.

Ben rolled on his side and draped his arm across Gwen's hips. "I'd like to redeem my raincheck now. May I?"

Oblivious to the ominous sky and the increasing breeze, Gwen curved her body toward his. "You may, sir."

Before his lips touched hers, raindrops pelted them both.

Helping Gwen to her feet, Ben shouted above the rising wind. "Gotta love New England weather." Stretching the blanket above their heads, they raced along the sand, across Powder Point Bridge, and finally made it to his Corvette.

Running his hand through his damp hair, Ben laughed as he clicked the remote to unlock the doors. "Glad I decided not to buy the convertible."

***

Mindful of the late hour, Gwen snuck in at nearly midnight by herself. Ben had suggested he return the following day after she'd received the deliveries from both Jeremy and the mail carrier so he could view all the snapshots at the same time.

As Gwen tiptoed through the foyer, Jenna rushed down the staircase and came to a stop. "Do you know I've been pacing back and forth thinking you were in an accident? And you didn't answer your cell phone."

Hiding her amusement at their role reversal, Gwen sensed Jenna was only half-kidding. "Sorry. Ben and I turned off our cell phones while we were on the beach. If I'd known you'd be waiting up for me, I would've texted you."

"Well, I'm relieved you're back safe and sound." Jenna stomped up the staircase.

Chapter Forty

… early morning, Saturday

A knock on Gwen's bedroom door wakened her from a pleasant but blurry dream. Opening her eyes to see the time of eight-thirty, she threw off her lightweight blanket, placed her feet on the floor and called, "Come in."

Jenna peeked through a crack in the door before swinging it wide. "You see what happens when you stay out past midnight, sleepyhead?"

Groaning, Gwen said, "Are you scolding me again?"

"Not scolding, but we *are* going for our morning walk. And I won't take no for an answer. Let's get outside before the day warms up. Sally said she'll feed you before we go."

"You've already eaten?"

"Yep. Pancakes with the yummy topping left over from last night's pork roast dinner. You missed a great meal, but you had other priorities."

"You can stop teasing me now," Gwen sassed as she headed for her bathroom. "I'll take a quick shower and be downstairs in ten minutes."

***

As promised, Sally prepared pancakes topped with the apple cranberry compote. Serving Gwen, she said, "Jenna tells me you were out with Ben on the beach until midnight. And now late from your bed this morning. Do you think you're still a teenager?"

Gwen lifted one eyebrow. "Nope. I guess I've graduated to active adult."

"Eat up, smarty pants," Sally quipped. "Your pancakes are getting cold. And Jenna's waiting for you."

Her appetite satisfied, Gwen swallowed her blood pressure pill and followed Jenna down the front granite steps. "Where to?"

Jenna pointed beyond the village green. "We haven't visited the harbor boardwalk for a few days. Let's go down there."

They maintained a steady pace until Gwen blurted, "I want to apologize again for my words to your grandfather."

Jenna lifted small hand weights in time with her strides. "I've never seen either of you so angry. You should know I've finally given up on the two of you ever getting married." Jenna looked up beneath lowered eyelashes. "But is there any chance you can mend your friendship, even if it's long distance?"

Gwen searched for the gentlest way to explain. "Maybe with the passage of time. I treasured your grandfather's friendship until he insulted me last December. I can't see us ever being more than acquaintances now."

Jenna seemed to absorb Gwen's words. "That's sad, but I guess I have to accept your decision."

Gwen gripped Jenna's jacket sleeve to slow her down. "Even if I will never marry your grandfather, I'm glad you accepted me as your sort-of grandmother."

Jenna transferred both weights to one hand and reached over for a one-armed hug. "A sort-of grandmother is the next best thing." A mischievous grin transformed her previously serious expression. "Since there's no hope for you and Granddad, at least Ben seems like a nice guy."

Gwen couldn't restrain a smile. "He *is* a nice guy. Besides, we have a lot in common."

By this time, they'd crossed North Street, and were fighting gravity as they eased down Harbor Hill.

"Like solving mysteries?"

"Exactly," Gwen confirmed.

"I have an idea," Jenna announced, tapping her temple. "You and I have never dueted on our flutes. Should we give it a try one day soon?"

Gwen's smile broadened. "We should. Before Sally moved in, I practiced every day, but I haven't picked up my instrument for over a week."

"And I used to play for Allison every evening in our dorm room, but not since graduation. How about when we get back from our morning walk?"

***

In Gwen's music studio, she located a folder of flute duets in the piano bench and rummaged through until she came upon *'Ode to Joy'*. "Let's begin with this easy one until we're warmed up for more complicated pieces."

Sally strolled in from the kitchen, wiping her hands on a kitchen towel. "When does the concert begin?"

"Right now." Raising her flute, Gwen nodded at Jenna.

At the end of the third duet, Sally clapped. "Wonderful."

The chime of the front doorbell echoed to the music studio.

"I'll get it," Sally volunteered. An instant later, her squeal bounced around the first floor. "Allison! Cole! Welcome back from your honeymoon!"

Delaying a few minutes to allow Sally time to deliver the bad news, Gwen and Jenna placed their flutes on the top of the Steinway before making their way to the foyer. Allison was crying in Sally's arms. Cole stood to one side.

Between sobs, Allison managed to say, "Cole and I drove straight here from New Hampshire. Ashley told me on the phone that Frank died, and our mother was arrested."

Sally pushed her granddaughter to arm's length. "I know this tragedy is upsetting, but we'll get through this together."

"I want to hear all the details," Allison demanded, "and what we need to do to get my mother out of jail."

Sally led Allison and Cole to the living room, waving them to sit as she handed a tissue to Allison.

Deciding she wouldn't interfere with the family reunion, Gwen said, "Why don't I bring drinks?"

"Yes, thank you, Gwen. I made lemonade. There's a pitcher in your fridge." Sally settled in the upholstered chair.

Gwen gestured for Jenna to follow her. They didn't speak as they retrieved the glasses and poured the lemonade, both listening to Sally's voice as it carried clearly through the open floor plan.

253

Allison blew her nose. "After yelling at me for turning off my cell phone all week, Ashley told me to come here to Gwen's so you could explain what happened in more detail."

When she began to cry again, Cole took over. "We were already driving to the Cape from the White Mountains, so detouring to Harbor Falls was no big deal."

In an awkward move, Sally hugged Cole. "Thanks for bringing my granddaughter to me."

Trying not to disturb them, Gwen set the drinks on the coffee table and returned to the kitchen. Taking the stool next to Jenna, they both listened to Sally's explanation of events.

"First of all," Sally began, "Gwen and I haven't uncovered the person who fought with Frank on Saturday night, but I'm determined to prove it was not your mother."

Allison grabbed another tissue from the nearby box. "How did Frank die, Grandma?"

Sally stumbled through a hitch in her voice. "On Sunday morning, Gwen and Jenna found him draped on a half wall in her new garage."

"But if my mother was arrested," Allison analyzed, "Frank must have died of something besides a heart attack or liver failure from his drinking."

"You're right. Neither of those reasons," Sally confirmed.

"You're not answering my question. Just tell me."

Sally heaved a lungful of air and scooted closer, laying her hand on Allison's knee. "Your stepfather was lying face up with a rebar spike protruding from his chest."

Allison gasped and more tears flowed. "How horrible. Do you know if he suffered?"

"I'd guess he died instantly." Sally rushed to add, "I don't believe your mother was involved. Gwen is helping me find the real attacker."

In the kitchen, the lid on a large pot began to rattle, begging for attention. Being closest to the stove, Jenna hopped off her stool, lifted the noisy lid, and stirred the contents with an oversized spoon. The savory aroma of rotisserie chicken soup filled the air.

In the living room, Sally sniffed. "Oh, my goodness. I forgot I'm making soup. It's a little early, but you kids must be starved. Let me feed you while Gwen and I explain what we've been up to."

Chapter Forty-One

… mid-day, Saturday

After lunch, the five of them remained seated around Gwen's island counter.

Cole draped his arm across Allison's shoulder as she wiped her eyes, but otherwise displayed little emotion while Sally recounted the day by day activities as they failed to find a snapshot to implicate someone besides Robin.

When Sally finished, Cole rubbed his forehead. "Nice try. Now what?"

Gwen raised her forefinger. "We're not done yet. The photographer found a few more photos, and the last guest mailed additional prints and a video. I should receive both sometime today."

"So, there's still a chance you'll come across a picture of the guy?" Cole asked.

"We only need one incriminating photo to exonerate your mother-in-law, Cole," Sally chimed in.

Allison took a shuddering breath. "I want to see my mother, Grandma. Can you arrange it?"

"Sure, honey. I'll call Ursula right now." Sally hurried to the music studio, quick-walking back to them minutes later. "Ashley is with your mother right now. If we hurry down to

Plymouth, the guards might let you share your sister's time, but Ursula is not making any promises."

Allison jumped off her stool and snatched her purse. "Let's go. Why don't you come with us, Jenna, so we can catch up?"

***

Alone in her library home, Gwen basked in her solitude. A feline meow drew her attention and she glanced up to see Amber meandering down the staircase.

"Hello, you little traitor. Sally's not here to spoil you, so you'll have to settle for me."

In response, the cat lifted one paw for a thorough licking before deigning to hop down the remaining treads.

Gwen grabbed her pet before she could scamper off and buried her face in the soft golden fur.

Amber soon struggled to be released.

"Oh, all right, you little devil. Let's go check your food and water bowls."

Pulling the bag of cat food from a lower cabinet, Gwen continued her one-sided monologue. "Where's that Jeremy?" she asked the cat. "He told Sally he'd drop off those extra prints this morning and now it's after lunch."

She glanced at the kitchen clock. The mail carrier wasn't due for another half hour. This was her first free time since discovering Frank's body nearly a week ago.

Searching for a minor chore, Gwen recalled the ruts in her lawn left by the guests who'd ignored her no parking signs. She headed for the shed where she filled the wheelbarrow with three bags of soil, a shovel, and a three-toed rake before trundling the patching supplies halfway down her side yard.

As she loosened the compacted soil, she considered Cole's lack of emotion during the earlier revelation of Frank's death and Robin's arrest. His questions about a snapshot to identify a different attacker had sounded more concerned than hopeful.

Wait. Was it possible Cole had snuck back across the village green last Saturday night after depositing Allison at the B&B? Had he intended to bring Frank back to their lodgings? In Frank's drunken stupor, had he resisted Cole's assistance? Could Frank's death be the accidental result of their struggle? Or had Cole taken advantage of the opportunity to rid his bride's family of the abusive stepfather?

Had Cole convinced Allison to leave town the next morning so he'd be out of sight? Their quick departure to elope did seem a bit too convenient.

Gwen shook her head. She was again grasping at straws.

Lost in thought, she tamped a thin layer of soil to cover the grass seed as the mail truck pulled to a stop beside her.

"Good morning," the delivery lady called. "I have a special package for you." She waved a padded envelope in the air.

Struggling to her feet, Gwen dusted off her hands. "Thanks. I've been waiting for that. But my hands are filthy. Would you mind sliding it into my mailbox?"

"Sure. I have bills and junk mail for you, too. At least I can get to your box today. It's been blocked all week."

"Sorry," Gwen said. "The extra vehicles will be gone soon."

The mail lady gave Gwen a thumbs up and proceeded around Library Lane, stopping in front of the old library to fill Gwen's box.

Reloading the wheelbarrow, Gwen returned her tools to the shed and the empty soil bags to the recycle bin. She washed her hands before hustling through the flower beds and down the driveway to retrieve the anticipated envelope.

Chapter Forty-Two

… mid-afternoon, Saturday

Tucking the miscellaneous flyers and bills beneath her arm, Gwen inspected the envelope labeled *Priority Mail* as she sauntered up her driveway toward the new garage. With Matt's crew at another job, the scene of the crime seemed the most appropriate place to view these new images.

Before tearing open the padded envelope, she gently squeezed the contents, confirming a hard object about the size of a thumb drive. Not that she didn't trust Gabriel's promise, but she didn't want to be disappointed.

Finally ripping the tab, she expanded the cavity. In addition to the thumb drive, Gabriel had included a stack of prints and a note card. Gwen flipped it open and read:

Mrs. Andrews,

I regret we didn't meet last Saturday, as I wanted to compliment your gardening skills. I'm saddened about the turn of events that cancelled the wedding and ruined your flower beds.

On a happier note, what a splendid idea to create a memory album for Robin's daughter and her new husband, even though the planned ceremony never took place. Years from now, they'll look back on the images

*without sadness. I hope some of the photos snapped by
my girlfriend will qualify for the album. Those pictures
are also included on the enclosed thumb drive. Luckily,
we're still old fashioned enough to enjoy prints, so we
had dropped off her Sim card a few days ago and are
able to supply you with the enclosed prints. The video is
a bonus, but I'm not sure you could print a frame. You
might be more computer savvy than me.*

    Best wishes, Gabriel Taylor

Removing the prints, Gwen placed the envelope and the
note on the leftover lumber pieces piled in the far corner of the
garage. One by one she inspected every detail of each image.

The first snapshots captured individual guests, an obvious
attempt to record which relatives and friends had shown up.
There were several shots of Allison and Frank, taken both
before he collapsed and after, one of Cole and Brodie hauling
Frank to the upper deck, a few blurry photos of people
scrambling when the fires broke out, and several groups of
guests heading away from the picture-taker after the wedding
was cancelled. These most likely coincided with Gwen's
escape to the birch trees.

And then she came upon the evidence she and Sally had
been seeking. Frank lying on the chaise lounge. The next print
had captured a man with his hand under Frank's arm, helping
him to his feet. The last print disclosed the two men further
along the upper deck toward the driveway steps.

That was the last photo. Gabriel's girlfriend must have stopped snapping pictures thinking Frank and the other man were the last guests to leave.

Gwen placed the stack of prints atop the lumber and pulled the thumb drive from the envelope. She'd have to go inside to view it on her tablet or laptop. And then it dawned on her that she was wearing the same jeans she'd worn during the drive back from the Cape. She patted her pocket and felt a lump... the transfer cable.

Wasting no time, she plugged it into her cell phone and popped the thumb drive into the other end. Within a nano-second, the contents came into view.

Barely able to contain her excitement, Gwen ignored the backup photo file, anxious to view the video. The scenes jumped sequentially as the wedding progressed.

First, location shots of Gwen's gardens. The guests mingling and murmuring on the decks. Taking their seats. Jenna, then Ashley marching through the French doors. Jenna playing the wedding march on her flute. Not the best recording of her performance, but satisfactory for the occasion. Allison supporting Frank as they made their way toward the groom, best man, and Justice of the Peace at the decorated trellis.

And then Frank's collapse, followed by Cole and Brodie carrying him to the lounge chair near the outdoor grill on the upper deck.

Gabriel had also recorded the hubbub of the fires. The guests running about and screaming, the arrival of the firemen, the hoses sprawled everywhere. He must have walked in circles around the back yard as the flames were extinguished. Finally, the fire truck driving away.

Unknown to Gwen, Gabriel had captured her strolling past the rental tables and down her side lawn, her figure shrinking as she approached the birch trees along North Street.

The next clip was obviously zoomed-in from a distance, as the decorations on the trellis were used to frame the sequence. Frank grumbling in the lounge chair as he struggled to his feet. Another man tucking his hand beneath Frank's arm, and their slow progress as they stumbled along the upper deck to the steps at the driveway. Though the video camera had recorded sounds throughout all the scenes, the conversation between the two men at that distance was too muffled to understand.

The video ended. Disappointed it didn't follow Frank and the other guy into her garage, she rewound to view the final scene again, this time paying attention to the details. The man with Frank wore a pale summer jacket like many of the male guests. With his back to the camera, his face and tie were out of view, and too many darkening shadows to describe his hairstyle. Few people would be able to identify Frank's companion in the dimming light.

Though the incriminating prints and the video backup would not identify the other man, they did prove one especially important fact. Robin had not been the last person with Frank.

Her fingers shaking, Gwen texted Ben. She'd found the proof they needed to free Sally's daughter from jail.

Chapter Forty-Three

… late afternoon, Saturday

Placing her cell phone with connected thumb drive near the three incriminating prints on the wood pile, Gwen sorted through the first snapshots one more time to be sure she hadn't missed anything. Concentrating on the images, she only half-heard the uneven footsteps making their way up her driveway.

A man's voice made her jump. "What have you got there?"

She whirled around to see the wedding photographer regarding her. "Oh, it's you, Jeremy."

"Sorry if I startled you."

Gwen chuckled. "I'll survive. I've been wondering when you'd stop by. Didn't you tell Sally you'd be here this morning?"

"I did, but I lost track of time in my darkroom."

"No problem. You're here now. Sally's out so you can give the extra wedding photographs to me."

He removed a small envelope from a pocket of his flak jacket and held it out. "Here you go. You seemed preoccupied by those pictures in your hand. They don't look like mine."

"They're not," Gwen confirmed. "We asked the guests to send us their snapshots. This is the last batch."

He reached out. "May I have a look?"

"Sure." Gwen placed them in his outstretched hand.

He sifted through them, finally commenting, "Not bad."

She suspected he was being kind about the amateur skills of Gabriel's girlfriend.

As he handed them back, he asked, "Were any of my professional photos chosen for the memory album?"

"You bet," Gwen answered, sensing his ego might be a bit bruised by the competition from the guests. "Yesterday, Sally and I selected our favorites from both your photos and the snapshots we've been collecting. I'm curious to see the extra ones you brought." She lifted the flap on Jeremy's envelope. Removing his prints, she quickly sorted through them, expecting pictures from a different angle to be useful for identification purposes. But there were no images of Frank with the other man.

"You went through those fast. Were you looking for something specific?" Jeremy asked.

Had her disappointment been so obvious? Even if Jeremy was aware of Frank's death, he'd have no idea she'd been hoping to find an alternate culprit. Deciding to tell him what had happened, she inhaled before speaking. "The bride's stepfather died in my garage last Saturday night."

Jeremy jolted. "How awful. I haven't read anything about that in the paper."

"This week's edition of the Harbor Falls Gazette didn't carry a notice." Gwen explained. "Sally and I assume Frank's twin submitted his brother's obituary to the Cape papers because that's where most of the family and friends live."

"Makes sense."

"There's more, Jeremy. Robin was arrested for the crime."

"Crime?" Jeremy's forehead wrinkled. "He didn't die of natural causes?"

"Far from it," Gwen answered, her voice shaken by the memory. "When Jenna and I came upon his body on Sunday morning, he was splayed on top of the cinder block wall with a rebar spike protruding from his chest."

Jeremy blanched. "I witnessed some gruesome deaths when I was shooting war footage for the Army, but nothing this personal. Do you think Robin is guilty?"

"I had my doubts," Gwen began, "until I looked through the snapshots that arrived a little while ago."

"Wait a minute," Jeremy pressed. "What do they have to do with Frank's death or Robin's arrest?"

Her leg muscles suddenly fatigued, Gwen shifted her weight. "When Sally and I requested the pictures taken by the guests, we told them we're creating a memory album, which is true. But we were hoping to find visual evidence of someone else with Frank. I spotted that person just before you arrived."

She sidestepped to the leftover lumber pile, snatched the three incriminating photos, and returned to Jeremy, fanning them out. "See here? There's a man helping Frank up from the chaise lounge and then leading him off my upper deck. Unfortunately, the guest stopped snapping pictures at that point, so there's no image of them entering the garage. But I think this is enough to convince the authorities that Robin was not the last person with her husband. She'll be a free woman as soon as I can get these into the hands of the police."

"Asking for those candid photos was clever." Jeremy pointed at her phone sitting on the stack of leftover lumber. "Was the thumb drive mailed with the prints?"

"Yep," Gwen answered, pride coursing through her veins. "A video, too. The final frames confirm the man with Frank from a slightly different angle. Do you want to see it?"

"Sure," Jeremy said, his enthusiasm obvious.

Retrieving her cell phone with cable and thumb drive, Gwen pulled up the video and pressed the fast-forward arrow, pausing as it neared the end. "I can't wait to show Sally when she gets back." Gwen played the final few frames again, angling it for Jeremy to see. "Is that other man limping?"

Jeremy peered at the image. "Hard to say. Frank appears to be quite a burden." In one smooth move, he ripped Gwen's cell phone from her hands and yanked out the thumb drive before tossing her phone and the transfer cable onto the lumber.

"I'll take those snapshots, too." He gripped the three prints.

Gwen's stomach clenched as awareness set in. Frank's killer stood right beside her. She glanced down at Jeremy's feet. He was wearing Army boots with dried patches of pale concrete clinging to the outer edges of the soles.

Her mind racing at warp speed, unspoken questions tumbled over each other. Did Jeremy suffer from PTSD? Was his Army disability compensation for more than his injured knee? Had he somehow considered Frank a threat?

Jeremy's now-cocky voice interrupted her efforts to understand his crime. "I can see you're trying to figure out why I did what I did, Gwen. You have to admit Frank deserved to die. I noticed the bruises on Robin's arms when she hired me, and then a fresh bruise on her cheek the day of the wedding. She tried to cover it with makeup, but she didn't use the proper shade for camouflage. Don't you see? I had to come to her rescue. My buddy Kyle would never have forgiven me if I hadn't tried to save his wife. He wouldn't be pleased about Robin's arrest, but there's no evidence to convict her."

Jeremy's eyes grew distant. "Frank was weak. I had no problem lifting him up and dropping him onto the rebar. By the way, thank your crew for providing such a handy weapon. Frank barely grunted when the spike punctured his heart."

Controlling the urge to throw up, Gwen struggled with mind over body.

Seemingly unaware of his one-way conversation, Jeremy kept analyzing his crime. "No one is ever going to find out I was the guy who eliminated Frank from Robin's life."

Gwen opted not to attempt logic with a madman.

Jeremy wrinkled Gabriel's prints. "I should burn these." He laughed, the sound disturbingly manic as he turned his wild-eyed expression on Gwen. "And then I need to deal with you."

Gwen's knees threatened to buckle. Another lunatic threatening her life. Chief Brown was right. She needed to retire from sleuthing. There were too many unbalanced people out there in the world.

Should she call out to Parker? Last December, his ghost had distracted a criminal, providing precious seconds for Gwen to react. She opened her mouth to call his name, but terror seized her throat.

Chapter Forty-Four

… late afternoon, Saturday

Ben walked into the chief's office, holding up his cell phone. "Mike, news from Gwen about the Hennessey homicide."

The chief looked up from his never-ending stack of paperwork. "Did Gwen and her cousin find something?"

"Her text didn't specify, but I'd bet one of the snapshots or a video she received from the last wedding guest provided a clue. Plus, the photographer was supposed to drop off extra photos he misplaced."

"So, you think our Gwen cracked the case?"

"I wouldn't be surprised. She's out-sleuthed the department before. If you don't mind a delay on the report I'm preparing for you, I'll drive over and see what she's got."

"The report can wait." The chief waved him off. "Get going. Be sure to keep me informed."

As Ben hurried to his desk for his keys, he placed a call to Gwen's cell phone. She didn't pick up, which was unusual, because her cell phone rarely left her jeans pocket. As he entered the elevator, he dialed her home phone, expecting Sally or Jenna to pick up. Again, no answer. The hairs on the back of his neck bristling, he texted a message. *No answer on your cell or house phone. On my way.*

When the elevator doors opened, Ben sprinted past the officer at the front desk and out of the station.

***

Gwen's cell phone signaled an incoming call.

"Don't answer that," Jeremy warned.

Seconds later, a jaunty tune announced an incoming text.

"Nope," he warned again. "No texting for you."

Her phone glared at her from the lumber pile, too far away to see who was calling and texting. Was it Ben? Gwen crossed her fingers, hoping he was on his way and not delayed by another crime scene.

She opened her mouth again to call Parker's name, emitting only a squeak. Jeremy didn't seem to hear her pitiful attempt.

Gripping Gabriel's wrinkled prints, Jeremy positioned himself sideways at the garage entrance, gazing down the driveway, but able to flip his head in a flash to check Gwen's whereabouts. "So, Sally is off somewhere in her van. When are you expecting her to return?"

Jeremy's flak jacket strained at his wide shoulders. He'd obviously been keeping himself in shape since retiring from the Army. Gwen would be no match for him physically. But maybe if she concentrated on his bad knee...

"Well, are you going to answer me?" Jeremy demanded. His head began to turn toward her.

***

Jumping into his unmarked sedan, Ben tossed the rotating red light onto the rooftop and squealed out of the police station parking lot, breaking the speed limit during the short drive to Gwen's place. Taking a right onto the cobblestones of Library Lane, he was forced to ease up on the accelerator to avoid circling the village green on two wheels.

He screeched to a stop behind Gwen's little sedan. The construction truck was not blocking the driveway as it had for the past week. Sally's white van was nowhere to be seen. Further along sat a panel truck Ben didn't recognize. The photographer? Ben leaped out and hot-footed it toward her front door.

***

In the garage, Gwen swallowed and choked out an answer. "I expect Sally to drive up any second." Was the threat of a witness enough to convince Jeremy he shouldn't harm Gwen?

Seeming to have forgotten his question, Jeremy smoothed out the wrinkled prints, grumbling incoherently. Without making eye contact, he said, "Gosh, Gwen, you're such a clever lady. I'm bummed I have to get rid of you."

Get rid of her? Of course, Gwen was the only person who knew Jeremy had killed Frank. Why had the photographer confessed? She found herself involved in similar circumstances to many movie scenes, where the villain tells his about-to-be victim of his plan. Gwen decided Jeremy was totally unhinged. Again, her stomach roiled.

Thoughts ran through her head as she tried to think of some way to stall. She closed her eyes and said a quick prayer to be rescued by Parker, Ben ... anyone.

What was Jeremy planning? Strangulation with his oversized hands? Toss Gwen in the air to land on her head and break her neck? With his muscular build, the photographer could do anything to her he pleased.

Gwen wondered if her last day on earth had arrived. Was this the hour when she'd join Parker in the afterlife?

"You seem like such a nice lady," Jeremy cooed. "So willing to help your cousin prove her daughter didn't do away with her no-good husband."

He began to explore the garage, his limp more obvious as he inspected the work completed by Matt's crew. "This is going to be a pretty little garage, Gwen. Too bad you won't be around to enjoy it."

He paused near the wall where Frank's blood stains remained visible on the lower cinder blocks. The bloody rebar spike was now covered by the upper wall. If the rebar had been visible, would Jeremy have speared her like he did Frank?

"Yep," Jeremy mumbled, moving his eyes away from her. "This is where it happened." He pointed at the concrete floor. "See these shoe impressions?"

He didn't notice her failure to answer. Lifting his booted foot, he placed it in the mishmash of overlapping imprints. "See?" He couldn't hide the pride in his voice. "My boot fits perfectly into the largest outline. No one could identify the pattern on my boots, though. Too many impressions from Frank's smaller feet. He put up a good fight, but I wouldn't let go. I told him to stop struggling, but he wouldn't."

Jeremy resumed his exploration, all the while spouting his twisted justification for murdering Robin's husband.

Gwen calculated the number of steps from where she stood to Matt's leftover lumber in the far corner and began to close the distance. Whenever Jeremy's heavy booted foot took a step, she advanced without detection. She feared he'd discover her inching toward the pile of slats and planks, but Jeremy lingered at the perimeter of the garage.

He swiveled in her direction, unaware of her progress. His next words chilled her. "Time to take care of you, Gwen. I've probably been boring you with my chatter, but I can do two things at once. The other half of my brain has been deciding the best way to get rid of you."

Now within feet of her, Gwen harbored no doubt he could move swiftly. She made an exaggerated head nod down the driveway. "Is that Sally's van?"

When he changed direction, she lunged for the wood pile, her heart hammering against her ribs. Gripping a 2x4 with both hands, she crouched low and swung at knee height with all the strength she could muster.

Chapter Forty-Five

… late afternoon, Saturday

When an ear-piercing scream reverberated from Gwen's back yard, Ben charged down her front steps and catapulted over the rose-covered fence. Realizing the sound came from the area of her new garage, he sprinted up the driveway, coming to a dead stop when he spotted a man writhing on the concrete floor. Gwen was staring down at him, a 2"x4" stud dangling from her hand.

Relief flooded through Ben… Gwen was alive.

Rushing to her side, he eased the piece of wood from her fingers and tossed it several feet away before gripping her arms and searching her stricken face. "Are you okay?"

Nodding that she was, Gwen pointed at the wailing man. "He said he had to get rid of me."

The man howled, "She broke my friggin' knee."

Ben didn't doubt Gwen's action had been self-defense. Resisting the urge to retaliate, Ben squatted down and cuffed the man's wrists before dialing 911.

The guy rocked back and forth, whimpering.

Ben placed his finger on Gwen's cheek and forced her to look away. "Who's he?"

Her voice hoarse, she stammered, "He's…he's the photographer Jeremy."

"And he threatened you? That's why you smacked him with the 2x4?"

Her mouth opened, but no words came out.

From his prone position, Jeremy spat, "Bitch."

"Shut up," Ben hissed.

Gwen fisted one hand, pointing at Jeremy with the other, anger restoring her voice. "He said he was going to kill me."

Ben draped his arm across her shoulders. "But you stopped him. I'll need a statement from you, but not this second."

She threw off Ben's arm and stepped toward Jeremy. "We need the thumb drive and snapshots from his pockets."

Snagging her sleeve, Ben held her back. "I'll get them. You stay here."

Despite Jeremy's attempts to roll onto his pockets and block the search, Ben rifled through the flak jacket, holding up the items for Gwen to see. "Is this the proof you mentioned in your text?"

"Yes. Those show a man… not Robin… walking Frank along the deck. It would have been difficult to identify the man, but now I know he was Jeremy." She pointed at him again. "Jeremy attacked Frank. He even bragged about it."

Glaring up at them, Jeremy sneered, "I want a lawyer."

Sirens wailed as emergency vehicles rounded the village green. An ambulance, two patrol cars, and the police chief's SUV squealed to a stop at Gwen's curb.

When the two EMT's passed Gwen, the taller one looked over at her. "Weren't we here last Sunday?"

Ben shooed the tech toward the garage before leading Gwen down the driveway.

Chief Brown met them halfway. "Are you all right, Gwen?"

"I am now," she managed.

Squinting into the garage, he asked, "What happened?"

Her face pale, Gwen furnished the basic details in as few words as possible.

When she stopped talking, the chief commented, "I would hope this is the last time you volunteer to find a bad guy."

Her back stiffened. "You think I end up in these situations on purpose?"

Chief Brown grimaced. "Well, no, not on purpose. But you're a magnet for trouble, Gwen. A sucker for a sob story. Always rushing to someone's rescue. One of these days, your luck might run out."

The EMTs rattled past Gwen with their stretcher.

Jeremy raised his cuffed hands for them to stop and struggled to his elbows. "I won't forget what you did to me, lady," he snarled.

Ben snapped, "Shut the hell up. You've made enough threats for one day."

Jeremy crumpled and the EMTs hurried him toward their waiting ambulance.

"Never mind him, Gwen," the chief said. "Ben, give me the thumb drive and the prints. I'll have a look back at the station while you take Gwen's statement. Come and see me when you're finished here."

***

Entering the safety of her home, Gwen made a beeline for the kitchen.

Ben hurried to catch up. "Where do you think you're going?"

"I need a cup of tea."

"Stop right there," he ordered. "I'll make it. Sit on your loveseat and organize your thoughts. I'll be right with you."

Gwen couldn't make herself relax. Nervous energy and excessive adrenaline kept her pacing until Ben walked in.

"Here you go." He placed a steaming cup on the coffee table as he sat, patting the adjacent cushion. "Sit, Gwen."

Gwen sat and risked a cautious sip of the tea. "This is good." As the brew warmed her body, her shaking subsided.

"I found a bear filled with honey and added a dollop," Ben added. "They say honey has soothing qualities."

"So it does." The tension drained from her shoulders. "Okay. I'm ready to give you my statement."

He removed an ever-present notebook, flipped to a blank page, held a pencil aloft, and waited.

"First of all," she began, "I don't know Jeremy's full name, but Sally has it in Robin's wedding file."

Ben made a note.

Gwen resumed her narrative. "Jeremy's interest in Gabriel's prints didn't seem unusual. He asked if any of his photographs had been chosen for the memory album. I sensed his professional pride was challenged, so I assured him we'd included many of his prints, which Sally and I actually had. When I sorted through his additional images, he noticed I was looking for something that wasn't there. That's when I told him about Frank's murder and our search for an alternate attacker. I was so proud to share the three snapshots that would free Robin." Gwen bit her lip. "I can't believe I was such an idiot."

"You had no reason to suspect him," Ben soothed.

Gwen sipped the tea again and swallowed. "When I showed Jeremy the video confirming a man with Frank, I said I didn't think anyone could identify the second guy. Then I pointed out the other man was limping. That's when Jeremy snatched the thumb drive and prints. Said he'd destroy them."

When Gwen stopped speaking, Ben filled in the blank. "He threatened to get rid of you so you couldn't tell anyone he was the limping man?"

"Yes," Gwen whispered.

Ben wrapped her in his arms. "You must have been scared out of your wits."

Gwen disengaged. "You're the master of understatement, Ben. When you called and then texted, Jeremy wouldn't let me answer. I didn't know if you were on your way or stuck at a crime scene."

"When did you decide to hit him with the 2x4?"

Gwen tried to remember. "I'm not sure. When I looked around for a weapon, the leftover lumber seemed to be my only option. I'm so glad Matt's crew was called to another job before they had a chance to clear it out."

Ben scribbled. "When did you make your move?"

"Off and on, Jeremy stood with his back to me. When he took a step, I took a step. He moved closer and closer to where I stood as he inspected the garage construction and didn't catch me inching toward the lumber pile. When he was a few feet away, I sensed he was about to turn around and grab me. I dove for that 2x4 and aimed at his bad knee." A nervous laugh escaped her. "I guess I disabled a disabled veteran."

"I guess you did." An admiring grin brightened Ben's face. "You said the prints and video might prove Robin was not the last person with Frank?"

"There's no might about it, Ben. They clearly show a man leading Frank along the upper deck toward the driveway."

"So there's no question the second person is *not* Robin."

"None at all," she confirmed. "I wish the chief hadn't taken everything back to the station. I'm not making this up."

"I never said you were."

Ben tucked his notebook into his pocket. "Based on your photo evidence and Jeremy's confession, I can't imagine the D.A. will object to Robin's release."

Gwen threw her arms around Ben's neck. "Tell the D.A. to compare Jeremy's Army boots to those shoe impressions. There's also dried concrete on his soles as extra evidence."

"The proverbial nail in his coffin." Ben kissed her cheek.

Gwen tightened her grip. "I'm so glad you showed up when you did. I don't know what I would have done if Jeremy managed to get to his feet. He's bigger and stronger than me."

"But you're smarter, Gwen," Ben whispered into her hair. "You knew better than to try to fight him as an equal, so you recognized his weak spot and hit him hard."

"I can imagine the lecture I'm going to get from the chief next time I bump into a local crime."

"How about you stick to gardening? Seems safer."

"That's a great idea, Ben. I'll see what I can do."

He lifted her chin and planted a kiss on her lips. "You know, we're both getting too old for this drama, Gwen. I'm thinking it's time for me to retire."

"Another great idea," she agreed, anxious to begin the next phase of her life with this white-haired man.

Releasing her, he stood up. "I've got to get back to the station and submit your statement to the chief. I'll call when I know the details of Robin's release." As he headed toward the foyer, he glanced at her, "Are you okay alone? I can have one of the officers stay until Sally and Jenna get back."

Gwen shook her head. "I'm fine. You go along."

He smiled, winked, and closed the door behind him.

Chapter Forty-Six

… late afternoon, Saturday

Not long after Ben left, the sound of approaching vehicles pulled Gwen to her door. Sally's white van parked at the curb, followed by Brodie's mud-splattered Jeep, and Cole's SUV.

The passengers emerged, blinking in the afternoon sun. From their doleful expressions, they could have been mistaken for pallbearers.

As they approached Gwen's front door, she called out, "I'm so glad you're back. Wait until you hear what you missed!"

Shading her eyes, Sally said, "What?"

"The real killer has been caught. Robin will be freed soon!"

Sally's face lit up like Fourth of July fireworks and she nearly stumbled as she hurried up the granite steps. "What are you talking about? What happened?"

"Come inside and I'll tell all of you at the same time."

After everyone was settled on the living room furniture, Gwen once again shared the chain of events.

Allison clung to Cole.

Brodie rested his hand on Ashley's arm.

Sally and Jenna listened with rapt attention.

When Gwen signaled she was finished, Sally jumped up and came at Gwen with both arms open wide. "You did it. I knew you'd help me prove Robin innocent. So sorry you were here alone. But, geez, why do I always arrive too late to witness the drama?"

"Bad timing, I guess." Gwen's cell phone buzzed. She listened before responding. "Everyone is here, Ben. I'm putting you on speaker."

His voice boomed, "Good news. The Harbor Falls police chief agreed that the snapshot and video evidence, plus Jeremy's confession to Gwen and his boot prints finalize his guilt. The chief called the Plymouth D.A. a little while ago." Ben paused, then said, "Sally, are you there?"

Sally scooted forward on the couch. "Yes, Ben, I'm here."

"Your lawyer was still at the courthouse, so they found a judge available for a quick hearing and explained the new evidence. The judge suggested the D.A. drop the charges and authorized Robin's release. Your lawyer is driving her to our police department if you'd like to come and pick her up."

Whoops of elation echoed throughout Gwen's home.

Sally said, "Come on, kids. Let's go get your mother."

As the family rushed out the door, Jenna hung back with Gwen, a lone tear rolling down her cheek. "Don't you ever again volunteer to hunt down a criminal."

"What a great idea," Gwen said, surrounding her *sort-of granddaughter* with loving arms.

Chapter Forty-Seven

... early evening, Saturday

Once again, Gwen responded to the doorbell. Standing on the top step, Sally held out her key. "You'll be happy to hear I won't be needing this anymore."

Reaching for the key, Gwen chided, "Get in here."

Sally stepped through the foyer.

"Where's Robin?" Gwen asked, glancing around Sally.

Pausing at the staircase, Sally smiled. "The kids took their mom to the bank's parking lot so she could retrieve her car. I'm here to pass along her gratitude, pack up my things, and get out of your hair."

"How's Robin handling her freedom?"

As the cousins ascended the staircase, Sally answered. "She's a bundle of contradictions. One second, she's elated to be out of jail, and the next she's dealing with mixed emotions about Frank's death. She's relieved he won't abuse her anymore, but sad the girls lost their stepfather. Despite his drinking, Frank was good to the twins."

"Your daughter's been through quite an ordeal," Gwen commiserated. "She'll bounce back."

Upstairs in the sitting room, Sally began to empty drawers while Gwen retrieved the suitcases from under her craft table.

Sally tossed her clothes willy-nilly into the luggage, all the while beaming. "I have more good news."

Gwen slipped items from hangers and passed them over. "Tell me."

"Robin's going to call Trevor and resume her job in his Cotuit mansion."

"A happy ending, Sally. More or less."

Sally dropped onto the daybed. "Sit for a minute, Gwen."

When Gwen settled beside her cousin, Sally squeezed her hand. "You're the only one who noticed those guests taking snapshots and suggested we chase them down." Sally's eyes glinted with emotion. "You saved my girl, Gwen."

"Any cousin worth her salt would have done the same," Gwen murmured.

"Oh, I beg to differ. You're no ordinary cousin."

They sat in silence until Sally spoke. "Well, the kids are waiting for me at the bank. We're going to form a caravan back to the Cape."

On the other side of the mezzanine, Jenna emerged from the guestroom. "I thought I heard voices." She soon joined them in the sitting room. "Leaving, Sally?"

"I am, Jenna. So nice to have met you. Please take good care of our Gwen."

"Don't worry, Sally. She's in good hands. Let me help you with your luggage."

After securing her many suitcases in the back of the van, Sally stepped toward her driver's door and turned. "I'm serious about you visiting me in Falmouth, Gwen. Time for you to stroll the Grey's Beach boardwalk once again."

Gwen laughed. "I'll email a few dates. Drive safely."

As Sally's white van disappeared, Ben's red Corvette took the turn onto Library Lane and circled the village green. As he parked, he beamed at Gwen and Jenna through his windshield.

Unfolding himself from the leather seat, he brandished a white package. "I bought steaks for dinner."

"Yum," Gwen said. "I'll bake some potatoes. Sally showed me a faster way."

"How's this instead?" Ben tossed out. "You relax while Jenna and I do the cooking."

***

Gwen sank into Parker's recliner near the empty fireplace and listened to the pots and pans clanging in her kitchen. Even if she'd wanted to, she didn't have the energy to cook, especially after being spoiled by Sally all week.

She tried not to doze off, but her eyelids kept drooping. She whispered Parker's name.

"Gwen, sweetheart, I'm here."

Her eyes flew open to see Parker's translucent spirit hovering, a broad smile on his face.

"You heard me call you?"

"Our connection has become stronger. Are you okay?"

"I'm not sure," she answered. "My body keeps reminding me I'm getting old." When a burst of energy coursed through her, Gwen hopped up from the recliner.

Parker wrapper her in his surprisingly solid arms. When he angled her to face his old chair, she stared down at herself. Her body sagged; her eyes were closed. She appeared to be asleep, her smile angelic.

"What...what?" she stuttered. "Is that me? Have I died?"

Ben and Jenna entered the living room. The instant Ben saw Gwen slumped in the chair, he rushed over, checked her pulse, and shouted at Jenna to dial 911.

Parker whispered in Gwen's ear. "It's not your time, sweetheart. I'll always be here if you need me. But it looks like you're in very good hands." He gave her a gentle shove and she fell backward.

***

Gwen's eyes fluttered open. A white-coated stranger held her wrist as he glanced at his watch. Ben and Jenna stood at the bottom of the bed, their expressions somber.

"Where am I?" Gwen asked, confused.

"In the emergency room of the Harbor Falls Clinic," the be-speckled man said. "I'm Dr. Jameson. You're going to be fine. Based on your vital signs and what your friends here told me, I'm guessing emotional stress more than anything."

"Not my blood pressure?" she asked, curious.

"Your levels were normal, so no. But you'll likely need to stay here at least twenty-four hours, maybe even forty-eight until we receive your test results." He tucked her hand beneath the bed sheet. "You lie here and rest. I'll be back in a little while to check on you."

As soon as the doctor slid the curtain closed, Jenna rushed to Gwen's side. "Don't you ever scare me like that again." She eased onto the edge of the bed and laid her head on Gwen's shoulder, flinging her arm across Gwen's body.

Knowing the courage required for Jenna to remain in an emergency room, surrounded by the repulsive smell of antiseptic, Gwen pulled her own arm from beneath the sheet and placed it across Jenna's back, feeling her sort-of granddaughter quiver from crying. This was not the time for the *we all will die one day* speech. Not everyone possessed Gwen's inside track to the hereafter. Parker would be waiting.

Or had she been dreaming?

From Gwen's other side, Ben tilted her chin toward him, meeting her gaze. "Welcome back. I thought we'd lost you." Though his words lacked emotion, the tears in his familiar grey eyes glistened. "The chief told me to take the rest of the day off and watch over you. I'm glad I listened."

"Me, too," she said, genuinely grateful.

He leaned closer. "You know what else Mike said?"

"No idea," she whispered, smiling up at him. "Guess you'll have to tell me."

"Our chief reminded me I've built up unused vacation time and suggested I whisk you away so you can relax."

Jenna eased herself off Gwen, wiping the tears from her cheeks. "Can't wait to hear your answer."

Imagining herself and Ben wandering the dunes of Cape Cod, Gwen focused on Jenna. "Can you look after Amber?"

"You bet. And I won't throw any wild parties."

"That will be appreciated."

As Gwen grinned at Jenna, Ben uncovered her other hand and clasped it between his. "There's something else."

"What could be better than a vacation?" she teased, thinking Ben would share an update about her confrontation with Jeremy in the garage.

A half-smile brightened his face. "If you haven't guessed, Gwen, I find you fascinating. And we're not getting any younger, so you and I need to make the most of the time we have left. One day soon, I'll get down on one knee and ask you to marry me. But I'd hate to embarrass myself, so I need to know now... will you consider accepting my proposal?"

Delight bubbled from the depths of Gwen's being. If now wasn't her time to join Parker, Ben was the perfect man to share her remaining years. "I'd most definitely consider your proposal, but only if you make me one promise, and this is non-negotiable."

His expression wary, Ben said, "Lay it on me."

Winking at the amused Jenna, Gwen squeezed his hand. "We tie the knot somewhere other than my back yard!"

THE END